Raif reached in, grabbed her arm and dragged her out of the tent. He spoke in an urgent whisper. "Don't dance."

"What?"

"Don't dance. Whatever I do, whatever I say out there, don't show yourself to them." He laughed harshly. "Come on, Sweetheart. Dance time."

He jerked her towards the fire, but his voice hissed in her ear. "Think of something, but don't dance if you value your life."

She began to resist, making him drag her. It was a relief to be able to fight.

The ring of outcasts laughed as they approached, throwing catcalls and lewd comments.

"What's wrong, Raif? Is she modest?"

"I hear she dances nice enough in your tent."

He tossed her into the firelight, a hateful grin on his face. "All right, Sweetheart. Show us what you can do." He motioned with his hand, and the musicians struck up a raucous tune.

Aleria stood, her head bowed, shoulders slumped, trying to make herself as unalluring as possible. Watching him through the fringe of her hair, she could see his expression change.

"Come on, girl. Dance!"

Still she refused to move, her pleasure in the defiance drowning her fears as to where this scene might lead.

The crowd waited hopefully, soft jibes and sloshing bottles circulating.

"You heard them, girl. Entertain us."

Again, she did not move. It seemed easiest. His face changed again, anger pulling at his brow. He strode to her, grabbed both arms and pushed his bristling moustache in her face. "Dance, girl, or you'll regret it."

"He's sure got a way with the women, ain't he?" The voice came clearly through the murmurs. The soldiers chuckled.

"Dance, you slut!" He shoved her, spinning her around. She stumbled and sank to the ground, cowering before him. As the crowd laughed louder, he hauled her up. She hung, limp in his hands, ignoring the way his fingers dug into her arms.

As the jeering increased, his breath came faster, his colour rose. He held her up to his face and shouted curses and insults. Still she refused to respond, only cringing lower. *He really doesn't mean this. It's part of the act. He's only trying to save my life.*

Finally he calmed, looking around at the crowd.

I think.

She peered up, and realized with a shock that he was grinning.

"Well, I guess she can't dance!"

Out of Mischief

Gordon A. Long

AIRBORN PRESS
Delta, 2014

OUT OF MISCHIEF

Published by
Airborn Press
4958 10A Ave, Delta, B. C.
V4M 1X8
Canada

ISBN - 978-0-9921243-2-8

Cover
Design by Dusty Hagerud and Gordon A. Long
Model Josie Buter
Photography by Gordon A. Long

Back cover painting "Henri de La Rochejacquelein at the Battle of Cholet in 1793" by Paul-Emile Boutigny

Gordon A. Long

Thanks

To Elizabeth Hull for her ideas and her editing
Dusty and Josie for their artistic assistance

CONTENTS

å

"Use brute force to solve a problem, and there is no going back. Violence will be one of your options for the rest of your life."
- Master Ogima

"Curiosity has killed of a lot of cats, but boredom comes a close second."
- Aleria

1. Caught!

Aleria crept along the hedge, her eyes straining through the faint dawn light for the gap that would allow access to the window. There it was, a dark splash against the light wood siding. As she pushed through the bushes, the bag clanked. *Oh, crap!* She froze and waited.

No movement. A sleepy bird chirped, and another answered. The smell of late spring flowers soared over the earthy tang of tilled soil. Reaching up, she clawed at the gap where she had left the window ajar. It gave reluctantly, and she swung the frame out. Slowly...slowly...it was a bit of a scramble to get up on the sill, so she sat, calming her breath and listening. Still nothing. *I could get good at this.*

As she swung her legs in, the bag caught on the latch and pulled from her hand, dropping with a loud clatter to the ground outside. *Double crap!* She held her breath, poised to fly in either direction. Silence. After an agonizing wait, she breathed again. She looked down. She didn't want to climb to the ground and back up again. The bag was leaning against the wall. If she could reach...

It was getting light. She'd better do something in a hurry; the servants rose early. Lying on her stomach across the sill and stretching down, she managed to get two fingertips on the bag. The rough cloth gave good purchase, and she wiggled it into her grasp. With a silent sigh of relief she slid backwards, lifting the bag ever-so-carefully clear, and stood up.

A scream burst from her lips as something sharp jabbed into her back, propelling her against the side of the window frame.

"Stand right where you are!"

She froze, staring at the wood in front of her nose. She was prodded again, not gently.

"All right. Who are you, and what do you think you are doing?"

Relief gushed through her. "Father?"

"What?"

She slipped away from the point and turned towards him. "Father, it's me. Put the sword away. That hurt!"

There was a suppressed curse, and a sudden beam of light blinded her. "Aleria? Aleria, what are you doing, crawling in the window at this time of the morning?" The lantern flashed downwards. "What's that in your hand?"

"Nothing." She put it behind her. *Stupid answer. Think, girl, think.*

"It doesn't sound like 'nothing.' Give it to me."

That tone in his voice; it wasn't often directed at her, but when it was, argument was not an option. She held the sack out towards the light. "Could you shine the lantern somewhere else, please, Father? I can't see a thing."

"That's the least of your worries right now, young lady." The light swooped down. "What's this? Hammers?" He lifted one, peered at the head. "Dust? Marble dust?"

The light stabbed at her again." What have you been up to, Aleria? Is this another one of your stunts?"

She shaded her eyes. "Yes, Father, it's another one of my stunts. It's over, and it went fine. I didn't do anything illegal or immoral. It was just a joke, that's all. A rather good one, I think."

He swung the light away from her, and in the reflected beam she could make him out, tall and straight in his dressing gown, the sword leaning against his thigh. He stared at her one long moment more, then picked up the sword and turned away. "Come along. I haven't got much time."

She followed, trying to seem as meek as possible.

There was a lamp burning in the family lounge. He pointed the sword towards a straight-backed chair and she sat hastily.

"All right. The reason I'm up so early is that I have a long ride and an important meeting with anDennal at his upriver raft landing. I don't have time to deal with this now, but I will. Don't worry, I will. When I return in late afternoon, you will be here. Do you follow? No meetings, no friends, no school projects. You will come straight home after classes and wait. Am I understood?"

"Yes, Father. I'll be here."

"That would be wise." He clashed the lantern and sword together in one hand and pulled the door open. Then he turned back. "Just a stunt? Nobody hurt, nothing..." he glanced pointedly at the bag, "...broken?"

She put on her most earnest face. "Nothing important, Father, I promise you. It was just a joke with the girls, that's all."

"Hmph." He seemed about to turn away, when suddenly his head came up and he stared full into her eyes. "Aleria, you are going to be attaining your Cumulato from the Academy in six weeks. You will be then considered a mature young woman, ready to take her place in society. I thought by now you would be thinking about...I don't know, marriage or something. Why are you still doing this sort of thing?"

He held the stare for a moment longer. Then without another word he was gone.

She sat there a moment, considering. *A minor setback, come to think of it. After all, we didn't actually do anything wrong.* She grinned to herself. *Well, some people aren't going to be exactly happy about it, I suppose.*

She rose, swung the cedar-panelled door wider and strode towards the back stairs. *At least it wasn't Mother. That doesn't bear thinking of. Of course, she'll find out, now. Hmm. I'm going to have to plan this afternoon very carefully...*

2.   Confined to Barracks

Aleria sat as primly as she could on the hard seat. The plain wooden chair, rather than the padded, brocade-covered lounger she usually used. She checked her dress. Chosen with care as well: blue, Father's favourite colour – it also set off her eyes and blonde hair – and a modest calf-length. As she watched her father pace, she tried to look the picture of a young woman ready to take her place in society. *The last thing I want, but at the moment...*

She regarded her father, boot-heels rapping, deep in thought, but smoothly avoiding the numerous chairs, tables, and other delicate bric-a-brac crafted of beautifully grained hardwoods that made the family lounge one of the cosiest rooms in the house. *He's slowing down. Here it comes.* She schooled her features to a pleasant smile, trying to control the quaking inside.

He spun to face her. "You realize I'm going to have to let you get away with this."

Aleria's heart lurched, and she examined her father's face. He wouldn't be joking about something as serious as this. *Did I hear that right?*

"Yes, that's what I said. You chose your cohorts well for your little escapade."

She thought of Hana and Gita, probably going through a similar experience at their own home this very moment. They had done their share: planting the sculptures perfectly, not getting caught. Surely that couldn't be what he meant. He didn't even know the details yet. Hopefully, some of the details he would never know. *Especially how I persuaded the Temple guard to look the other way.*

Her father was staring at her as if expecting a response. Coming up with nothing, she shrugged in what she hoped was a helpless manner. "I don't know what you mean, Father."

He threw up his hands. "Aleria, I don't expect you to understand all the intricacies of my position. But surely you realize that the Dennal family would be rather upset if they thought that my child had led their darling daughters into any sort of indiscretion."

"Father! We did nothing indiscreet!"

"You consider putting up statues in the Artists' Corner of the Temple Garden to be the model of prudence, do you? And what about smashing them apart afterwards?"

From the look in her father's eye, she realized it was no time to argue. *Wait it out. He'll give me more information.* She sat a bit straighter, tried to look attentive.

"You have, I assume, heard about the Shaeldit situation."

Then it all clicked: the last time the Dennal family had visited. As usual, she and the Twins had hardly been listening to their fathers nattering on. Policy decisions were often made around the banquet table, and that evening had been no exception. Thinking back, she remembered her father's earnest discussion with his ally, and the reluctant admissions the senior Dennal had made.

"Yes, of course..."

"I don't think you realize how serious it is down there." He flung his hand towards the south. "There are people being killed. Murdered. And why? Because they're people like us. People of Rank, with enough property that others are jealous. I probably shouldn't be telling you this, but I want you to understand how serious this is. The leaders of that rebellion were carrying Mechanical weapons."

She frowned. "You mean guns? They aren't allowed to have guns. Nobody is except the Royal Army. They aren't safe!"

"Nobody told the rebels that. I don't know how they smuggled them into Galesia from Domaland, but they had them." He paced a few steps away, then turned back. "That's the sort of problem I'm dealing with, and anDennal has become my strongest supporter, in spite of the fact that all his river shipping is from the north, where there hasn't been any trouble."

Her father dropped to the settee in front of her and leaned forward, a sudden flush coming to his face, and she realized how upset he was. "Did you choose your accomplices because you knew their father's status in this project would protect you?"

She had rarely seen her father angry, especially with her, and she thought quickly. A protestation of complete innocence would work, but she rejected the idea. He would never know if he could believe her. *Perhaps the truth will work.*

"Not exactly, father. I chose them because they are good friends and because I knew they could handle their end of the task. I don't suppose I considered their family positions, as such, but I knew they would be safe. They wouldn't be my friends if they weren't. If anything went wrong, it wouldn't make us politically vulnerable."

"What did Mito have to do with this?"

"I couldn't involve her in even that much risk. Some of those moss-beards on the Board would just love an excuse to throw her out of the Academy because of her uncle's so-called disgrace. It's unfair, but that's the way it is, so I never even told her."

Her father sank back, and she could see he was mollified. "So you did, in spite of the evidence, show a smattering of judgement. Perhaps you realize what you have put in jeopardy?"

Exasperation took the place of fear, and she jumped to her feet. "Oh, Father, I haven't put anything in jeopardy. It was just three schoolgirls playing a prank, that's all. We didn't do any real harm. Your precious contracts to move wood from the North and coal from the East will continue, as they always have."

"That was more good luck than anything else."

"No it wasn't. I planned it all carefully. There was very little chance of getting caught, let alone causing any harm." She moved towards him. "Come on, Father. It went perfectly!"

She could see her father's mouth twist, and she knew she had him. He rose and ran a hand along the teak sideboard. She had seen that gesture before, and knew that the smooth curve of the wood seemed to comfort him. Then he turned back to her. "You realize you have caused a certain amount of embarrassment to the Royal Artists' Guild of Galesia."

"Oh, that stuffy bunch." Relieved, she sat again, in a more relaxed pose. *If I can get him going on art criticism...* "You know as well as I do that Ralule can sculpt as well as any of them, but he uses too many Mechanical tools, so they won't let him sell any of his work in the Royal Gallery."

"Ah. So that's where you got the sculptures."

"I did not! I got them from a trader. I happened to see him unloading them from one of our wagons down at the yard. He only had the four – imitations of Wotahg works from Sixth Century Aesmark – but they were probably made in Domaland."

"How could you tell?"

"The stone was polished, but if you looked at the bases, they weren't chiselled by hand. They were done by Mechanics. Aesmark doesn't have that much industry. In Domaland their machinery can turn out that sort of stuff by the cartload."

"Why did the trader bring them here? He must have known he wouldn't be allowed to sell them."

"He didn't know, and when I told him, he couldn't think what to do with them. That's when I though up my plan. I bought them before anyone else saw them. That way no one had any idea who the artist was. That was the real fun part of the whole thing. The Artists' Guild thought the Temple had put them up, and the Temple thought the Artists had. Once they had been there for a while, people started to say how good they were, and both the Temple and the Artists started to stick out their chests about the whole thing. They were quite good, actually. For copies. The hardest part of the whole thing was when we had to smash them."

"And what do you expect me to do now?"

"I don't expect you to do anything."

"So you plan to leave this uproar going on? The Temple, the Guild and the King's soldiers all looking for the sacrilegious villains who smashed the art work in the Temple grounds? How can I go to them and admit that it was all a childish prank by my daughter and her friends? I can't even mention the friends, because then I will expose their family to public censure. Not a particularly good gift for a new ally."

"Father. There you go again, taking all the responsibility for everything." She leaned forward with enthusiasm. "You don't have to do anything. Everybody knows by now what really happened. They finally looked at the bases and realized they weren't properly made Art. Word was all around the Academy by noon today. I was told the whole story by three different people." She grinned. "They even had most of the facts straight."

"You mean everyone knows it was a hoax, but no one knows you did it?"

"So far."

"What do you mean, 'so far'? Is anyone going to find out?"

She shrugged. "Not as long as the people who know keep their mouths shut. Perhaps you should contact the Twins' parents, in case they go off on a tangent."

Her father's face hardened. "I do not choose my allies, young lady, from people who might 'go off on a tangent' at the first sign of trouble. I will be hearing from the Dennal family soon. Was there no one else involved?"

She considered. "The merchant is long gone. The Temple has no idea when the statues went up. We put them in when the repairs were going on, so no one used that area for weeks. I don't see any problems. If you hadn't caught me coming through the window with the hammers, no one would have been the wiser."

"I can think of several other 'ifs' that could have happened."

"True, so can I. But you have to remember, we weren't breaking any laws. The statues were my property and I could smash them if I wanted to. Think of the positive side, Father. If you get anDennal's daughters out of this, you'll be a hero and it will help the relationship."

"Except it was you that got them into it."

"His pride won't let him believe they were followers."

Her father shook his head. "I know, I know. I just wish you wouldn't get involved in this sort of silliness."

"It wasn't silly, Father. I had a point to make. I think I made it rather clearly, don't you? Those so-called "artists" in the Guild can't do anything original. They only copy the Ancient Masters. For example, what do you think of this new fad that they are so proud of?"

"Which 'fad' is that?"

She smiled at him. "You obviously don't follow the Art scene. The latest philosophy in Art circles is that it's conceited to think that anyone could make a work that is perfect. Only the Gods can create perfection. So they say every work of Art should have a small flaw inserted, so as not to anger the Gods by trying to achieve perfection."

"That sounds very pious to me."

"But it isn't. It's the opposite!"

Her father cocked his head. "What do you mean, the opposite?"

"Think about it, Father!"

He considered for a moment. "I see. If you have to insert a flaw, it means you think you are capable of creating perfection. Which is challenging to the Gods."

She leaned forward, pleased. "Exactly. If you truly believe that only the Gods can achieve perfection, you try your best, knowing that there will be flaws, no matter how hard you try."

Her father smiled and shook his head. "That's pretty complicated thinking."

"That's the kind of thing artists discuss all the time, Father. They taught us about it in Aesthetics class last term. But the established artists are so devoid of creativity, they spend all their time talking about things like that and they don't have any idea of what true art is or how to create it. That's why it was so easy to fool them."

"But why did you need to fool them?"

She shrugged. "I don't know. It isn't just the artists. It's everyone. All these rules about what is Mechanical and what is

9

not, because somehow inventing Mechanical things challenges the Gods. It always sounds to me more like Mechanical things challenge everyone who is making a lot of money with the old ways."

"Like horse-and-wagon transport?"

"Yes, even Dalmyn Cartage. And it's going to destroy us all in the long run. We learned about it in Evolutionary Science last year. A species that doesn't adapt to a changing environment is doomed. Same with a business. Especially a business like ours."

"You think I should be importing one of those steam-engine tractors we saw when we visited Domaland last year."

"It pulled seven full cartloads of coal, twice as fast as a man can walk."

"And did you see what it did to the road?"

"Obviously we would need better roads."

"And can you see carrying the parts of one of those monsters around the Chanaan Canyon Rapids?"

She shuddered at the memory. "With the road hanging out hundreds of feet above the river? I wouldn't want to be the one driving that wagon."

"And a bigger obstacle than the rough country is the incredible weight of popular sentiment in Galesia. For most of our population, 'Mechanical' equals 'Sinful,' and that's an end to it."

She threw up her hands. "I know, I know. It would cause more trouble than it's worth. I just can't help but wish...I don't know. That I could see some hope of change."

He shook his head again and smiled wryly. "So you don't think I should do anything about this."

"I told you, it's all taken care of."

"I don't mean the matter of the sculptures. As I told you, I have to let that ride for political reasons. I mean the matter of my daughter doing such a prank. Don't you think some punishment is in order?"

"Oh, Father. It was so funny, and it worked so well! I thought you would be proud of me." She hung her head. It wasn't hard to seem disappointed. She had hoped that he would at least laugh a bit.

"Well, I suppose I'm going to have to think about it."

Aleria's heart gave another leap. When her father started thinking about something she had done, it usually meant no more action. She was about to throw her arms around his neck when a strident voice cut her off.

"Think about it? Kensel anDalmyn! Is that all you're going to do?"

She spun to face her mother, heat rushing to her face. *How much did she hear?*

"Well, my little schemer. What have you to say for yourself? There are all sorts of stories going around the market, and I can see your meddling in every one of them. This is a pretty mess you've got us into."

"But I haven't, Mother. It's all going to blow over. No one at the Temple or the Guild will dare to let on that the statues were fakes and they didn't recognize it."

"And you think the Dennal family won't do anything about it because they don't want the publicity. And you have persuaded your father all this, and he's going to let you off completely free." She turned and glared at her husband.

He smiled gently, warding off her stare with a graceful wave. "Now, Leniema, it's not that bad. She is right about the political implications. And at the moment it wouldn't be wise to punish her overtly, in case someone starts asking why."

Good old Father. I hadn't even thought of that angle. She sat back to enjoy watching one of the most respected politicians at Court turn his considerable talents to her benefit. She could see that her mother was already softening before that gentle smile, that 'don't worry, everything is in hand' calm.

Leniema accepted her husband's invitation to sit beside him, but frowned. "Well, we have to do something!"

"Of course. But perhaps we should wait to see how this all turns out. Did any of the stories point towards Aleria?"

11

"I was listening for that, let me tell you! No, as far as gossip goes, the main suspects are the Guild apprentices and the students at the University."

"So no one would even think that a few schoolgirls could manage something so complicated."

Aleria's mouth opened, but a warning twitch of his finger silenced her. She was surprised to see a touch of a smile on her mother's lips.

"No, I suppose not."

Her father settled back, pulling his wife into the crook of his arm, and Aleria felt suddenly lonely. *They are so handsome together. I don't want them angry with me. Come on, Father, make this work!*

"So there we are. If nothing else happens, we have a little story to go down in the private family annals. 'The Day Aleria Became a Critic.' That has a ring to it."

Her mother pulled away. "Don't treat this lightly. If they get caught..."

"It doesn't look as if they are going to, and if they do, we can pass it off as a childish prank. After all, those stuffy Artists are going to be even more happy to keep it under wraps if they find out it was children who fooled them."

"We aren't children!"

Her mother's head snapped around. "You will be happy enough to hide behind your childhood if it means you can duck the responsibility for your childish actions!" Her mother controlled her expression. "Aleria, I know you are not completely insensitive. I know you think that at the proper time you will grow up and stop doing these things. But what if one of your stunts now has an outcome that will affect the person you will become? That worries me."

"What do you mean?"

"Well...what if you hurt yourself and are crippled for life? No, don't bother arguing. I know you think you are more careful than that. It's impossible to predict the results as long as you refuse to show enough responsibility to stop of your own accord."

Her father frowned as well. "Yes, I think our young schemer has not demonstrated proper contrition for her deed. Some small punishment is required. I will think on it between now and supper."

Her mother jumped up. "Supper! This whole situation put it clear out of my head. I'll have to go down to the kitchen to supervise, or those girls will never get the sauce seasoned properly. Why did the cook's mother have to get ill just now?"

"The cook's mother is a very nice old lady, and I'm sure she would have arranged her illness to suit your schedule if you had let her know ahead of time."

Leniema tousled her husband's hair. "You know what I meant. Now I'm going to the kitchen to do my duty. You do yours." She jumped up, turned to look down at her daughter. "I am not pleased with you, young lady." She continued the turn towards the door.

"Mother?"

"Yes?"

"Could I help? With the dinner, I mean. If there were some vegetables to cut, or something…"

Her mother's face softened. Slightly. "You had too much fun with those hammers this morning. I'm not going to let you anywhere near a knife. I recall what happened the last time." With one meaningful glance, she swept out of the room.

Aleria's father looked up at her. "What did she mean by that?"

She felt her face get hot. "Oh, nothing. It was years ago. I was just practising, you see…"

"Practising?"

"Yes. You know…throwing them?" She flicked her wrist.

Her father shook his head. "Let me guess. With the kitchen knives."

She shrugged and grinned. "There weren't any others around."

"At least you know when to keep your mouth shut."

She glanced up to see her father smiling. "Oh, I know Mother better than that. I never cross her when she's angry."

13

"You mean you haven't recently."

She winced at memories of a few years ago, when broken crockery and scattering servants had been the order of the day. "I guess I've grown up a bit."

"Well, I could wish you would grow up a bit more. I don't like it when the two of us have to gang up on your mother. It isn't fair."

"You two gang up on me all the time."

"We're your parents, dear. That's how it's supposed to work. Now come and give me a kiss, and then trot off and do whatever you need to before supper. We will be having company."

"I didn't know anyone was invited."

"No one was. But I had a feeling that anDennal was going to want to talk to me and I thought a good meal would smooth the conversation. I sent to him before I talked to you."

"Shall I ask the major-domo to bring out some of the Lodim wine?"

He smiled up at her as she stood over him, and she knew she was forgiven. "A very wise thought. Make it two bottles." He held his cheek up, and she kissed it softly, holding the hug a little longer than usual.

"Thanks, Father."

"Thanks for what?" His voice was grumpy, but she could tell when he was putting on a show. She bounced from the room, determined to be extra mature and gracious to anDennal tonight.

3.   Hawk's Egg

Mito stretched out her arms and lifted her face to the sun. "This is so beautiful. I love getting out of the city." Then she turned to look at Aleria. "If you're confined to the house, why are we out here on this cliff?"

"Because I need these eggs for my Biology Final Project. They have to be around here somewhere. Dr. Anville said raptors always nest on the highest riverbanks. I saw a pair spiraling down just below this tree. They must have a nest. Here. Hold this rope."

"What is the rope for?"

"Safety. I'm not a complete idiot, you know."

"Do I?"

"Just put the rope around that tree, and stand over here."

"And do what?"

"Pay out the rope as I go over the edge." Aleria was looping the rope around her chest under her arms.

"Pay out the rope. What if you go over the edge for real?"

"Then you hold onto the rope, of course."

Mito looked down at her slender hands, then up at Aleria.

"The tree provides enough friction. You can hold my weight easily."

The smaller girl tugged experimentally. "And if I want more friction, I just move farther around the tree."

"Good idea."

"If the tree holds." Mito pushed experimentally against the trunk, which flexed slightly. "That's not a very big tree."

"Don't worry. These trees have their roots knotted into the cracks in the rock. They're very tough."

"Aleria, you <u>have</u> done this before?"

"Not really." She tugged the knot in front of her to be sure it was tight. "I heard the boys talking about it. It sounded very logical."

"Until we find out something we forgot to think of."

15

"Don't be a spoilsport. I need those eggs." Aleria started down the rocky slope, but it soon steepened to the point where she turned and backed down on all fours.

"All right. I'm at the edge now. It isn't that steep below me. Lots of ledges and broken rock. This ought to be easy."

Mito's voice came to her faintly, swept away by the breeze. "What did you say?"

Louder this time. "I said, I hope so!"

Aleria backed down farther, peering around below her for footholds and any sign of a nest.

Nothing. She climbed down more, aware that the rock was getting smoother and steeper, and the full drop to the riverbed below was a long way down.

"How's it going?"

"Fine. How much rope left?"

"Lots. You haven't used half yet."

"Good. I'm going down more."

"Be careful."

"You said that before." She stretched one leg down, found solid footing, followed with the other. As far as she could tell, the nest wasn't much lower, just around that bulge of rock. She shouted up loudly to be sure Mito could hear. "I'm moving along the cliff to the east, now."

"Who said anything about a cliff?"

"Just hold the rope. Be ready."

"For what?"

"In case I slip. I don't have good handholds at this point."

"All right. I'm holding on."

"You have to let go a little or I can't move."

"All right. I'm letting go. A little."

Slowly, Aleria edged sideways, leaning outward to see what was around the corner.

"There it is!"

"What?"

"The nest, of course. Give a little more."

"All right."

"Whoa! Pull in. That was too much. I'm going another way." She climbed a bit higher, but soon ran out of handholds completely on the smooth rock. "No, that didn't work either."

She worked farther down, but try as she might, Aleria could get no nearer to the nest. The bulge pushed her out too far, and she was afraid she might overbalance.

"Pull in the rope. I'm coming up."

She scrambled back up the rock face, surprised at how short the distance was. Mito kept the rope taut as she came.

"What's wrong?"

"The nest is on the far side of a big smooth spot that sticks out sort of, like this." Aleria gestured with her hands. " I can't get at it from this side without swinging my weight on the rope."

"I don't think that's such a good idea."

"We'll reserve it for a moment of desperation. But I want to try from the other side, and maybe straight down from the top, as well."

Mito shrugged. "You're the one on the end of the rope."

"Away I go."

"Don't you want a rest?"

"Not really. It's only about four yards down, you know. Until I get over the rim, it isn't really climbing, just scrambling." She started down farther to the left.

She tried several ways down, but no matter how she clambered and stretched, she could not find a path to the nest. Always it sat there looking rather smug on its tiny ledge, just out of reach. When she climbed straight down from the top, she could see three mottled eggs in it, but they were almost straight down and the ledge was very narrow.

"I'm coming back up. I need a rest."

Once again she scrambled to the top.

"No luck?"

"None at all. The only way is to go straight down over the edge, using the rope."

"But I can't hold you."

"Of course you can. If you need more friction, just move around the tree more."

"And what about when you want to come up?"

"I'll just hand-over-hand up the rope like we do in the gymnasium. As I said, it isn't far."

Mito shook her head. "I still don't like it, but you're the one out there. I trust you not to make any mistakes."

"So do I. There's a couple of sandwiches in the bottom of the pack. Let's take a break."

The sandwiches were rather squashed, but they ate them with pleasure anyway, sitting shoulder-to-shoulder against the narrow tree trunk and looking out over the river canyon below.

After a while, Mito glanced over at her. "So how is this 'punishment' of your father's going to be a punishment?"

"Well, I'm confined to the house until we start our Quest, except for school and the official Cumulato meetings. How mortifying."

Mito looked concerned. "But what about the Departure Gala? You'll miss that."

"I wasn't too concerned about it anyway. I was going to come home early to get rested up for the next day's travel. No chance I'm going to start my Quest with a hangover."

"Do you think your father would let you have company?"

"Mito, don't you even think about it! You go to the parties, have some fun."

"You may have noticed. I'm not that popular at the parties."

Aleria frowned at her friend. "Don't be ridiculous. The Twins like you. Several of the boys are interested, if you'd only let them be."

"The Twins are the Twins. They'll be nice enough, but they always have their own agenda, which nobody except you can break in on. And you know I can't afford to get mixed up with boys. I have to get my education."

"I know, I know. We've been through it a hundred times. It suits me just as well, since I don't find any of them interesting enough to bother about."

She rose, dusting her hands together. "Let's figure out this rope. I'm going to back down, with my feet against the cliff. You're going to let the rope out slowly, and I just walk down."

"Sounds easy. It won't be."

"It slopes gently at first. You'll be able to test it out before it gets steep."

"Let's do this before I think about it too much."

"That's my girl."

"I hope you're still here to own me when this is all over."

Aleria walked to the edge of the drop, and Mito took up the tension. "I'll turn around now. Start holding some of my weight. Remember, if it starts slipping, just move farther around the tree."

Mito merely nodded, her face serious, her knees bent as she took the strain.

Confident of her friend's ability, Aleria leaned back against the comforting strength of the rope and started down. Soon the slope became steeper, and she began to feel a tightening around her chest. Her foot slipped, and the weight came harder.

"Ouch!" She scrabbled with her feet. "Well, we learned something there."

Mito's voice came faintly over the edge. "What did we learn?"

"The reason why they put several loops around their chests. That rope really cuts. In tender places."

"How are you going to get back up?"

"I'm not ready, yet. I haven't got to the nest. Let me down some more."

Soon she was leaning back horizontally, and more and more weight was coming on the rope. She looked down. The nest was just below her.

"Wait! Aleria, stop!"

"I'm almost there! Give a little more."

"You have to stop. Now!"

Something in her friend's voice brought her up sharply.

"What's wrong?"

19

"Come back up. Slowly. Don't put any more weight on the rope than you have to."

"Is something wrong?"

"Come up!"

"Coming. Hold it tight." As smoothly as she could, and very aware of the steep drop at her back, Aleria hauled herself, hand over hand, back up the cliff. It took much longer this way, and by the time her feet began to get a decent purchase she was sweating and her fingers ached.

When she got to the top, Mito was all the way around the other side of the tree, pulling away from her.

"What's going on?"

"The tree was bending."

"Bending?" She put a hand to the tree and pushed. It gave, but not that much. "That's not a problem."

"Push the other way. Look!" Mito pushed the tree out towards the cliff, and, sure enough, there was a slight movement in the moss at the base, as if a root was trying to push out of the ground.

Aleria tried the same move, thinking. "When I pull down on this side, and you pull down over here, we're both trying to pull the tree over. But when I came up, you were all the way around on the side of the tree opposite the cliff, and you were pulling against me and helping the tree. It was working fine."

Mito did not say anything for a moment, and Aleria kept testing the pull, watching the moss heave over the root.

"Aleria. Look at me."

She obediently met Mito's eyes, which dark and slitted. Her finely drawn features were harsher than Aleria had ever seen them.

"Don't think of me as your quiet little friend Mito who follows along and does almost everything you ask. Think of me as Mito from a poor family, who spends all her school breaks at home, where there is a mill, a farm and a cartage company, without enough people to do all the work, where a willing hand is always welcome. Someone who knows ropes and weights and the strength of things."

"And?"

"And someone who has seen accidents, and blood spilled and bones broken, because the equipment is too weak or too old or not used correctly. You are not going over that cliff again."

Aleria considered. "And if I tie the rope to the tree and just go down it hand-over-hand?"

Mito's eyes narrowed. "Then I will have it untied before you get two steps, no matter how tight you do the knot." She dove into her rucksack, came out with a paring knife. "And if that doesn't work, I will cut it."

Aleria nodded. "You're rather serious."

"I'm glad you finally figured that out. I tell you, I have seen men injured, and I will not be a party to you doing the same."

Aleria sighed and shrugged. "All right. You've convinced me." She put her back against the offending tree and slid down. "What do I do now for eggs?"

"You use hen's eggs like everyone else."

"I suppose. How boring."

Mito's attention wandered, and she strolled over to the edge of the drop-off. Then she turned back. "You went about this backwards, didn't you?"

"What do you mean?"

"You didn't find this nest, then go looking for a way to get down to it. You heard the boys talking about the rope method, and went looking for an excuse to use it."

"Sort of."

"So you didn't check all the routes."

"What routes? What do you know about climbing?"

"I've been watching you. Now there's a frightening thought." She grinned and turned her attention to the rope. "Give me a moment." With a quick flip of her wrist, the smaller girl tied the end of the rope to the tree and checked her knot with a strong tug. Then, using the friction of the rope across her lower back to steady herself, she eased down to where the ridge began to steepen, looking all the while over the edge.

21

Then she clambered back up and lowered herself on the other side of the bulge.

When she returned, she looked satisfied. "You never looked at it from the bottom, did you?"

"Of course not. It's four times as far, and steeper."

"But over on the left there is a lot of broken rock that looks like an easy scramble, and a ledge that gets you right across to the nest."

"There is?"

"Take a look."

Aleria took a turn on the rope. Sure enough, there was a route. "Looks like it might work."

"So, do you really want these eggs, or are you satisfied with your little adventure as it stands?"

"I really want them. I know I could use chicken eggs, but if I get some hawk's eggs I might be able to raise them after they hatch so I can hunt with them."

"All right." Mito pointed. "You go down into the bottom over there, where the cliff drops away. I'll sit up here in the sun and have a nice rest and enjoy the view. When you get back up to the ledge, call out and I'll throw the rope down so you can use it as a safety while you crawl along to the nest."

"You seem to have it all figured out."

"It's just an idea. You do whatever you like."

Aleria grinned, picked up her rucksack and strode away, whistling. Everyone always said ladies shouldn't whistle, but it always gave her such a lift while she walked.

She arrived some time later – hot, sweating and without the breath to whistle – at the top of the rockslide. Sure enough the ledge was a short scramble above her. She called out and sat to rest until the rope slithered down.

A faint voice came from over the top. "One more thing."

"What's that?"

"How many eggs do you really need?"

"Just one, but I'll take them all just in case."

"No. Just take one."

"Why?"

22

"You'll find out."

It wasn't worthwhile carrying on an argument at such distance, so she shrugged and started along the ledge. She walked the first part, but soon it narrowed, and she turned her face in and sidled along. The rope was almost more hassle than it was worth, catching on the overhanging rocks as she tried to flip it around them. However, mindful of her friend's warnings, she fought grimly on.

Soon the ledge narrowed even further. She could no longer stand, but she could see the nest. She lay face to the cliff, wriggling her body forward, left hand outstretched, right hand twisted in the rope.

Suddenly there was a sharp cry, and a whoosh of wind blew past her. With difficulty, she twisted her head around to see. Another whoosh, and a fury of feathers lashed at her with sharp talons, catching her sleeve and tearing the cloth like paper. The next time there was a strong tug to her pack, almost overbalancing her, and she scrabbled for a grip on the smooth rock.

This is getting serious. I have to move. Well, here goes...

She launched herself forward, ignoring scratched knees and bruised ribs, and snatched one egg from the nest. The hawk screamed again in rage and attacked, catching her hair this time, its talons tugging painfully.

"All right, little lady. I get the point. One egg."

She began to edge backwards, but she only had one hand in front to push with, and it was occupied with her treasure. Trying not to think where the egg had been, she put it in her mouth and squirmed back. It tasted foul and made her mouth water, but she determined not to swallow. As she retreated, the bird swooped past several times but did not make contact. *Perhaps birds can't count*

Once again, a faint voice from above. "How are you doing?"

She grinned around the egg and did not answer, merely flipping the rope again. Soon she was able to stand up, and she pulled the shiny-clean egg from her mouth so she could shout upward. "I'm fine. One egg. Thanks for telling me."

23

"I thought you'd figure it out. You finished with the rope?"

"It's all yours." She untied the knot and watched her safety line swing away. Suddenly the rocks below seemed sharper, farther down.

"See you at the bottom."

The rope snaked upwards. Aleria took off her knapsack, noting a couple of deep slashes across the leather flap, and placed the egg in the cotton wool she had brought. A quick scramble down through the rocks and she was striding along beside the creek, heart high.

Mito was waiting farther down. "How did you get along with Mummy?"

Aleria turned around to reveal her packsack.

"She could have pulled you right off the ledge!"

"I was holding on pretty tight." She displayed her torn fingernails. "There are equal slashes dug into in the rocks up there."

Mito merely shook her head and led the way back to the trail, Aleria following with a light step, her mind full of the swoop and soar of a hawk in flight.

* * *

After they had bathed and changed they relaxed in her study, and Aleria's euphoria faded. She strolled around the warmly lit room, waving an arm to include the comfortable lounge chairs trimmed in dark teak, the matching bookcases created by the very best of Galesian artisans. Numerous souvenirs of her travels and accomplishments lined the shelves and covered the walls.

"Just look at all this. You know, in one way you are very lucky."

"I am?"

"You're the only girl in our whole class who has a real purpose in life, a real problem to solve."

"It that's the case, I could wish I wasn't so lucky."

"No, no, you don't understand. When I take on a challenge, when I try something and then I succeed, I almost always look back on it and say to myself, 'Well, that wasn't so hard. What was the big whoop-de-do about that?' And it takes all the fun out of the success." She swept her hand around at the trophies and mementos again.

"So the girl who has everything wants more."

A pang of sorrow shot through Aleria and she stopped, her arm dropping.

Mito sprang to her feet, her hand outstretched. "That was so unfair of me, Aleria. I do understand."

Aleria shook her head and went over and sat on her swivel chair, elbows propped on her desk, staring at the garden outside the bay window. *Drooping lace curtains, bright crystal vase of cut flowers languishing on the varnished oak sill. So beautiful. So...empty.* "That's what makes it even worse. Who am I to complain? I know that it isn't fair for me to feel that way, considering all the other people and all the problems they have." She turned to her friend again. "But I do feel that way. No problems, no challenges, no way to prove myself. You know what my parents want? 'A young woman ready to take her place in society.' And why shouldn't they? They haven't done anything wrong. They love me and give me everything I need and more, and I repay them with stunts and ungraciousness.

"Not you, Mito. You had a problem from the start. You had to fight for everything and you succeeded. You must be so proud of yourself."

Mito shrugged. "I wish I could call what I've accomplished a success. Certainly, I've completed the curriculum despite what some people expected and wanted. But what now? This Cumulato is a two-edged sword for me as well, you know. I don't know what I'm going to do next, either."

Aleria felt a rush of love for her friend: so different, yet so much in tune with her thoughts and emotions.

25

"All right, you've persuaded me. I'll get Father to let you come by after the Gala. But only if you go to the party for a while first. Hana and Gita can come, too, if they want."

"How do you know your father will let them?"

She smiled and flipped her hair back. "He will, if that's what I want. Father and I have that kind of a relationship."

"I don't know if I'd like that."

"Why not?"

"He's your father, and you're supposed to have some respect for him. How can you have respect for a parent who does anything you want?"

Aleria was silent for a while. Finally she nodded. "I see what you mean. I'm sure I have respect for Father. I must. I love him dearly. Now that I think about it, he doesn't do absolutely anything I want. He gives me what I ask, as long as I don't ask for the wrong things. Sometimes I push a bit, just to see what I can get. You know, if I do get what I ask for, I always feel a little disappointed, like I'm missing something. Maybe that's what it is."

She dropped the thoughtful look. "But not this time. I'm quite pleased with the whole thing. I'll spend most of the next two weeks at home, and guess where I'll lounge around? In Father's office, where I love to be. He'll give me some of the payroll estimates to calculate, I'll tell him about those new accounting methods we learned in school, and we'll both have a lovely time. So it was definitely worth it."

She grinned over at Mito. "It was worth it just to see the look on Praetor Marmen's face when he discovered the statues. Oh, was he horrified!"

"Do you think you should have been there when they discovered it? Wasn't that risky? Someone might put two and two together."

"We had to be there. There was such a hubbub, half the city showed up. We stayed out of the front row. No one even noticed us. I just wish I were a mouse in the corner when they hear about it all being a hoax. I would like to see his face then!"

There was a long silence, and Aleria looked over to see Mito's face working. "What's wrong, Mito?"

"Well, I..."

"Come on, you can tell me. What's bothering you?"

"Well, I don't want to seem jealous or anything, but why didn't you ask me to join in?"

"I thought about it, but you wouldn't have gone."

"How do you know?"

Aleria just waited.

"All right, I wouldn't have. It would have been nice to be asked."

"Mito, you wouldn't have gone, and even knowing about it might have been a problem. Even if you would have done it, you shouldn't have. It would be too much of a risk for you."

"What do you mean for me? Why me more than anyone else? Am I that inept?"

Aleria put her arm around her friend's shoulders. "Of course you aren't inept. Whatever gave you that idea? No, I didn't dare bring you in because if anything went wrong I would never forgive myself. Now, don't get your feelings hurt. You know you can't afford to get into trouble. If I get into a mess, my father has the money and the influence to get me out. You don't have that luxury." She had always spoken casually about her friend's hardships, because she felt it made them less important, made the differences between them smaller.

Mito was silent for a moment. Then she sighed. "I suppose you're right, as usual."

Aleria slapped her shoulder. "Don't let it bother you. Think of how much strength of character you're building with all these tribulations."

"Strength of character?"

"My father's very words. You know why he was upset about letting me off? Now, try to understand this. He said that it would help my strength of character to accept responsibility for my actions. He thought this would have been good for me, but he couldn't let it happen because of political considerations. So, for the good of the family, I was going to

27

have to miss out on a valuable learning experience. Can you figure that?"

"I suppose, since you explain it so clearly."

She glanced over, relieved to see an impish grin on Mito's face. "Good for you. I didn't try to follow too closely. I was just pleased that he was letting me off."

Mito shook her head. "So even the chance for a lecture was missed. Your poor father."

"Whose side are you on?"

"You don't need any help, I don't think."

4. Challenge

Aleria's equipment bag hit the tiles of the change room floor with a clatter. "Gita, you have told me seven times this week about the Samnian silk you ordered for your Spring Ball gown." She shook out her barehand tunic. "From your description, that cloth is so beautiful, you could make a fighting smock out of it and wear it to the Ball. Couldn't you just let it rest for a while?" The moment she said it, the crestfallen look on the other girl's face made her wish she could take it back. *But really*!

"What's wrong with you, Aleria?" Twin sprang to Twin's defence as usual. "You haven't said a word for hours, and now you get insulting. Are your monthlies on the way?"

"I am not having my monthlies, Hana. There is nothing wrong with me except that I am tired of all this gabble. Gowns and teas, boys and parties, it's all just so boring." She tossed her dress over the peg in her usual cubicle, the one nearest the door. "If half of our outings came out a quarter as interesting as our chatter ahead of time pretends they are going to be, our parents would lock us up in our rooms until our hair turned grey. But they don't. They turn out to be the same old boring parties, with the same old boring boys, and the same old boring jokes being told, and not one of us with the gumption to get out and do something truly interesting."

Hana's nose came up. "And what do you consider 'interesting', since we're all so dull?"

"I don't know. Anything that doesn't involve the dubious thrill of dancing around the rules of etiquette, pretending we're going to do what everyone knows that nobody has the nerve to try."

Her friend pulled on her padded leggings and tied the laces more firmly than usual. "I suppose you think these personal defence lessons are boring as well."

"Not at first. They were quite a lot of fun at the beginning. But now I realize that when we get out on the floor, I am going to be able to beat Mito, and you can beat me, and any of the boys could flatten any of us any time they wanted, but they don't, because they have to follow the rules of the combat. If one of those mercenaries we met in the street yesterday tried to grab me, or hit me or something worse, I wouldn't have a chance of fighting back, and we all know it. Those are tough men, and the world out there is full of people like that, and some of them are *not* polite."

"I thought he handled it very well, when you ran into him at full speed. He was very polite."

Aleria hesitated, sorry she had brought up the topic of soldiers. "I had no idea there would be a whole line of them right around that corner." She rubbed a bruised rib. "He certainly was well armed. I think I caught his sword hilt or something even harder."

Hana giggled. "If he had known you were coming, it might have been something else you ran into. You should have seen the look on his face when he reached down to pick you up and realized what he was holding."

Aleria shook her head in disgust, her face heating. "There you go again with your silly jokes. He just helped me up, that's all. It was polite."

The other girls let loose a peal of laughter. "And when he realized that you were only wearing a light summer dress with very little underneath it, he dropped you so fast you almost fell down again. I never saw a man look so embarrassed."

"He was frightened, I think."

Heads turned to Gita in surprise. She was the smaller and quieter of the two sisters, but Aleria often found her ideas worth listening to.

"Frightened?" Aleria flopped down on the bench and began to lace her leggings.

"Yes, I think so. Hana and Mito were busy laughing at you, but I noticed his face. He looked straight at his sergeant, sort of putting his hands behind his back like a boy caught stealing a cookie. I think he was afraid of causing trouble."

Aleria took a final tug on the laces, then nodded. "You're probably right. Those mercenaries may be necessary because of the revolt in Shaeldit, but they aren't exactly popular locally. I imagine they have strict orders not to cause any trouble." After a subtle pause she sighed. "Too bad."

"Aleria! Whatever do you mean?"

Mito's eyes were wide, but Aleria wondered if her friend was that shocked or just putting on the expected act. "I mean that the boys we go to school with have no idea what life is all about. Those mercenaries are men, experienced men. If you met one of those soldiers on a secluded forest trail, he might do more than kiss your ear and grope at your shoulder, like Knaren did to Hana the other night after the party."

Hana giggled, but Gita looked more serious. "Yes, if you met one of those ruffians alone he might just do whatever he wanted, and leave you with a little memento for the rest of your life."

"Nonsense! There are ways of taking care of that as well. Not that I'm likely to need them, if things go the way they have been." The bitterness in her voice was only partly feigned.

Mito's face became serious. "You don't have something planned, do you?"

"Don't worry. I'm not the kind to do something stupid."

"Not the kind to do something stupid!" The other three burst into laughter again. "After all the stunts you have pulled this year?"

They bundled out onto the practice floor with the rest of the girls and continued their chatter as they warmed up. Master Ogima was not on the floor yet, leading Aleria to conclude that he was spending only the bare minimum of time with them, probably because the whole thing was worthless.

Aleria dropped to the mat and started her exercises. She was rather proud of the fact that she could do pushups and speak at the same time. "What's the point? You lot spend much more time worrying about the Arrival Reception than you do

31

on whether you're going to have any trouble completing your Quest.

"Why worry? Everyone always makes it."

"Then it's not much of a test, is it? It isn't any accomplishment to do something that everyone always succeeds at."

"You just want to make things difficult. That's easy for you. You'd make it anyway."

"Yes, Aleria," Mito was smiling, but there was a serious note in her voice, "what about the rest of us, the normal ones?"

Aleria's retort was cut off by the arrival of Master Ogima, who started with his usual remarks about them exercising their jaws too much and ignoring the rest of their muscles. She half listened, more concerned with what the other girl had just said. *'Am I that much different from the rest? I always knew I was a leader, but not different. Not that different.'* Her preoccupation kept her from making the best use of her practice time, and even the Battle Arts Master, whom she knew enjoyed working with her, asked her if she were in love or something worse.

In the changing room after practice she paid more attention than usual to the conversation of the other girls. As she came out of the shower they were going on about virginity. After a moment, she had to speak out.

"The reason you aren't having any success, girls, is that you're not really trying."

"What?" They all turned on her, not quite the effect she wanted.

"Considering the number of men out there and their general attitude towards sex, it would seem that any girl who seriously wanted to lose her virginity could manage it pretty easily. Especially anyone as pretty as you, Plendinta."

The other girl's frown showed she was unsure whether to accept the compliment or reject the challenge, as Aleria had intended. "Thank you, Aleria, but I don't see it that way. Sure, you listen to the boys talking, especially when they think we aren't listening, and you'd think they would accommodate a girl at the drop of a shoulder strap. Not a chance."

"You mean, not a chance under your terms. You don't just want sex. You want romance, with the right person. That's why you haven't succeeded."

The Plendinta's head came up. "Who are you to be telling me what's going on in my mind?"

Aleria laughed. "All right. I apologize. I was just telling you what I want. I thought that was pretty normal. Sorry if I'm not normal."

That got a chuckle from all of them.

"You're saying that if you wanted to lose your virginity, you could do it, no problem."

Aleria regarded the other girl. *Is there a setup here? Doesn't look like it.* "Probably. But I don't want to. Not just like that, for no reason."

"That's right. You want romance, the right man, the right place."

"Is there something wrong with that?"

"Not at all."

Aleria took a good look at the other girl's eyes. "But...you still don't agree. I can hear it in your voice."

"I just think it's kind of unfair, you telling us how easy it is, then making all sorts of reasons why you can't do it yourself."

Aleria laughed. "Nice try, Plendinta. You know I said nothing of the sort. I certainly didn't say I couldn't do it myself."

"So you think you could, and under your conditions."

"Sure. Take a boy like Kalmein adWoling, for example. Take a time like after the Spring Ball. And a place like the Sailor's Delight. Those would be conditions I could handle. Especially after a few glasses of the new spring wine."

Several girls sighed. Kalmein was the acknowledged heartthrob of their year, much in demand socially, even by girls two or three classes ahead. Aleria knew she had an advantage because he had always shown a preference for her, although she had never acted on the possibility.

"It's a bet, then. None of us will say anything, of course. You have free rein. If you can get him to the Sailor's Delight after the Ball, and if you can get him into one of those cosy little alcoves and use it for what it's there for, then you win. If not, then..."

"Then I lose, in several ways. Good enough!"

The other girls left at this point and Aleria, who had been too busy talking to change into her street clothes, sorted her equipment while Mito waited.

"You don't have to prove anything, you know."

"It looks like I do."

"That's not what I mean. I saw how you butted into their conversation. You usually ignore that sort of foolishness. It didn't matter what they were talking about. Whatever it was, you had to jump in with both feet."

"But you're the one who said I was different."

"You're not proving that you're one of them, you're just proving again that you're better than anyone else."

"I suppose it could be interpreted that way."

"Can you think of another interpretation for someone who always has to go one step farther, make one move grander than anyone else?"

"Am I really that bad?"

"Who said anything about good or bad? That's just you. I don't hear anyone complaining about it. Most of us accept you that way." She grinned. "We've had enough years to get used to it."

She received a clout on the shoulder for her pains. "You know, for a while there, I thought you were going to be nice. Why'd you have to go and spoil it?"

Mito shrugged. "Wouldn't want you to think you could get away with being you, without at least a token resistance from someone."

"Ah, I give up."

"I doubt it."

Aleria smiled at her friend. "I suppose not. Giving up isn't in me." She sighed, staring off down the street to where the western hills rose in gradual waves. *Wild and free, with no restrictions, no pressures to be anybody you aren't.* "But don't you wish sometimes, you could just let down and relax?"

"I can. Any time. You can't. You'd get bored and start some kind of foofaraw to liven your life up."

"I suppose you're right."

"Oh, I am. I most definitely am. And I'm going to be very interested to see how you manage to liven it up in this instance."

"At least I have guaranteed company at the Spring Ball."

"That's for sure. Although Kalmein might wonder why he's suddenly so unpopular with the other girls."

"I'll make it up to him!" She had a sudden thought. "Mito, did she set me up?"

Mito glanced at Aleria's face and sobered. "I think if there was any setting up, you did it yourself, Aleria. You don't have to do this, you know. Not if you don't want to." She paused. "Do you want to?"

Aleria shrugged. "I don't know. It sounds like a lot of fun. And I do like a challenge."

"Is it the kind of thing you should be doing on a dare? How do you think Kalmein is going to feel?"

She wiggled her eyebrows. "Oh, I think he'll feel just fine."

But her friend's face remained adamant.

"All right. I'll think about it. Honestly, I will. I won't do it if I think I'll be hurting anyone. All right?"

Mito shrugged. "It's not for me to say."

"Fine."

Mito stopped. "Does this mean you don't want me to stay overnight afterwards, then?"

"It means nothing of the sort. It's not going to change anything."

"That's fine, then."

As they walked on, Aleria reviewed the conversation. *Why do I want to do this?* At the moment, there didn't seem to be an easy answer.

35

5.   Disaster

Her father looked up from his reading as she passed through the family lounge. "So, my dear. Which fortunate young man is going to receive your attentions at the Ball tonight?"

Aleria winced inside. "Who says any specific young man is going to be that lucky?"

He smiled. "I say so. If I hadn't already known how important it was to have some designated swain at the Spring Ball, I would be enlightened by this time. It has been the subject of conversation in this household for two months."

"It has not!"

"Not when I could avoid it, it hasn't. So who is it going to be?"

"Kalmein anWoling."

"Hmm."

"Father!"

"What, dear?"

"That was hardly an enthusiastic response."

"You make your own social arrangements, my dear. I don't interfere, I don't expect to have any influence, and I don't expect to be asked for approval."

"Oh, Father. I know you don't think much of his family. But he's not that bad."

"Not that bad? Not an impassioned defence of your chosen one."

"Father!" She spun around and glared at him. "I'm not mating for life, here."

"I am glad to hear that."

She sat beside him on the sofa, frowning. "Look. This is an important social occasion, whether it means anything to you or not. Kalmein is very popular, and it will add to my status to be seen with him. He is also a rather nice, if not too intelligent, young man."

"If that's all it is, I suppose I don't mind too much."

She stood and curtsied, hiding her flush of guilt. "Thank you, Honoured Father. I am so glad you deign to approve my choice."

He smiled. "Don't be a ninny, Aleria. You know I trust you not to do anything silly. Go ahead and have a good time with your friends."

"Thank you, Father. I promise not to do anything silly."

When she thought back on it later, that conversation was what spoiled everything. Up until then, she had no doubt she was going to go through with the challenge, and was looking forward to it with great anticipation. But a tiny seed of doubt had been planted.

Still, the Ball was a great success. The huge arc of coloured lanterns over the door was a new and very impressive addition to the usual decorations. Aleria noted that the bright lights looked suspiciously Mechanical, but set the thought aside for a more appropriate time. The chandeliers sparkled, the mirrors echoed multiple reflections of swirling lace, and the men provided an upright contrast in their uniforms and formal tabards.

Aleria knew she was not the most beautiful girl there, nor was hers the most expensive or daring dress by far, although the red velvet did bring up some auburn highlights that didn't usually show in her hair. Instead of the daring scoop to the neckline that some of the girls affected, she had gone for one bare shoulder and arm, set off engagingly – at least she thought so – by the single rose at her wrist. And no beautiful girls were matched with the fantastic gowns, so she turned as many heads as anyone. Her three friends enjoyed themselves in their own styles. The Twins, as usual, had no interest in any individual, but were surrounded by their choice of young men. Aleria thought privately that Hana had rather overdone the black-and-white checks, but they certainly drew the eye to her statuesque figure. She had to admit that Gita's subdued, tight-fitting blue silk suited her slim form perfectly.

At one point in the evening, she looked around to see how Mito was doing. The girl sat off to one side, her long, dark hair drifting over her left shoulder and her soft eyes sparkling in the coloured lights. Her dress, though one of the more modest by far, had an embroidered bodice that was the envy of the more affluent girls. Only Aleria knew that Mito had done the work herself. With a start, Aleria realized that, by some standards, her friend was the most beautiful woman in the room. Not pretty. Not bold or stunning. But there was something about her...

The young man speaking to her certainly appreciated it, by the tilt of his head and the lean of his body. Then Aleria's attention was attracted elsewhere, and when she looked again some time later, Mito was alone.

Aleria raised her glass in a silent toast. Mito smiled dreamily and returned the gesture.

"How are you doing? As if I need to ask. Was that Trien who was mooning over you?"

"Don't be silly, Aleria. He's a good friend. I like to dance with him."

Aleria regarded Mito with her head to one side.

"He is! He understands!"

"I watched him, and he is definitely more than friendly. Are you sure how you feel? You're fooling somebody. I hope it isn't yourself."

The dark head tilted up. "We have had our dance, and he won't be back for the rest of the evening. Just you watch."

Aleria grinned. "Oh, well, I suppose you'll survive. In fact, I believe I see someone else glancing your way. A friendly and understanding sort of glance. "

Another young man approached, this one in officer's uniform, and Mito was swept into the dance again.

Aleria noted with satisfaction that their table was the centre of a constant eddy of the best and brightest of their class. As the evening wore on, she spent more and more time with Kalmein, finally turning down any others who wished to dance with her. It was the first time she had ever really tried to be charming, at least in such a formal context. Considering her boasting, she shouldn't have been surprised at how effective she was, but it seemed very easy, even so.

She had always flirted with Kalmein in a friendly way, and it was simple just to push it a touch farther, to allow him a bit closer each time, when before she had held him off. In response, he was becoming more attentive, ignoring the others in their party, sitting closer to her so that their thighs always touched. His arm was thrown across the chair behind her, and by leaning back she could brush her bare shoulder against his fingers at any time.

Usually the first to note the subtle changes in the crowd, she was so wrapped up in her little game that it took her a while to realize that the Ball was starting to settle. Immediately she straightened and looked around. Yes, the signs were all there.

"Time to move on, Graduates!" She clapped her hands and dragged Kalmein to his feet, managing to swing herself into the circle of his arm as she did so. "The Sailor's Delight awaits, my friends."

There was a chorus of assent and they swept from the room, conscious that their departure would signal that the Ball was as good as over.

The Sailor's Delight was a traditional spot for after-hours parties. It was just a local drinking establishment, near enough to the docks to carry a certain thrill but far enough away that few real bargemen or raftsmen ever entered. It had several "deluxe" rooms, all satin furnishings and faded gilt trim, which could be rented, with lavish and unobtrusive catering. No one ever mentioned the secluded alcoves that led off the party rooms, and couples who disappeared behind the curtains were studiously ignored.

Aleria, at the head of the group, surveyed the premises and gave her opinion, as if it made any difference. "Very nice, young man. It will suit us quite well, I think." She swept her shawl over the arm of the attendant and made a slow circuit of the room, choosing the most comfortable and central seat. It was a low divan, long and softly upholstered, and she semi-reclined against the arm in a classic pose. Patting the seat beside her, she glanced up at her suitor and smiled, ever so slightly.

He grinned and sat at the other end, leaning against the arm. "Lots of room on this one!"

Slipping off her dancing pumps, she slowly stretched her legs, one at a time. She laid her feet, not too high, not too low, in his lap. "My feet are sore, darling. Rub them, please."

His strong hands began to massage her toes, more a caress than a rub.

"Oh, that feels so nice." She slid her free foot a bit higher up his leg, wiggled it a bit. He smiled wider, worked his way up her foot, over her ankle.

While this had been going on, the others of the group had gathered on nearby lounges, chatting and ordering drinks. Aleria noted with satisfaction that every one of them was seated in such a way as to be able to see Kalmein and herself. It was time to be gracious.

"So, Plendinta. What did you think of the orchestra?"

Plendinta was the most competent musician in the class, and her good opinion of the band was necessary to acknowledge the success of any party. She smiled cheerfully. "Oh, I think they did very well. It was the usual group, you know, but I noticed a couple of additions. Did you see the percussionist?"

Several of the girls made swooning gestures. "He must have some kind of tribal background. I've never seen hands move that fast, and that dark skin, well, it's just sooo..."

One of the boys snorted. "I suppose some of you girls would call him handsome. All I know is, he put an incredible beat in to that Rambala."

There was general agreement. Talk swirled in different directions, and Aleria turned her attention to her partner. Pulling her feet from his hands, she reversed her position to lay her head on his lap instead. "What are you going to do now?" She looked up at him through partly closed lashes. He really was handsome.

"Since I've just been playing with your feet, I suppose you don't want my dirty hands messing with your face, do you?"

Sitting upright in mock pique, she managed to rest her hand farther up his thigh than was strictly necessary. His leg was firm, well muscled. "Why Kalmein, how unromantic of you!"

He raised his hands in innocence. "Just trying to keep you happy, my dear." When he lowered them, they slid down her shoulders to rest on her waist, his thumbs just under her breasts, but not quite touching them.

She leaned forward. Viewed from this angle, the bodice of her gown left little to be imagined. "Then I suppose you're forgiven." She looked straight into his eyes for a moment, then away again.

She looked back at him, seriously this time. For that one moment, when she had looked in his eyes, the game had disappeared. He was a real person, someone she had known for years. How could she go through this charade with him? Did she really want to take him into one of those perfumed alcoves, with everyone else politely and enthusiastically looking the other way?

Then his left hand, the one hidden from the rest of the room, slid upward, and she realized that he, too, was playing the game. And enjoying it immensely.

She waited just long enough to let him know that she didn't mind, then slipped away. "I have to make a little trip."

"Don't be long."

She let her fingers trail down his leg as she rose. "I couldn't bear it, darling."

In the women's functionary, she gave herself a once-over. She looked pretty good, taking into account the wavy and stained nature of the mirror. On an impulse, she slipped out of her undergarments. Tying the strings of her gown back up, she regarded her profile. Not bad, if she tied them just a bit tighter. Not too noticeable, except at close range, which was right where she wanted the most effect.

Picking up the discarded items she realized that, scanty as they were, there was no room for them in the small pouch, all

41

that the designer had allowed for a purse. She considered other alternatives: leaving them behind, putting them with her shawl...

Then she laughed. *What a ridiculous thing to be worrying about.* With a quick twist, she opened her gown and re-dressed herself. This whole evening was beginning to take on an aura of unreality. Recalling that she had actually said, "I couldn't bear it, darling," she looked around, wishing that Mito or one of the Twins was there to share it. Since she was alone, she just chuckled and headed back to her lover.

Her lover. She looked at him as she crossed the room. Could she consider this boy as a lover? In spite of his good looks and his fine evening dress, he still looked a whole lot like the kid who used to throw overripe plums at her every fall on the way home from school.

"Well, you two look pretty comfortable over there."

She grinned towards Plendinta, who was flanked by three young men. "It only gets better."

With that cryptic response, she slid back beside Kalmein, moving into the role, more aware of the audience, her hesitancy forgotten.

They chatted about nonsense while playing a delicious round of "put your hand where no one else can see," until Aleria started to feel distinctly stimulated. If she didn't do something soon, she felt that she might become indiscreet. The slight twinge that thought gave her allowed her the presence of mind to break away.

"Let's walk around a bit."

He looked into her face a moment, then grinned. "I don't think I'd better."

She looked down. "Oh. I see."

"Right. So would everyone else."

"Why don't you just sit there for a while and calm down, and I'll see what kind of wine they have." She made a show of moving casually, stopping to talk to several people on the way to the bar. There, she asked for two small glasses of a dry red wine that she especially enjoyed. Holding them carefully, she returned to their couch.

"Ready to move now?" She held his glass high enough that he had to rise to take it.

"If you'll stand in front of me."

"Not too close. I don't want to make things worse."

"Oh, don't you?"

"Not quite yet."

Laughing, they set off around the room, visiting the groups who were talking, avoiding the couples that weren't. Bottles stood on every table, and even though her glass was small, she sampled a good portion of them.

As they circulated, Aleria kept moving in a certain direction. She had been keeping her eye on an alcove, less luxurious than the rest but more secluded. She knew it was unoccupied, and that there was a group lounging a short distance away from it. As the conversation flagged where they were talking, she pulled Kalmein's arm, steered him to the back of that group. They approached casually, not attracting attention. At the last minute she tugged him aside and they slipped, unobtrusively she hoped, between the curtains.

A single, tall candle was burning on the dark wooden table, and it was difficult to see any details of the furniture, which consisted mainly of a low, wide couch of midnight blue velvet. Aware of a slight dizziness, she sat herself down, carefully placing her glass beside the candle. There was a splash of wine left in the glass, and for a moment she watched the flame flickering in its depths.

She turned and looked up at Kalmein, his face half-hidden in the darkness outside the candle's range. Why was he hesitating? "Joining me?"

"I suppose." He slid in beside her, his hands pulling her towards him, moving across her body. It was so easy to relax against him, to feel his body so close. When she tried, it seemed that her arms would not move to reach for him, but he did not seem to notice.

It was pleasant enough to feel him touching her, his hands light on her body, his lips at her ear and neck. She lay back, drifting on a current of sensation, her eyes half-closed, the candlelight flickering on the ceiling.

So this was what it was like. This was love. At least, it was lust. She knew she didn't love him, but that didn't matter. All that mattered was the feeling smouldering in her. She sighed, knew she was smiling, and hoped he would notice.

She opened her eyes a bit, focused more clearly. Kalmein's eyes were half-closed too, his face slack and vacant, and she realized with a start that the expression, in any other context, would look incredibly stupid. Did her face look like that, too? She stifled a giggle.

His eyes cleared, his face took back expression. "Is something wrong?"

She lay back again, wondering what to do. What was wrong with her? Maybe she did need a bit of persuading. It was becoming obvious that she wouldn't get through this on her own. As he pressed himself down on her, she closed her eyes and lay still for a moment, to see if it helped.

It didn't. It felt more and more as if someone was pushing her, forcing her to do what she didn't want to do. She opened her eyes.

His face, close above her, had that same vacant expression, but there was an underlying bestiality that chilled her. "Wait a minute, Kalmein."

"I don't want to wait." His knee slid between hers, his hands pulling more firmly at her gown. "You've been keeping me waiting all evening."

She twisted, her body tensing. "But Kalmein, it isn't right. I don't feel..."

He stopped moving, staring directly at her, but his eye sockets were shadowed to dark pits in the wavering light. "Listen, girl. You are not going to lead me on all night, right up to the final moment, then shut me out. You don't play that kind of trick with me!"

His hand reached behind her neck, pulled her face close to his. He kissed her roughly, pressing his lips against hers, his tongue searching.

It was too much. The dizziness was gone, leaving a queasiness in her stomach that threatened to increase, and quickly. She tried to break his hold. "No, Kalmein..."

"Yes, Aleria!" His knee jammed up into her crotch, and a jolt of pain surged through her. Then she was back on the practice floor, her hands in the proper position, her enemy unaware of the danger, just as the instructor had said. The power of her anger flared with the pain, but at the last moment she managed her rage enough to keep the blow under control. Her fists landed on either side of his neck just below the ear: not too hard, just enough to show she was serious.

A stifled shout broke from his lips, and he jumped up from the couch. He stood a moment, staring at her, his fingers massaging the sides of his neck. She had a moment of fear, then, as his anger showed. She sat up, pulled her feet beneath her. She cringed as he leaned over her, but all he did was hiss in a hoarse whisper.

"What in the name of all the Gods do you think you're doing?"

Reassured, she glowered up at him. "I said I didn't feel right."

He sneered. "You didn't feel right. You certainly made sure that I would be feeling right. What's your game, anyway?"

"It isn't a game. I just don't think it would be such a good idea." Even as she spoke, she knew how weak her words sounded.

There was a moment's silence, and she was aware of laughter and the clink of glasses from outside the curtain.

"It's just power, isn't it? You get a kick from making a man want you so much, but you're not ready to come through with your side of the bargain!"

A gush of indignation shot through her. "That is not true!"

He had calmed some, and his contempt was somehow more frightening than his anger. "Then give me another interpretation. Prove to me that you're not just a spoiled child, wanting everything, not wanting to pay for it."

How dare he speak to her like that, like she was a child! "Spoiled child? You're one to talk about spoiled children! I said I didn't feel well, and did you have any concern for me? No! All you could think of was that you weren't getting what you wanted, so you decided to take it. If I hadn't hit you, you would have, too. I know what that's called!"

His face paled, even in the ruddy candlelight, but his voice was low. "You bitch. You would lead me on like that, and then cry rape? And they'd believe you, wouldn't they, because your mother comes from one of the gods-bedamned Exalted Families. Do you know what that would do to me? I'd be ruined and my family shamed. And all so you can have your twisted fun. To think I've known you all these years, and I never suspected you were like that."

The justice of his words slapped against her, but she refused to waver. "If you're so worried about your precious little family, then act accordingly. Save your strongman act for the girls down on Lime Street, if they like that sort of thing, or if you can pay them enough to put up with it. Don't try it in polite society."

He laughed shortly. "Polite society! Look around you, Aleria. This isn't a polite place, and you knew it when you brought me here."

"I brought you here? I didn't see you hanging back any."

"No, I didn't, and neither did you. Not at the beginning. You have to admit that, Aleria."

She sighed. "Yes, Kalmein, I admit that. I was thinking, when we first came in, that maybe..." The thought was repugnant to her. "Well I was thinking about it anyway. But it didn't work out. Why did you have to be so mean?"

"Mean? I wasn't mean. I just though you wanted to be persuaded a bit more."

"You call that persuasion? It might work on a horse that won't jump a fence. I suggest you take it out of your bag of tricks for the persuading of young ladies."

46

"Somehow you keep making this sound like it's all my fault."

"Well, accept your share of the blame, then."

"Then you accept yours."

She glared at him. "We both know that a woman has the right to refuse a man at any time, and no gentleman will force his attentions on her."

He turned away for a moment, and his shoulders stiffened. Then he turned back. "Aleria, I'm going to try to be nice about this. I'm going to assume that you really do believe that you didn't do anything wrong, and that you really aren't the kind of person to play that kind of games with a man's affections. I'm going to assume that you will some day grow up and realize what you have done tonight. I have to do this, because otherwise I have to assume that you are not a very nice person, and I hope I have a better judgement of people than to get mixed up with someone like that."

Having made this little speech, he bowed. Then, with a quick motion, he tossed the curtain aside and stepped out. She heard his boot heels fading across the floor, and then silence. Then the sounds of the room started again, the murmur of voices, the sound of cutlery. Had everyone really been watching him leave?

She waited until she was certain of her composure, then left the alcove. To her surprise, the room was almost empty. All the single boys were gone. Only a few couples remained, and a small group of girls, gathered together in a corner. She knew what they were waiting for. They were silent as she approached, making no pretence of conversation, just watching her. She put on a bright face.

"So have you all finished celebrating?"

Plendinta did not respond to her smile but looked at her quizzically. "Yes. How about you?"

"I think so. Shall we depart?" She turned and walked to the entrance, where an attendant was passing out shawls.

The other girls scrambled to join her, Hana in the lead. "I think I noticed Kalmein leaving a moment ago. In a bit of a hurry?"

"Probably."

"Come on, Aleria. We're dying to know. What happened?"

She shrugged. "Oh, I lost interest. He's not..." she paused. He had treated her abominably, but he didn't deserve to have his reputation ruined. "Oh, he's just not what I was looking for. You know." She turned to Plendinta. "So you win. I lose. You happy?"

The other girl's eyes studied her for a moment. "No, I'm not happy, Aleria. It can't have been much fun for either of you."

The accuracy of the comment rocked Aleria for a moment, but she rallied with her brightest smile. "I don't know. It was pretty good for a while, there."

She spun into her shawl and skipped down the steps, hoping her laugh didn't sound too forced.

* * *

It was very late, but a yawning servant brought them a warm drink. Relaxing in their robes, the two girls lounged on their beds and summed up their evening.

"It wasn't a good situation, Mito. I don't know why, but it just didn't seem right. Why did I do it?"

"I suspect that you just got smart before you did something stupid."

Aleria sighed. "I have to agree with you there." She leaned forward. "I'm expected to be good at diplomacy, and I really messed it up. Sure, he was an idiot as well. But I'm supposed to be able to handle people. Even idiots. Why did it have to go so wrong?"

"Probably because you're young and you've never had to deal with that situation before."

"Mito, you sound like a dear auntie, forgiving me my youthful waywardness. How old are you, tonight?"

The other girl's smile was even softer than usual. "I don't know. I've just had the most beautiful evening of my life, and I didn't get into any trouble, so it's easy for me to be gracious. Can you forgive yourself? And will Kalmein ever forgive you?"

"Him forgive me? After what he did?"

"Are you being fair to him? Either you were in control, or you weren't. If you were, as you just said, and you messed it up, then you've just lost a friend."

"Kalmein and I were never friends. That was what made it easy at the beginning, but impossible at the end."

"I see, I think. So you weren't friends." Mito's dark eyes gained intensity. "But do you need to make him your enemy?"

She thought a moment, then nodded. "When you put it in that perspective, no. The next time I see him I will attempt to make amends. Is that good enough?"

Mito smiled. "You're not doing it for me."

Aleria stared at her friend for a moment. "Did you realize that you were one of the most beautiful girls there tonight?"

There was a stunned silence. "What are you talking about?"

"You were. No, not the prettiest. The most beautiful. I'm pretty; I know that. But I looked at you, and you were beautiful. Trien noticed it too. I know he did. He just didn't dare do anything about it."

"Why would you say a thing like that?"

"Because it's true. Why shouldn't you know it?"

Mito flung up her hands in surrender. "All right. You said it because it's true. Thank you. It means a lot to me to hear that you think it's true." Her hands dropped, and a smile quirked her lips. "And also because it got us off a topic that was uncomfortable to you."

It was Aleria's turn to surrender. "I should have known better than to try that with you. You must admit, it worked for a while."

Her friend laughed. "I guess."

Aleria placed a hand on the other girl's shoulder. "You still were beautiful. Don't ever forget that."

Mito shook her head. "If you say so."

"Oh, but I do! And some day I'm going to make you believe it, too."

6. Quest

In spite of her pose of disdain, on Quest morning Aleria felt a certain amount of jumpiness in her movements that no amount of willpower could control. The ceremony was simple, and the girls then climbed into the plain, hired carriages, each anxious for her own reasons to get away from the crowd. Aleria sat back on the lumpy upholstery watching the outside scenery, her mind on other things. She had drawn a longer trip to her starting point than most. Abret was a small transport hub to the south of the Goncelin River, which flowed in from the western mountains. It occurred to her to wonder how arbitrary the choices were. Would they have given her Quest to a mama's girl like Envelune, who blubbered through most of personal defence class? She thought about the other two girls sharing her ride. Both were competent, but not brilliant. They gossiped away, and she was glad that they would be getting out within the next few hours. Today of all days was not a time for chitchat.

Not that it was going to be too difficult. She might have to save a bit of extra cash for a ferry crossing or two, but her assigned route, like all the others, lay through populated farming country with enough small towns an easy day's walk apart to provide accommodation every night.

She took out her map. There was a short, probably low, spur jutting out of the western mountain range that she would have to detour around, but that was all. She wondered about the possibility of cutting across the hills. Probably slower than going around, if there was no road. Better to stick to the populated areas. Still, she would keep an open mind until she saw the terrain. Much dryer and more open than the forest they were driving through, if she remembered her Geography lessons. She leaned back, closing her eyes. Now that she was on the way the tension in her eased, and she could make up for the sleep she had lost the night before.

She awoke twice, each time to wish one of the other Questers luck as the girl descended, wide-eyed and breathing quickly, into the central square of a strange western village. A glance back, a wave, and each was gone, standing in the middle of the open space with her pack beside her, vulnerable and small.

Once Aleria was alone her sleepiness left her. She banged on the carriage wall and asked the driver permission to ride up top with him. The lean, leathery man granted it willingly, pleased to share the boredom of his job with a willing ear.

In between his far-fetched but entertaining stories she was able to squeeze out a few drops of reliable information. He travelled this route often and knew the country well.

His comment on the mountains was both optimistic and discouraging.

"Sure, there's paths through there. Lots of 'em. Too many, if you're thinkin' of cuttin' across. If you don't know your way, you could end up losin' more time than you'd save. Why I mind once…" and he was off again on another of his stories. He couldn't know that her interest was not for his exciting exploits but for the morsels of factual information that dropped through the mass of questionable plot.

By the time they reached Abret it was past mid-afternoon, but the driver was turning around immediately. "Oh, I'll get back down to Valencone before dark, no problem." He winked. "I let the ponies loose a bit when there's no passengers." Then he became serious. "You're better to stay here the night, though. The first place to the north is Charavin. That'd be, I don't know, maybe two hour's walk. Best to rest up and get a nice fresh start in the morning."

Smiling, she thanked him, tipped him the traditional coin and watched him whip up his team and head east. She looked around. Not a bad town, but no place to spend a quiet evening. There must be two hours of daylight left. If it got too dark she could always camp. Shouldering her pack, she took the road south.

After the long day in the carriage it felt good to be moving, but she was careful to keep a good watch all around her as she had been taught. The street had been deserted when she had arrived, and she was sure that few people had watched her leave. It was better that way. The sooner she slipped into the anonymity of the road, the better. She had chosen her clothing with great care – sensible shoes, medium brown, calf-length dress with a short jacket – and felt that she looked much less like a rich girl in costume than most of the others. Except Mito, of course, who seemed so comfortable in her outfit that it could almost be her own clothing, although Aleria had never seen her friend dressed like that. Aleria's one concession to comfort was a thick woollen cloak with a hood, which cushioned the bottom of her pack, ready to hand for a rainy day or a cold night camping out.

Charavin was an easy stroll along level terrain in the cooler part of the afternoon. As she approached, she decided that it was even smaller than Abret. She wondered if there would be a decent inn, then caught herself. She didn't want what her friends would call a decent inn. She wanted a cheap, safe, preferably clean place to sleep; that was all. With this objective in mind, she looked around.

In the main square, if you could call it that, there was one fair-sized place, almost as large as the two-storey, half-timber building beside it that must serve as the town hall. Sure enough, when she asked, it was twice what she could afford, and she left with regret. It had looked very comfortable.

There were just two side streets, one lined with more prosperous houses, the other deteriorating towards sheds and stock pens. She took the first, but found nothing. Returning to the lower street, she started along cautiously, trying to keep aware of everything, assessing the nature of the people she saw. To her inexperienced eye there seemed nothing threatening, so she continued.

A sign so small she might have missed it caught her attention by creaking in the breeze that warned her she was getting too close to the stockyards for comfort. No words, just a crudely painted bed. The house was a low place with tiny, deep-set windows and dormers peeking through a shaggy roof. She knew about thatch ... full of vermin and not always waterproof ... but she had to try.

To her surprise, she entered a common room that was neatly swept, if not exactly spotless. The furniture and walls were dark with age, the ceiling blackened above the fireplace. There was no one present, so she shut the door firmly. Immediately a small head popped around the door behind the bar, then disappeared.

"Maw! There's som'un here!"

"I'm coming in a moment. You go out and do what you're supposed to."

"All right."

The figure reappeared, straightening her dress and smoothing her hair. She reached the bar and stopped, her chin just above the plank top. Reconsidering, she hopped aside, dragged a bench over, and jumped up. Taller now, she stood, placed her hands on the bar with a studied gesture, and leaned forward.

"Good evening, Miss. What can we do for you?"

Aleria smiled across into the perky eyes. "I'm looking for a place to spend the night."

"I believe we might accommodate you. Will it be just yourself?"

Aleria kept her face serious. "Just me. What sort of rooms do you have, and what do they cost?"

A slight frown wrinkled the diminutive brow. "Let me see. I think the upstairs left would do. The price? Now let me see." A rather grubby set of fingers tugged a straw-blonde pigtail. Then the girl shot Aleria a shrewd glance. "What were you expecting to pay?"

So it was going to be a bit of a game. "Well, I don't have that much. I was sort of hoping to find a nice, clean room, it wouldn't have to be too big, for about half a crown." She watched, noted the girl's reaction. "With supper included, of course."

The girl retained her poise, but her eyes were jumping. "I'm afraid I'll have to check that with the propri...etress. Just wait here a moment, if you please." A flash of flying braids, and the "innkeeper" disappeared round the doorpost. After a patter of hurried feet, she could hear a jumble of whispers, coming closer and getting louder. Finally the girl reappeared, a small, stout woman in tow.

"Now, Mirette. What kind of a lady do you say..." The woman stopped, looked Aleria over, seemed to look again. "Oh. I see."

She stepped forward smiling. "Good to see you here, young lady. I'm sorry I couldn't be out to greet you."

Aleria nodded in return. "Oh, your assistant did an admirable job. Would you have a room at that price?"

The woman shook her head. "Not a room for one person. I think you'd have better luck finding your sort of room back up near the square."

"I already looked up there. The inn on the square was much too expensive. I want something a bit plainer, I'm afraid."

"Oh. We...we don't have too many places in town..."

She wondered why the woman hesitated. "Well, then, what kind of room do you have, and what is the price? I don't have to have supper."

Then the woman smiled in realization. "No, no. I don't mean that. I mean...well, our rooms with supper are a quarter crown. With breakfast in the morning, and a good one, if I say so myself, who cooks it."

"I guess I should take a look at this room, then."

"If you wish. Right this way."

There was a harsh whisper. The woman leaned her head down to listen, then nodded. They started up the stairs, the small girl leading the way with her head up, her braids bobbing. At the top, the hallway was close under the ceiling, as high as a tall man. The girl turned down the short passage and threw open an even lower door.

"This way, if you please."

Sharing a hidden smile with the mother, she ducked into the room. It was small and the ceiling sloped to halfway down the window, but the floor was swept and the coverlet on the bed looked clean. Not that it mattered, since she could always wrap up in her cloak. Her small hostess turned down the cover and bounced on the bed, which seemed firm enough for her weight at least.

"So what do you think, Miss?"

Getting a confirming nod from the mother, she turned to the young hostess. "The room seems fine. Now, what about supper?"

"The supper will be fine, of course. We have a very good cook."

"And what's on the menu?"

"I will consult. Mother?"

"Stew and bread, just like you helped me put on the hearth an hour past."

With a look of disgust for her mother's lack of discretion, the girl turned to Aleria. "My mother's stew is always very good. Plenty of big meat chunks, and the vegetables cooked just right, not all mush like some people make. She is also a dab hand with the spices." This last must be a quote from somewhere, and Aleria again had to fight to keep a straight face.

"It sounds great to me. I think I'll stay."

The girl's eyes sparkled, and it looked as if she could hardly keep her feet still. "Very good. A quarter crown, then." She looked to her mother, received some sort of prompt. "And what name shall I put down, Miss?"

"Aleria. Um...Aleria Dalmyn.

With a glance to her mother to make sure that someone would help her with the spelling, she skipped out of the room, leaving the two women helpless with suppressed laughter.

The older woman found breath to speak. "Pleased to make your acquaintance, Miss Dalmyn. I'm Tamina Bouchage, and your elegant hostess is Mirette, my daughter.

"She's doing a fine job."

The mother held her hands in a helpless gesture. "She's nine."

"Well, she'll be a formidable assistant when she hits twenty."

The mother smiled. "I'll leave you to settle in, then." She indicated the wash table and basin. "I'll send Mirette up with water so you can get the road dust off. Have you come far today?"

"Only from Abret. I started late."

"Ah." From the tone, it seemed that this explained something. The woman turned in the doorway. "You can eat any time after you wash. No need to rush, though. Supper won't be busy tonight. Just a few regulars."

The woman left, and Aleria was alone in her room. She investigated as she had been taught, checking the window for security as well as use for a fire escape. No problem there. It was too small for anyone dangerous to get in without a fuss, but large enough for her to get out and slide down the thatch to where it came within her own height of the ground. Satisfied with the window, she tested the bed. It was solid enough; it had no springs, only boards with a straw mattress. The coverlet and sheet were clean, but she knew she would be happy to have everything beneath her for padding and use her own blanket next her skin.

She lay back on the bed, gazing around the little room. Not too bad a start. Probably lucky, though. Take the same space, give it several months of bad management, and it would become a foul hole. She doubted if many establishments at this price were this clean. Going on the basis that nothing was ever perfect, she glanced around. The inside latch on the door looked sturdy enough. No lock, so she would have to take her valuables with her. Not a serious problem, as she was well prepared, with a hidden pocket for money and an inner purse in her coat.

So she had offered too much the first time. Well, an understandable mistake, one that she wouldn't repeat. At a quarter crown, she could afford places like this for most of the trip.

She was interrupted in her musings by a knock on the door, and the straw-haired girl staggered in, a jug of water steaming in her hands. She was barely able to lift it to the tabletop, but she managed. Then she stood back proudly. "Will there be anything else, Miss Dalmyn?"

"Do you usually supply towels?"

Uncertainty clouded the brow. "I don't think so, Miss. Would you like me to check?"

"No, I'm sure that if you did, there would be one here. I have my own. That's all I need. Thank you very much, and tell your...tell the kitchen I'll be down for supper in a moment."

The lips were working, and Aleria realized that the girl was trying the phrase, "tell the kitchen" a few times. She schooled her expression, nodded in response to the bob of a curtsy, and then she was alone again.

It took her longer than expected to tidy up and arrange her belongings to her satisfaction, so her young hostess was skipping with anticipation as Aleria entered the common room. She played along to the hilt, allowing herself to be escorted, seated, arranged and pampered. Clean linen appeared from somewhere, in spite of the fact that none of the other diners had anything of the sort. She exchanged smiles with the patron at the next table, an aged but formally dressed man who might be a clerk of some sort. He must be a regular, and seemed to enjoy watching the little girl bustling about.

"You're getting real service tonight, Miss."

She shook her head. "I guess I can't complain. It's better than I'm used to."

He eyed her a moment, then returned to his meal.

As she ate, Aleria scanned the other diners, but all three were intent on their fare, which was wholesome but plainly spiced. The jug of light ale she tasted first and set aside. Later she tried again and found that, while bitter by itself, it suited the meal well enough.

After Aleria had eaten and her waitress had bustled the dishes away, the landlady came out of the kitchen to survey the room. Satisfied that everyone was taken care of, she strolled over to Aleria's table. "Do you mind if I sit and talk awhile?"

Aleria slid her jug aside, motioned to the opposite chair. "I'd be happy to chat. Perhaps you can give me details of the road north."

"I'd be glad to, but it would be better if you wait. My man's coming down from Sermerey tonight, should be in any moment. He'll have the newest news, so to speak."

"Good enough. So your daughter is fixing to run the place, is she?"

"Oh, yes. A regular little organizer. Always has been. It's only lately that I've allowed her to deal with strangers, so she loves to practice."

"She's been getting a real workout on me. I hope you don't mind, I've been sort of gently giving her hints as to how to do things."

"Mind? I should hope not! I'll be thanking you. I do my best, but it's not often she'll get the chance to practice with a true lady."

"True..." her protest was cut off by the woman's knowing smile. "How can you tell?"

"A lot of little things. For example, not many girls of my class, even with the money to have your haircut and manicure, would know or care to have such a subtle touch around the eyes. I worked in the big houses when I was a girl."

Aleria nodded. So her disguise wasn't too obvious. Still, the eye makeup would have to go. "Do you get many like me here?"

"On their Quest? No, not usually. We're too close to Abret, where they always start, and they usually stay there the first night. Even at that they don't stop here. Most use the inn up on the Square."

"I asked there. If I stayed in a place like that every night, I would run through my allotment about half way."

The woman smiled. "Then maybe they learn as they go along." She glanced sidelong at Aleria. "Although I don't suppose there's many going by with only their allotment on them." Her look became questioning.

"I must admit I have some emergency money hidden away, but not much, and I certainly don't plan to use it. That's for real emergencies, not for a better inn."

"Good for you. I can see you've entered into the spirit of the thing. Not all do, from what I've heard."

They were interrupted in their chat by a squeal of delight from the far corner of the room. "Show me again! I don't believe you did that. Show me!"

The landlady turned a wry smile on her guest. "I think our young hostess has forgotten her proper deportment." She rose slowly from the bench, and Aleria realized that the woman must be tired, if she had been cooking and cleaning since before breakfast. "I had better get back to my own duties. It was a pleasure to talk to you, Miss Dalmyn. I'll send my husband over when he gets in, to let you know about the roads."

Aleria thanked her and allowed her eyes to stray to the daughter, who was being entertained by a young man in the corner. He was doing some kind of magic trick, making a card appear and disappear. He looked tall and big-boned but not clumsy; his hands moved smoothly through the routine. His clothes were rough and a bit dirty, although he was clean-shaven and his hair was almost neat. He showed the trick again with high good humour and then slid the deck away, scooting Mirette back to the bar with a wave of his hand. As she left, his head came around and he caught Aleria's eye, smiling and nodding to her. She nodded back, then looked elsewhere. She had been taught about the danger of making eye contact, but he was evidently known and trusted to some degree by Tamina, judging by her lack of reaction to his byplay with her daughter.

Then their attention was distracted by a clattering in the street outside, and Mirette scooted out the door, waving madly. The man on the cart outside saluted her with his whip as he pulled into the yard. The innkeeper had returned.

A few minutes later he entered the common room, a short, smiling man with a curly, black beard, trimmed neatly. Introduced by his daughter, he welcomed Aleria politely, and she invited him to join her and tell her about the road north.

'I'd be pleased, Miss, but there's not much to tell. Firm and dry the whole way through to Sermerey, and I'd guess a good way past. A bit rough for the cart, but you won't be troubled by that if you're walking. 'Course, you might pick up a ride with a carter if you're out of here at a decent time in the morning. Least as far as Magnin. After that, there's less traffic and you'll probably have to walk it."

"I'm planning to walk most of the way," she grinned, "unless I find out I'm not as tough as I thought. I can actually make better time than the average loaded cart. I've tried it with my father's horses. I just don't know whether I can keep the pace all day."

"So your father does cartage, does he?" She could see the man's scepticism.

Her head went up. "Among other things. I won't say I harness teams or clean tack, but I've handled a quad rig on city streets, and I can back a four-wheeler into a tight shed if the team isn't too skittish."

His hands went up in defence. "I'm sorry, Miss. I didn't want to seem disrespectful. We don't see many young ladies like you around here."

"Are we that conspicuous?"

"Oh, no. At least not you. Country people pride themselves on being able to spot a Quester the moment she walks into the room. I wouldn't have picked you out unless my wife had told me."

"Good."

The innkeeper shook his head. "Might not be so good, Miss."

She made a wry face. "In other words, it would be much easier for me if I was obviously a Quester, because people would treat me better."

He glanced at her and frowned. "Is there something wrong with that?"

She leaned her elbows on the table. "Tell me. What do you think the Quest is for?"

He was taken aback for a moment. "I never really thought about it. I guess it's sort of a Cumulato ceremony."

"A ceremony. Not a test."

"Test? I suppose it might have been once..." He seemed reluctant to go on.

"But it has long ago lost any resemblance to a test, because it's so easy."

The man shrugged his shoulders. "Well, we are so much more civilized, these days."

She laughed. "You don't have to sound apologetic about it. I'm sure there are enough rough spots around that some of the girls will find it quite a challenge. Some of my class would find it difficult to even think of sleeping under a thatched roof. Why, a spider might pounce on them!"

He chuckled as well. "I don't know, Miss. Have you ever rolled over in bed and squashed a big spider?" He shivered. "They make quite a mess."

"I haven't had the pleasure. I guess this trip has some surprises in store for me." Then she became serious. "But tell me. If I'm not that obvious, how is it likely to be different?"

He considered a moment. "A girl of my class might be travelling alone, just from village to village, and thus known by most people in the area. A stranger with a pack is unusual, but not unheard of. As I said, we're pretty civilized in this neck of the woods. Nothing like they are down South."

She shuddered but did not respond, and he went on. "Nobody would touch you around here, because the local townspeople would string him up for it. However, you might lose your money to a pick-pocket or get pulled into any number of swindles if you're foolish enough to fall for them."

"Which ones have been doing the rounds lately?"

"The fact that you know to ask means that you're halfway there already."

"I listened in class, that's all."

"You took a class in how to spot swindles?"

"They don't send us out completely unprepared, you know."

He raised his eyebrows, but did not comment further. "Well, there's a bunch of gypsies around lately with a beggar kid. She looks all bent up and crippled, but if she has to she can run like the wind. I noticed her when she stole an apple in Magnin the other day. And there's a woman in Walibi who tells a sorry tale about being beaten by her husband and having to run away with nowhere to go. Problem is, she takes her 'earnings' home every night to her husband and the lazy sot drinks them up."

"The best swindles always have a bit of truth in them."

He nodded. "You do have some training, I can see that."

"Those sound relatively harmless. Any serious dangers?"

He thought again. "There was a pedlar had his pack stolen between here and Drummetar last spring, never found it, but we figgered it was somebody travellin' through got it." The man looked at her, grinned, "Fact is, there was a joke that one of the Questers took it. The poor fellow who lost it didn't like to hear that. Made him look a proper fool."

She shook her head. "We're just a joke to you people, aren't we?"

His face was immediately contrite. "No, Miss, not at all..."

She looked him straight in the eye. "'Not at all...' but what? What can you say? I bet that, to you people, the Quest is just another sport the Ranking Classes play, like hunting, except it's less objectionable because nobody crashes their horse through your farmyards or tramples your crops. I bet you rather like it, because it makes you a bit of money, with more travellers going through. In fact, as you said, it's a bit of a game for you, trying to spot us, but a bit important as well, because it could go pretty rough for a town if one of us came to grief there."

The man did not respond, his eyes wary, and she smiled reassuringly.

"I don't mind. In fact, you don't even have to answer. The look on your face is enough to tell me that I'm right. I suspected it before I came, I've been on the road half a day, and it's already obvious."

He shrugged, held up empty hands. "I don't know what to say, Miss. I wouldn't put it quite so harsh as you do. You have the right idea, but it isn't all bad, you know. If you think we treat it as a sport, I suppose you're right, but we enjoy it, too. We like to help out a bit, sometimes. We're proud that you go through our town. I'm proud that you stayed at our inn."

"And I've given you tales to tell for weeks."

He grinned. "Months, Miss. I bet no one's never heard any Quester talk like this," his smile disappeared, "unless you don't want me to say anything. I wouldn't want to get you in trouble."

She laughed aloud. "Master Bouchage, I don't think anything you could repeat about this conversation could get me into near as much trouble as I've jumped into many times, all by myself, with no help from anyone else at all."

He shook his head. "Come on, Miss. I'm sure you're not a trouble-maker!"

"And I'm sure you're not a good liar. You're an intelligent man and a good enough judge of character to have me figured out better than that."

He scratched his head and his smile disappeared. "I don't think I'll respond to that one, Miss. If you're as bad as you say you are, I'd just get into more trouble."

She laughed again. "Good choice. Now tell me more about the roads north."

He went on with his description until the evening customers started arriving and he was too busy to talk. She went to bed early, her long day taking its toll. As she left the common room she saw that the rough young man had departed. She smiled to herself. *Maybe he really is a magician and he made himself disappear.*

The bed was harder than she had expected, and with all the things she had to think about, she did not sleep for a long time. At least she wasn't joined by any spiders big enough to notice.

7. A Companion on the Road

It was later than she had intended when she buckled up her pack, made her final room sweep, and clumped down the narrow stairs to the common room. The only occupant was the magician from last night, looking as if he had slept in his clothes: in the stable, by the straw in his hair. He looked straight at her, and she nodded as she crossed to her table. He grinned back before she could break eye contact and banged his mug on the table.

"Mirette, she's come down!"

The small head appeared, disappeared, and returned, hidden behind a cloth-covered tray. "Fresh scones and tea, Miss!"

"They smell wonderful, Mirette. Did you make them?"

The little girl's eyes glowed. "I helped. Mother made sure I put in all the right things, but I stirred them all up, and I cut them and put them in the pan, too."

Aleria crunched into the crust, just catching a dribble of butter that tried to escape down her chin. She nodded in appreciation. "Very good, Mirette."

The girl beamed.

"Hey, Mirette, how about some of those for me?"

A small frown appeared on the girl's face. She turned to the other guest. "I don't think you get breakfast for a penny, Rheety."

"Aw, come on, my darlin'. Just one of the fancy lady's scones would set me on the road so happy."

The chin came up. "I will ask the kitchen."

As she marched away, the young man caught Aleria's eye and winked. She couldn't help but smile.

"Are they as good as they look?"

"Oh, yes. There's nothing like cooking in a stone oven to make them crisp like this."

"Great. She'll get me one, just you watch."

"Another of your magic tricks?"

"You noticed."

"You held the card behind your hand, between your fingers."

"All right. I'm only practising. Fooled Mirette."

"So you fooled a nine-year-old. Well done."

"It's just in fun."

Considering his clothing, and noticing that he didn't seem to be going off to work anywhere, she wondered how much of it was just in fun.

He stared right back, appraising as well. "So...you headed north?"

"That's right."

"Hmm. Like some company on the road?"

She looked him over again, considered the possibilities. He was known by these people, and she could make sure they were seen leaving together. "Are the roads well-travelled between here and Sererey?"

"Sure. No worry about being out on a lonely road with strangers, this area."

"I wasn't thinking about strangers."

He thought a moment, grinned. "You mean me? I'm pretty harmless."

"I'd like to think that."

"So shall we stroll along together?"

"If you can keep up."

"Right." He leaned back, satisfied, to wait for the promised treat. Sure enough, soon Mirette appeared with one small scone, a dab of butter in the middle, all alone on a large plate. She brought it to him with ceremony and he received it with dignified thanks, spoiled by another wink at Aleria over the girl's head.

"Are you finished, then, Miss?"

Aleria nodded, and the Mirette cleared the dishes, returning to scrape the last crumb away with a rag. "Will you be travelling on today, Miss?"

"Yes, I will. Should we settle up, now?"

"I will call the proprietress."

With precise steps, the little girl paraded behind the bar and out the door. Then the patter of running feet could be heard, and a call of "She's leavin', Maw."

Aleria waited at the bar, and soon Tamina appeared, drying her hands on a towel.

"Sorry to pull you away, but I have to get moving."

"Right. Looks like a nice day for walking. That kind of cloud seldom sends rain. Too thin." As she was making change for Aleria's crown, she noticed Rheety, standing with his pack at the door. "Company on the road?"

Aleria raised her eyebrows, received a non-committal shrug. She nodded. Probably no trouble, but it was up to her. Fine.

She said her good-byes to Tamina and Mirette, making sure that the little girl knew that the penny tip was for "service". Then she shouldered her pack and swung out through the door, which Rheety held gallantly open for her.

As they were leaving, Master Bouchage appeared around the corner of the inn. He, too, wished her a polite good-bye, but as he passed Rheety, he laid a hand on the boy's shoulder, spoke a few quiet words.

Aleria stood sideways, turned back enough to notice the glance her companion gave her, the sudden dropping of the shoulders, the nod. Then he moved towards her, and they strode off down the street.

It was a fine day, cool enough to walk at good speed, and they were soon out of town. She used the time to practise her story of a middle-level carter's family, and her journey to visit an old aunt in the south. They chatted on as travelling companions do, and she wondered, with a wry smile to herself, how much truth she was getting in return.

That made her remember her caution, and she dropped her own little games in order to make a better assessment of her companion. She listened, prompting him occasionally, and he talked on. Finally, she came to the conclusion that he had no legitimate occupation.

The possibilities of how he actually supported himself were just starting to occur to her when she realized how isolated the terrain was. The small farms bordering the road had given way to a deeper forest, and their way wound through a series of low hills. There were few other travellers, and she began to realize how large and tough looking her companion was.

However, he walked on at her side, chatting on, and soon she was relieved to see a line of smoke rising from the trees ahead and the fields of a small farmstead opening up on either side of the road. Glancing surreptitiously at Rheety, she noted the long knife at his belt, the scar that peeped over his ragged collar. This was no gentleman, she was sure. Yet he had offered her no harm. She was just lucky.

Or a good judge of character. She studied him again. A very tough young man, she decided. Maybe it wasn't luck, after all.

"You know, when we were leaving the inn this morning."

"Yeah?"

"When the innkeeper took you aside?"

"He did? Oh, yeah, I guess, yeah."

"What did he say to you?"

"Nuthin'. Just good mornin', have a nice trip."

"That was all?" She stopped, forcing him to turn and face her. "Nothing about me?"

"Not really." He walked on, but not before she saw the look in his eye.

She thought back to the incident, how Bouchage had glanced her way, then spoken to her companion. Then Rheety's quick reaction, staring at her, then turning away when he saw she had noticed. Had he been warned? It was possible.

"Rheety, I have to know."

She had stopped again, and he retraced his steps to her. "What's all the fuss about a friend sayin' good-bye?"

"I don't think that was all he said. Did he say something about me?"

He grinned, with a bit of relief, she thought. "Aw, don't be worried. You're not gonna run into any trouble from that guy talkin' about you. Just the opposite, I figure."

"What do you mean?"

"Look, we ain't gettin' anywheres standin' here. If you're tired, sit down. If you wanta talk, let's walk."

He started out briskly and she followed him for a moment, then hurried up beside him. "So he really did warn you."

He looked down at her, then away. 'Now, why would he warn a big fella like me about an itty bitty girl like you?"

"I don't know. That's why I'm asking."

He walked on in silence.

She had to know. "Do you know who I am?"

"Of course. Aleria. You told me."

"What else?"

He held his eyes steadfastly away from her, but she kept the pressure on. Finally, he glanced at her. "You're one of them Candidate girls, makin' that Quest thing to the Citadel."

"And that's what he told you?"

"Yeah." He shook his head, looked at her more directly. "Don't know why I didn't figger it myself. I've seen that type before, everybody has. Just they don't dress like you, don't act like you. I thought you was a tradesman's daughter or somethin'."

She smiled. "Why, thank you. That's what I was trying to do."

It was his turn to stop, facing her earnestly. "Well, it wasn't a good idea."

"Why not?"

"Because as long as everybody knows who you are, you're not gonna have any trouble. Everybody knows that they keep their hands off the Questers. You bother one of them, and like as not there'll be the father with twenty or thirty men come lookin' for you. A town gets the reputation for bein' too rough, they change the routes and you lose the business. Nope, you leave the Questers alone, you don't want a whole heap of trouble for yourself and everybody else to boot."

"So I can wander around here, safe as the streets back home."

His lip wrinkled slightly as he resumed walking. "I wouldn't say that. There's always them as don't care, or think it's a challenge. Or maybe they're so stupid they think they won't get caught. I wouldn't just wander along with my eyes closed, if I was you."

She nodded. "Thanks for the warning. It's important for me to do this right, you know. That's why I dressed so carefully."

He seemed interested, and for a while she chatted on, telling him about her life at school, about which he was interested, but had little idea. After a while a thought entered her head.

"You thought I was a tradesman's daughter, did you?"

He shrugged. "Somethin' like that."

"And if I had been, what then?"

"Whattaya mean?"

"You know what I mean. The innkeeper warned you. What were you going to do that you shouldn't?"

"Nuthin'."

"I'm sure."

He was silent, and for a while they walked along, unspeaking. Aleria knew that if she waited him out, he would give in. It had happened before. Sooner or later he would tell her. Sure enough, after they had passed another farm he cleared his throat. Time for a nudge.

"Look, Rheety. I'm on this Quest to learn things. If no one tells me anything, how am I going to learn?"

He considered this a moment. Then he turned to her, his palms upward. "I wouldn't have done nothin' bad, you realize. I mean, I'm not no murderer or nothin'. Just that, well, maybe if she's a tradesman's daughter, and goin' a ways, then maybe she'd have some money or jewels, or a nice length of cloth in her pack."

"So you would take whatever opportunity passed your way."

"Right. And then, if I got tired of her company, I might just disappear with somethin'. I wouldn't hurt her or nothin' like that." He grinned. "In fact, if I liked her, and she liked me, there's no tellin' what we might get up to. Only if she was willin', you understand."

He glanced over at her, noted her smile. "Well, it ain't completely unusual, you know, a girl findin' me attractive."

"No, no, I'm sure it isn't."

He walked a little faster, his back straight. "Yeah, it ain't unusual at all. And not only the servant girls, neither."

"Rheety, you've been straight with me, and I'll be straight with you. Put that thought right out of your mind."

"Hey, I can take a hint."

"Evidently."

"What?"

"It's not important."

"You know, you talk kinda funny."

"I don't speak exactly like you do. But I think we get the ideas across."

He grinned ruefully. "Well, you sure do, anyways."

She laughed. "Oh, Rheety. I'm so sorry I spoiled your fun. You don't have to keep walking with me, you know. As you have pointed out, I'm perfectly safe. You can go back and look for some cute little farmer's daughter with a chicken in her basket for you to lift."

"Aw, I don't think so."

"Go on. Maybe you'd get to lift more than the chicken."

He was silent, and she realized that he was blushing. After a moment he glanced at her. She was careful to be looking straight ahead.

"Nope, I think I'll keep along with you. I was thinkin' of goin' to Sererey anyways. And it's not that safe, you know. I told you. And there's bears and the like, too. Not often, but once in a while. And I like talkin' to you. It's different."

"I imagine. Well, it's different for me, talking to you. So I guess we can travel along together a bit longer."

"Suits me."

"Suits me."

It was a long, dusty walk, but the afternoon passed quickly in Rheety's company. He opened up as they went along, describing his childhood, which she could barely credit, his parents, whom she could hardly imagine, and his present life, which didn't sound half so much fun as he tried to present it. As far as she could gather, he was a seasonal labourer, picking up any work he could, trying to keep himself alive and independent. He made decent wages in the winter when he went logging in the north, but the summer was more difficult. Or he didn't try that hard. He would stoop to petty thievery if the occasion presented, but didn't consider himself an outlaw by any means.

Reaching Sererey, she found a strange reluctance to part from him, her first friend of the road. "Where are you going to sleep?"

He shrugged. "I got plenty of friends here. Where you're goin' to sleep is much more important. I know an inn. Just off the road, so it's not so expensive, but real clean and respectable."

He led her to a fine little place, a bit more costly than she would have chosen, but within her budget. Supper was included, and she invited him to share the meal with her, but he looked around, hesitated, then refused.

"Thanks a lot, Aleria, but I better be goin'. I gotta look up those people, make sure they're home, get me somewhere that suits me. You have a good sleep, so you can make good time tomorrow."

"So I won't be seeing you again?"

He tilted his head from side to side. "Maybe, maybe not. I figure you'll be up and gone before I even wake up." He grinned. "After all, we made it a good hike today. I'm gonna be tired."

"All right, then. Thank you ever so much for your company. I really enjoyed talking to you. Learned a lot."

He shuffled his feet, and she thought again how easy it was to embarrass him. "Good-bye, then, Aleria. Thanks for the company. Sure made the day go fast."

"Good-bye, Rheety. See you on the road somewhere."

He smiled, nodded, then turned away. She watched him go, his head high, and he didn't look back. Finally, she turned and went into the inn, feeling lonely.

8.   Reward for Hard Labour

The feeling of wellbeing that returned with the morning sun lasted all through the following day and well into the next, when a rain shower soaked her as she stood, undecided, at an unsigned fork in the road. Unfolding the sketchy map they had given her, she tried to protect it from the water that ran off her sleeves while she puzzled it out. There was nothing to indicate which way she should take. She knew she should be able to get to Dargilan by evening, but that was all.

With a shrug, she stowed the map and chose the road that looked like it might be used more often. As she walked along, she tried to relate this road to the one she had been travelling, and it seemed about the same, though a bit narrower. She resolved to ask someone.

She passed several small farms, but there seemed to be no one around. Then she saw a figure working in a field ahead. She would ask him.

As she got closer, he turned and worked his way up the next row of corn, hoeing with slow determination. By the time she reached him, he was far up the row, and it seemed a shame to ask him to come all the way back to speak with her. She waited to see if he would notice her and turn, but he didn't. She couldn't wait forever; she walked on.

There was no sign of life at the next few farms, and she was beginning to wish she had spoken to the first man. At the next place, she saw a man with a dog, herding a flock of sheep into a pen. He waved in a friendly fashion when she stopped to watch, but he was so far up the hillside she couldn't ask him to come down, and she didn't want to go up and disturb his flock while he was working them, so after leaning on the fence for a brief rest she continued.

There were no more farms for the next half hour, and she was getting quite upset at herself. If she was on the wrong road and she had walked all this way, merely because she was

73

too shy to talk to a peasant, then she probably deserved it. She resolved to speak to the next person she came across. The rain had stopped, and now the sun was doing a good job of drying her clothing, so her optimism returned.

This next person proved to be a wizened old woman sitting in her doorway in the sun, peeling potatoes with a well-worn knife. Her house was very near the road, and Aleria strode around the corner and came upon her quite suddenly.

"Oh. Hello." *That was creative, Aleria.*

"Hello, dearie." The woman's smile seemed vague.

"Nice day."

"Nice day, isn't it?"

Aleria nodded. "It is."

The woman nodded as well. Was she simple, or just hard of hearing? One way to find out.

"Is this the road to Dargilan?"

The woman's head tilted, eyes squinted a bit, and Aleria realized that she was standing so that the sun fell over her shoulder on the woman's face. She moved to the side and tried again. "Dargilan. Where is Dargilan?"

The old head nodded. "Dargilan."

"That's right. I'm going to Dargilan." She made walking motions with her fingers, mimed uncertainty, up the road or down.

A toothless smile was her reward. "Dargilan's that way." The knotted hand holding the knife rose, pointed back down the road.

Aleria sighed.

But then the smile got wider, and the hand swung "And Dargilan's that way."

"Pardon me?" She mimed again, spoke even louder. "Dargilan? That way?" She pointed the other way "Dargilan? That way?"

"That's right, dearie. You can get there both ways."

"Ah."

"If you go back down to the main road, where you just came from, and turn right by the big clump of cottonwoods, that'll get you to Dargilan." The weathered hand swung back. "But if you go up over the pass, there, through the pine forest, it's a steeper road, but much shorter."

"I see. Shorter but steeper. "

"Shorter but steeper. So it all depends on how much energy is left in those young legs of yours."

"I think there's still a bit." The old woman was watching her lips, and Aleria decided she must be hard of hearing. Once she started she had no lack of words.

"Then you go over the pass through the pine woods, dearie, and you'll be in Dargilan by suppertime."

"Are there any turnings I need to know about?"

"What's that, dearie?"

She mimed a join in the road. "Turnings. This way, that way?"

"Oh. Turnings." the old eyes roamed upwards as the woman thought. "Yes, just after the top there's a single trail to the east. Don't take that one. Keep to the cart track and you'll be fine. Once you get down along the river, though, take the first bridge, the one on the left. You can cleave to the right bank as well, but the left side is the shady side, and you'll be warmed after hiking the pass."

"Thank you." There was a pause. Aleria tried to think of anything to say.

"Have a nice walk, then, dearie."

"Thank you. Have a nice day."

"Thank you. So far I have." A brief, cackling chuckle. "The way I see it, any day my toes are above the sod is a nice day."

Aleria smiled, raised a hand in farewell, and strode away.

The track became steeper and soon she was slowed down to one foot in front of the other. She had discovered that on the hills the shorter steps she took, the easier it was, so she schooled her impatient head and let her aching legs control her pace. It was better in the shade of the pine forest, where the spicy scent of the trees filled her nostrils. She peered off into the depths behind their dark trunks, rank on rank, but her eyes could not pierce the dimness.

The pines thinned as she reached the top of the pass, and the last part of the climb was out in the blazing sun again. The idle thought came to her that perhaps the old woman wasn't quite right in the head and had just told her what she wanted to hear. Perhaps she was going to have to climb this mountain, climb down, find herself stuck, then climb back over it and walk all the way back to the other road.

Next time she wouldn't be so slow to ask directions.

It was with supreme relief that she crested the last small rise and saw the road begin to drop before her. She mopped her streaming face, took one more swig from her canteen and looked around for some shade. There was none, so she started downhill, placing her feet carefully on the rough track. The mountains around her weren't high, but their dry, rocky faces were uninviting. Not a place to spend the night. She looked for the next landmark.

Sure enough, a narrow path soon branched off to the east, and her doubt in the old woman diminished. When she reached the bottom of the valley and the road again divided, she was confident to cross the old stone bridge and swing along beside the stream in the shade of the trees that grew there.

The sun had just begun its final slide down into coolness when she saw the outskirts of the village. Realizing her condition, she glanced around to make sure she had no company, then left the road, dropping her pack beside the stream and using her headband to give herself a quick going over. There was no water still enough to see her face, so she wrung out the headband and stretched it around her tousled hair again. She wasn't in any competition for style and beauty anyway.

Refreshed at least, she swung up her pack and marched into the town. True to her new resolve, she stopped the first decently dressed woman she saw. "Excuse me, Ma'am, but could you tell me of a reasonable inn, not too expensive?"

The woman, a middle-aged, portly type in a good quality cotton skirt and apron, smiled. "There's several choices, young lady. How much were you planning to pay?"

Aleria shrugged. "I've been getting by quite well on a quarter crown, back up the road."

"Have you come far today?"

"Only from Magnin, but I couldn't figure which fork to take, back at the big cottonwood clump, you know?"

"I know the spot. And you came over the mountain."

"It's hot up there."

The woman regarded her with a faint smile. "You have a problem, then. Warm day like this, a hike like that, I imagine you'd enjoy a bath."

"I certainly would. I freshened up in the stream but it isn't the same."

"For a quarter crown, you aren't going to get a bath. The only hostelry in town with a bath will cost you three quarters."

Aleria winced. "I suppose I could afford it, but it seems a lot. Is it a nice inn?"

"Nice enough. Clean, and the food's good. I think they're asking a bit much, though, bath or no bath."

The woman looked at Aleria, frowned some more, looked up and down the empty street, seemed to make up her mind. "I tell you, young lady, I have an idea. I'm not in the business of making beds up for strangers, and I can't afford to let people stay for free, but I've got my son's old room, and a little bath house in the yard. You come and stay with me. I'll take your quarter crown and go out and buy a good cut of meat and a nice bottle of wine, and you and I can have a good meal, you can have a long soak, and we'll both be ahead of the game."

It was Aleria's turn to be cautious. Upon closer inspection, she could see that this woman was not perhaps as prosperous as she tried to look. The apron had light stains of the sort that cannot be washed out, and the collar and cuffs of her blouse were on the point of fraying. "Do you live by yourself, Ma'am?"

"I do. My son has his own place now, just outside of town, and I'll be honest, I don't get half the company I'm used to, now that he's moved out. It would be a pleasure to have someone to talk to for the evening."

Aleria nodded. "It sounds fine to me." She held out her hand. "My name's Aleria Dalmyn, and I'm travelling to..."

"To the Citadel, of course. I'm Lussan Solere. It is a pleasure to meet you."

They clasped hands, and Lussan turned her into a side street. "My little house is just up here. We'll get a fire going under the water tank and you can have a cool drink while you're waiting."

It was a pleasant little cottage, only four rooms on one floor, but there was a spacious yard out the back with a poultry coop, an extensive vegetable garden and, right by the house, a small wooden shed with a chimney on one side. Lussan bustled about, opening a spigot to let water from a barrel under the eaves run into the tank, and lighting a fire in the metal box under it.

"There. It'll take an hour or more. Come over here and sit down."

At the side of the vegetable garden, just by the kitchen door, there was a small area paved with odd-sized stones, sporting two weathered chairs, low of leg and slanted at the back. Aleria dropped her pack and sank into one of them. "Ah. That feels good."

"You just rest a moment. I'll get you a drink, and then I'll go shopping."

Aleria smiled to herself as she watched the older woman scooting back and forth arranging everything. She sipped the drink, which seemed to be made of some sort of berry, a watery but refreshing taste.

"This is nice."

"Thank you, Aleria. I make it myself, keep it cool in a special box I have in the kitchen...no, don't get up. I can show it to you later. My son made it for me." She waved towards the bathhouse. "He's a coppersmith, my son. Does pipes and drains and that sort of thing." Her chin rose. "You look around my house, you'll find water conveniences as good as most manor houses."

Aleria nodded. "That's very good of him, to treat his mother so well."

Lussan grinned, leaned closer. "To be honest, what I get are the ones that don't work as good as they ought to. When something goes wrong, he throws it on a scrap heap out back of his shop."

"That must be a real treasure trove. Isn't he worried it will get stolen?"

The woman laughed. "If it was iron, perhaps. But copper isn't so valuable, and only a bit of it's brass. So it just lies there. Then every once in a while he gets an idea, and he goes through the scrap and finds enough to put it together for me."

Aleria shrugged. "If it works, it works." She grinned up at her hostess. "If I'm getting a bath out of it, I'll be the last one to complain."

"Fair enough. Are you comfortable, now?"

"I certainly am." She took another sip of the cool drink.

"Then I'll just slip out and get some things."

"Right." Aleria had been prepared for this, sliding a quarter crown from her inside purse. "Here's my contribution."

The woman smiled. "You just relax, now. I won't be long."

She hustled herself out, and Aleria heard the front door close. She stretched her legs in front of her, took a longer drink of the juice and looked around the yard. It was very tidy: the kitchen garden in neat rows, well weeded, the raspberry canes tied up, the chickens and ducks looking well fed and healthy, as far as a city girl could tell.

Aleria's eye wandered from the rain barrel up to the eaves, noting the copper troughs, the downpipes running in different directions. Curious and not that tired any more, she investigated and discovered that the water from the roof was directed to three different barrels. One fed the bathhouse, one was used for watering the garden, and the other led through the wall of the house to an unknown destination. Not wanting to snoop, Aleria strolled back to her chair. It was a small house. She would find out soon enough.

Even in the shade it was warm, and Aleria was soon dozing in the comfortable chair. She roused, disoriented, when the front door closed. She felt fuzzy around the edges as she shook her head, not trusting herself to get to her feet.

"Hello!" The voice rose up and down in a singsong.

Aleria managed something that was not quite a growl.

"I'm sorry. Were you asleep?" Lussan poked her head out of the kitchen.

"Just drowsing. It's so peaceful here."

"Too peaceful for me. That's why I'm glad you're here."

Aleria nodded, content that there was no required answer.

"You'll never guess what I have for our supper. Of course you'll never guess. How could you know that Leuf Charnisay just butchered his best steer ? How could you know that he had saved some of the loin chops at the very end?"

"Loin chops?"

"That's right. I have to admit they cost almost the whole of the quarter crown. But they'll be worth it. Just you wait." Lussan had scooted out the door and was hunting around the garden, for all the world like one of her hens, pecking at a bush here, a twig there, filling her apron with herbs as she went.

"Have you checked the water?"

Aleria sat up with a start. "Was I asleep that long?"

"Probably. I was out a bit longer than I had hoped. I met some people who just had to talk. You know how it is."

"I'd better wake up and check the water, then." Aleria dragged herself out of her low chair, stumbled a few times as her stiffened legs protested, and hobbled over to the bathhouse. Steam rose from the tank as she opened the door. She dipped a finger in.

"It seems pretty hot."

"Just make sure the plug is solid in the tub, then open the gate at the bottom of the heating tank and let it run."

She did as she was instructed, marvelling at the skill of the workman who had created the system. Soon the tub was full and smoking. As she regarded it, her hostess' head appeared beside hers. "That's just about right. Now look here. Have you ever used one of these baths?"

"Not exactly like this, no."

"This is how it works. You sit on that stool over there and dip water from the tub to pour over yourself. Then you use the soap, here, and scrub yourself all over."

"And you rinse before you get into the tub."

"That's right. If you don't wash yourself in the tub, you see, the water doesn't get dirty."

"We have big bath houses in the Capital that work like that."

"So you soap up, scrub down, and rinse yourself all over before you get into the tub. Don't worry, it all goes down that drain, there."

Aleria nodded.

"You have a nice bath. Here's a towel. I have a dinner to cook."

Aleria followed her hostess back to the patio to retrieve her pack, then retired to the bathhouse. She stripped down, anxious to get into that wonderful hot water. As she lathered up, she realized that it wasn't just any soap. There were herbs in it that released their aroma as the hot water worked on them.

It wasn't long before she was slipping into the big cedar tub: slowly, because the water was so hot. She sighed and leaned her head back. "I could get used to this."

Once again, she found herself dozing.

"Aleria! Aleria?"

She rallied around, raised her head. "Yes?"

"I forgot to tell you. Don't stay in too long!"

Something in the woman's voice alerted her. "Why not?"

"It's not a good idea to stay in too long when you're tired, and the water is very hot."

"Why not?"

The door opened a crack, and a worried face appeared. "Because you'll get so tired, you won't be able to get out."

"Oh, I doubt that." Aleria straightened her back, raised her head. It felt very heavy. She tried to raise her arms to grasp the edge of the tub, but they seemed heavy too. It was difficult to care, though, because the water was so warm and she felt so drowsy...

A pang of fear shot through her. Could she even get out? She willed her arms to lift, her hands to grasp. She pulled herself upright, sat on the edge of the tub.

"Are you all right?"

"I...I think so. I see what you mean, though. My arms are like noodles. No, don't worry, I can make it." She pushed herself upwards, and slid over the edge of the tub, gripping as firmly as she could. When her feet hit the cool tiles of the floor, she straightened slowly, holding on until she had her balance.

Lussan reached in and handed her the towel. "That's better. You just dry yourself off, get into some fresh clothes. As soon as you're out, it's my turn!"

Aleria scrubbed herself with the rough towel, willing the strength back into her muscles. As she worked, her mind began to function again. Of course. You didn't waste firewood on one person's bath. Lussan would want to bathe as well.

Dry and tingling all over, she dug into her pack for fresh undergarments and blouse, decided to wear her better skirt, and stepped out into the cool of the evening. She stretched again, leaning her pack against the bathhouse wall, and looked around.

The sun was setting, and everything seemed crisp in the twilight air. She grinned as Lussan bustled by her, towel and clean clothes over her arm. Aleria returned to her chair, to find a fresh drink waiting. It was the same juice, but with a different tang. A touch of some sort of brandy, perhaps. It tasted far better this way. She resolved not to drink too much.

She slipped into the chair again, her head clear now, and assessed her situation. It had cost her the same as a night's lodging, but if this woman's cooking was anywhere near as good as her son's handiwork, she was in for a pleasant evening.

9. Old Women's Dreams

She was roused by a tapping from the cottage. She looked over to the bathhouse, but there was no response.

"Lussan, there's someone at the door. Do you want me to answer?"

The voice came faintly from inside. "Please do."

The rapping came again, and she hurried through the cottage and opened the door. An older woman stood looking up at her, a pot in her hands and a soft bag slung over her shoulder.

"You must be Aleria? I'm Preully." She pushed the pot into Aleria's hands.

"Could you put that in the kitchen? I'll just slip out to the bath house for a moment."

Bemused, Aleria complied, taking a moment for an appreciative sniff at the chops, sitting in their marinade. By the time she returned to the garden, the bathhouse door was closing behind the little woman. Shrugging, she returned to her chair.

She hadn't been sitting more than a minute when another knock came at the door. Glancing over to the bathhouse, where all she heard was a loud giggle, she shrugged again, and went to answer.

The caller this time was a once-tall older woman, stooped with toil, her face weatherworn and wrinkled. She held, cradled in her hands, a dark glass bottle. Slowly, ever so slowly, she held it out like an offering. "Here you are, my dear. Treat that with care, now. There's only three left."

With that cryptic statement, the aged woman slipped past Aleria and she, too, disappeared into the bathhouse.

Aleria looked the bottle over, could discover nothing except that the dust and the wax over the cork seemed very old. Moving with care, she placed the bottle in the middle of the kitchen table and went outside. With a wry glance at the bathhouse door, she started back to her chair. It seemed the hot water was doing its full duty.

Somewhat to her surprise, there were no further interruptions. Soon Lussana appeared, towelling her hair as she walked. She stopped and looked at Aleria hesitantly. "I hope you don't mind. I just invited the two of them."

Aleria smiled. "Can't let all that hot water go to waste."

Her hostess grinned as well. "Right. And wait till you taste Dusina's wine. Her husband was a master vintner, dead these fifteen years. We've been trying to get her to open another bottle of his best blend for a long time now."

She continued to talk, so Aleria followed her into the kitchen. "I wonder what Preully brought?" She lifted the pot lid. "Oh, good. Cold potato salad is so nice on a hot day." She started passing dishes and glasses to Aleria, who spread the table. As they worked, the two other women finished their bath and returned, glowing from the heat, to sit around the table.

"You sit down, as well, Aleria. There's no room for two to work in this kitchen."

Aleria gratefully complied, as there was a lassitude over her whole body. The women chatted about the news of the town and their families, regaling Aleria with the usual tales of eccentric relatives and impossible husbands. She was amused to realize that the conversation was not a whole lot different from that of her mother's friends when they got together over a cup of tea.

With this entertainment, it didn't seem long before Lussan was handing around plates, each centred by a thick and steaming piece of meat. Aleria deduced why the chops had cost almost a quarter crown. There were four of them. So this situation had not been completely impromptu.

Before she sat, Lussan reached out for the bottle of wine, presented it to her older friend, along with a simple corkscrew. "It's your wine, Dusina, you do the honours."

With a business-like flourish, the old woman opened the bottle, poured a drop in her own glass and tasted it, using proper technique, Aleria noticed. Then she nodded. "Just keeps gettin' better."

She poured for everyone, and they sipped appreciatively. Aleria was amazed. She backed up and started the full tasting ritual that this wine deserved. It was deep and heavy, not a summer wine, but the flavours were rich, and a smoky aftertaste seemed to linger and develop.

"I see you can appreciate a good wine, young lady."

She smiled at the old woman. "One this good, even I can tell. It's beautiful! Where did it come from?"

"Right here, from a vineyard just outside Dargilan. My husband, Jernit, put this down, oh, must be twenty years past. Died long since, and never had a taste of it, he did. Said to keep it for special occasions. So I have been. Then I did some figurin'. Figured there ain't too many special occasions left in my life, and I'll be damned if I'm gonna have anybody drinkin' Jernit's special wine to celebrate my funeral. So I decided to drink it when I felt like it. Today I feel like it!" She stared at each of them as if challenging anyone to disagree with her.

Aleria raised her glass. "Well, Dusina, I'll not argue with that decision. This is wonderful."

"It's awful kind of you to say so, Aleria, and you havin' better'n that every day of the week if you wants it."

"I think you have an exaggerated idea of how we live in the Capital. My family only drinks wine when we have company or on special occasions. Most of my friends do the same."

The oldest woman made a scoffing sound. "Aw, quit bein' so truthful. We're much to old to have our dreams tossed around like that."

Aleria grinned. "All right. I was just being polite. At home we drink nothing but the best wines every night of the week, and at lunch on Feastdays as well." She looked at the serious, nodding faces in front of her.

"And I still don't get to taste wine this good more than twice a year!"

They exploded into cackles of mirth at that. As they settled, everyone took another small, appreciative sip. All nodded in unison, and a brief silence settled over the group.

"So now tell us."

"Tell you what?" She looked at the three faces, leaning forward with anticipation.

"About your school."

"My school? Why would you want to know about my school?"

Lusson laid a hand over Aleria's. "Every woman in the realm knows about the Ladies' Academy. Every girl dreams of going there. The knowledge, the ideas..."

Dusina cackled, "...the parties, the handsome young men..."

Lusson continued as if she hadn't been interrupted. "And we see you all go through here on your Quest, and every woman wishes that it was her, or her daughter."

"And we all want to know what it's like." Preully clasped her hands in front of her, twisted them back and forth.

"But there's a barrier. You girls are supposed to be on your Quest, you're not supposed to be recognized. So we can't ask you, don't you see? It would spoil everything."

Aleria shook her head. "So all sorts of people let me know that they have recognized me, but the ones that dearly want to talk to me can't, because that would spoil their dream."

The three women sat back in unison, satisfied smiles on their faces.

Lusson raised her hands helplessly. "But then today, you came up and talked to me, and you were so friendly, and so natural, and so...beautiful, and I just couldn't help myself."

The look of anxious sincerity on the woman's face stifled Aleria's shout of laughter. She paused, shook her head, softened her voice. "Beautiful? I'm not beautiful. I'm just one of the pretty ones."

She nodded against their incredulous stares. "My face is too round. I'll never be beautiful, not like you're talking about."

She looked at the disappointed faces in front of her. "You want beautiful, you should see my friend Mito. Now there's the kind of beauty you want to see. Not because she's just well formed. She has the kind of beauty that just shines out from her heart, you know?"

There were three slight nods, as if her listeners were unaware of the need to respond. Taking another sip of the excellent wine, she began to tell the story of Mito at the Spring Ball, not leaving out the tragic element of her impoverished family, of their sacrifice to keep her at the school, and Mito's ethereal beauty as she sat, rapt in her dream, receiving the hopeless adulation of the handsomest of the young men.

As she spun out the tale to her entranced audience, the small idea wiggled through her consciousness that the best story is one that has a whole lot of truth in it, and she wondered how much of what she was telling was true, and how much was just her own interpretation of a mundane situation. Gazing at the three women listening to her, she realized that it didn't matter a whit.

When she had finished the tale, she sat back and took another sip, hiding the fact that she had finished her glass.

"But what happened next?"

"What did she do?"

"That's the story, ladies, up to the present. I don't know what she will do, and at the moment, neither does she."

There was a combined sigh, and the three women sat back in their chairs in silence.

Suddenly Dusina reached out and grabbed her glass. "A toast, dammit. A toast to the Royal Academy for Young Ladies, and for all that's good and beautiful!"

They all solemnly raised their glasses.

"And Aleria's glass is empty." The old woman raised the bottle to the light. "But so is the bottle. Dammit."

"I guess an about-to-become graduate of the Royal Academy for Young Ladies can afford to buy her friends a drop of wine." She fished out another quarter crown. "Lussan, let's go for a walk, you and me. The inn must have something good."

Lussan glanced at her friends and rose. "Don't you two go anywhere." They nodded and retained their places.

Aleria followed her hostess out into the street. It was dark down among the buildings, but there was plenty of starlight, and she knew from her walk in this afternoon that the street was clear of obstacles. As they walked, Lussan hummed a little tune to herself.

"That was a nice story. Where did you get it?"

"Get it?"

"Yes. Some wonderful writer must have written that story. It was so beautiful, yet so sad."

Aleria snorted. "You know what really bothers me? It's that I can't tell Mito what you said, because then I'd have to admit that I told a bunch of strangers about her, and she'd hate that."

"What? She really is real?"

"I said she was my friend. She is. And nobody would think that was a story by a wonderful writer, because if it wasn't real it would be just too sappy to believe."

"Sappy?"

"Yes, sappy. Oh, I know that a bunch of women sitting around telling their dreams would find it beautiful. It is beautiful, in a way. But the last thing I'm going to do is tack a 'happily ever after' ending on it, because that would make it even worse."

She could feel her companion looking up at her through the darkness. "I think I just learned something else about the young ladies going through here on their Quests."

"What was that?"

"That some of them are not as sweet and innocent as we would like to believe."

"Are you talking about me?"

"Partly. There's a sort of a sharpness about you."

"Huh! A sharpness. Yes, you wouldn't be the first one to notice that."

"You hide it well."

"Most of the time."

In the growing light as they approached the inn windows, she could see Lusson nod. "It's not an easy life, being like that."

"No, I guess it isn't."

"My son is like that. He just can't let things be. In his trade, it's a benefit. In his life, sometimes it isn't."

"Some day maybe I should find a trade like that. In my life, it has almost always been a detriment."

They were entering the inn, now, and her companion did not respond.

It was a pleasant little country hostel: nothing special, but well lit and freshly whitewashed inside. Aleria knew she would not have even asked the price, bathtub or not. Lussan did not seem affected by the opulence.

"Good evening, Perusse. Do you have any of that case of Chatelire wine left? We'd like a bottle, please."

The barman nodded. "Yes, we have a few left, Lusson." He glanced at Aleria, grinned at the older woman. "Special company tonight?"

"That's right, Perusse. A special friend from the Capital."

"From the Capital?" His second glance took longer, but he said no more, turning away to descend a set of narrow steps behind the bar.

Lusson grinned at Aleria and turned to survey the people in the room. No one ignored them, but there was a distinct lack of overt interest.

Aleria smiled back. "They don't have to be impolite enough to ask. They'll all know by tomorrow."

"That's about it."

The barman's head appeared up the stairs, and Lusson leaned closer for a moment. "The price ought to be three pennies, but he'll try for four. On no account give him five."

Aleria turned, feigning a lack of interest, and tossed a quarter crown on the bar. The barman set the wine down, picked up the coin, paused.

"There will be change, I assume?"

"Now, young lady, that's a nice wine you're getting there."

"I'm glad of it. How would it rate against a bottle of Jernit's Special Blend?"

Perusse raised his hands in defence. "Oh, it isn't in that class. If I could get my hands on some of that Special of Jernit's, I could sell it for three, maybe four crowns."

She nodded. "So we've just been drinking some of Jernit's, and our mouths are sort of set on that level, you know? So I'd be very disappointed if I were to open a bottle I paid, say three pennies for, and discover it wasn't up to standard."

"Three! Oh, come on, now, young lady. I'm sure you can get wine of this quality for three pennies in the capital, but there are shipping charges, and agent's charges, and..."

"But you have perfectly good vineyards around here, or that's what I've been hearing. Surely you have wines as good as this with no cartage at all."

"Perhaps, but I still couldn't let this one go for less than four pennies."

"I'll tell you what, Master Perusse. You slip the cork out of that bottle and we'll have a little taste of it right now. If it's worth it, I'll pay your four pennies."

The barman frowned. "But what if I open it and you don't buy it? What do I do then?"

She laughed. "Then you have an overpriced bottle of wine for dinner that your sharp dealing brought you. Don't worry. If this wine is as good as you say it is, I'll pay the money."

The barman shook his head and reached under the counter, bringing out three glasses and a corkscrew. By this time, considerable interest had been drawn to them, and several patrons sidled nearer. He frowned and, very carefully, drew the cork from the bottle. It came out with a satisfying pop, and he raised it to his nose, a bit hesitantly. Then he recovered with a professional smile and passed it to her. There was nothing wrong with the smell, and she nodded.

He poured three small dollops. It was a rich, dark, wine and it seemed to fall rather than to flow from the bottle. She took the glass and swirled it, watching the wine run down the sides.

She held it to the light, not that she was expecting anything but a clear, deep red.

She continued to go through the tasting ritual as she had been trained since she was young, aware that her knowledge was very shallow, although her sense of taste was acute. It was a good wine, although nothing like what she had just been drinking. She said so.

The barman slapped his hands on the bar in front of him. "I can't compete with old Jernit, I told you that."

"I don't expect you to. However, I must say, I would not pay three pennies for this wine in the Capital, or four for it anywhere else. It has a fine, rich nose, but there is a hint of sourness in the aftertaste that no amount of aging is going to get rid of."

The barman stuck his nose in his glass again, sipped, then stared at the ceiling as he swirled the liquid in his mouth. Finally, he swallowed, then breathed in, shaking his head. "I'm afraid you're right, Miss. The other bottles in the case weren't like that, I'll swear."

She nodded. "Of course, it's a Chatelire."

"That's right. It came highly recommended at the price."

"Chatelire mostly deserves it, but they had a problem a few years back, I'm not sure how long, when they changed Master Vintners. The new man took a while to get settled in, and their quality suffered. From what I hear, they're back on their form now, so their more recent wines will be fine."

The barman wordlessly slipped her coin across the bar to her. She pushed it back.

"I think we can agree that this is worth three pennies, what with the cartage and the agents and all."

A smile lit his face. "Well, Miss, your advice on the Chatelire is worth the extra penny any day." The quarter crown vanished and he handed her the two pennies change.

She nodded. "Then watch out for last year's whites from that area when they start coming around. I'm told they had way too much rain in mid-summer and the grapes grew too fast."

The barman nodded, as did several of the onlookers. "Thank you, Miss. I hope you two enjoy that bottle."

Lussan smiled. "Oh, I'm sure it will be fine. After Jernit's, nothing would be really good anyway."

"Say, do you think there's any chance Dusina would let any of that go?"

"I think she's saving one last bottle to drink on her deathbed."

They bid the barman good night and carried their prize away. Once they were well out of earshot of the inn, Lussan chuckled. "That was an interesting lesson."

"For who?"

"Everyone. For a young lady, you know wines. I didn't have any idea."

"Part of the training we get at school, and the rest at home. My father has a decent cellar, although we don't, as I keep trying to tell you, drink that much of it."

"I believe you. Let's get this back home. If we're lucky enough, those other two have fallen asleep and we'll get all this to ourselves."

Dusina had, indeed, fallen asleep, but she awoke with a snap and thoroughly enjoyed Lussan's telling of the scene at the inn. She slapped the table several times when the story was over. "I allus thought young Perusse took too much on himself, with his schooling and his hoity-toity wines."

"Give him his due, Dusina." Lussan pushed the bottle across. "The wine is pretty good, and he was willing to give Aleria her money back if she wanted it."

The old woman rolled the wine around in her mouth, sucked air across it. "You're dead right, Aleria. That aftertaste needed dealing with. A touch of Callot grape would have evened it right out."

Aleria laughed out loud.

"What was so funny about that?

She shook her head. "Not you, Dusina. I was just thinking. All of you people say you're getting stories about me that you can tell. I just realized I'm getting some of my own. Can you imagine? Here I am, out in the centre of nowhere, and I'm discussing wine with a woman more knowledgeable than most restaurateurs in the Capital."

There was a general chuckle, and they began to ask her questions again. She answered as well as she could, and soon the next bottle of wine was also gone. As she placed her empty glass on the table she was unable to hide the huge yawn that forced its way up from her chest.

"There, now, the girl's had a tough day on the road, and got another one tomorrow. We can't keep her up talking all night."

The other two women nodded and Pruelly rose. "I'm getting tired, too."

Dusina slapped her hands on the table in her predictable gesture. "You young folks sleep too much. I'll be up milkin' goats with the sun, no matter when I go to bed." But she, too, rose and made her way to the door.

They said good night and wished Aleria good roads and dry weather on her Quest. Soon they were lost to the darkness, and Lussan and Aleria turned back into the house.

"Don't start cleaning up. I have plenty of time to do that tomorrow."

"I wouldn't dream of letting you clean up alone. We can talk some more while we work."

That swayed the older woman, and they made quick work of the dirty dishes. After a moment, Lussan paused, turned to Aleria. "Can you tell me, now? How much of those stories were true?"

Aleria took a moment to think back. "I didn't tell you anything that wasn't true, at least for me, at the time it happened. I realize now that I had a pretty slanted view."

"But all the events really happened?"

"That's right. It wouldn't be fair to tell you lies."

"But you knew about our dreams. Weren't you worried about spoiling them?"

"Ah, you're all old women." Aleria grinned. "Your most cherished dreams don't spoil that easily, just because some young nothing tells you some questionable facts. No, I thought you would be happier if I told you the truth. The only dishonesty may have been in what I didn't tell you."

"What didn't you tell us?"

"The usual stuff nobody wants to hear. The everyday drudgery, the nastiness, the social climbing, that sort of thing. It happens everywhere, and with pampered young girls it's probably worse than most. But tonight wasn't the time."

"No, it wasn't. And I thank you for that." She hung the drying cloth over the oven handle. "And since we've stopped coddling our dreams, I should tell you; we notice all the girls who come through. We can tell that some of them are perfect twitters. We just smile and take the money they throw around."

Aleria nodded and grinned. "Just like always."

"Just like always. And now I suppose you need to see the last waterworks wonder of my house and then your room."

She opened a small door, which Aleria had assumed was a pantry, to reveal an indoor toilet. Aleria inclined her head in appreciation.

"I suppose you have these at home."

"You couldn't manage a city as big as Kingsport without a sewage system. At least, you could, but can you imagine the smell?" She leaned into the little room, angling her candle to see all of the brass and porcelain. "It's very well made."

"My son does good work, I'll give him that."

"And treats his mother wonderfully."

"He does. But now I'll stop talking, because it's been several hours and two bottles of wine, and I'm sure you'd like to make use of his handiwork."

"That I would."

After that, Lussan showed Aleria to her room, which was rather small because of the space taken up by the toilet. It was cool and the bed was more comfortable than any she had used lately, so she was soon drifting off. Her last thought was that, in spite of a free room, somehow the evening had cost her almost half a crown: a bit over her usual budget. Worth it for several reasons.

10. Journey's End

As the days went on and she neared the end of her journey, she felt a strange conflict inside. Always, she looked ahead to the completion of the Quest, the enjoyment of success. But creeping in was a sadness that it would end. She worried less now about where and how she was going to sleep each night. She looked forward to each new town, wondering whom she would meet and what she would learn from them. Sometimes the inns she chose were too rough, but her status always protected her, if her forthright interest in the patrons might have failed.

The incident in Snowe was a typical, if extreme, example. She had stayed too long talking with the farm wife who had given her lunch, so she came into the village late, with darkness falling and no clear idea of where to stay. Because of this, she had taken a room at a small, rundown place. The innkeeper probably recognized her, because he made every effort to be polite and told her that he was expecting a quiet night. He was wrong.

Perhaps because of the season, or maybe the day of the week, about fifteen itinerant farm workers decided to make this the headquarters for their evening celebration, and they stormed into the tiny common room while she was eating. The innkeeper shot her a worried glance, but it was too late to do anything. She leaned forward, let her hair fall over her face, and concentrated on her meal.

She listened, though, and soon realized that the men were far from happy. Something about the payment for their time on the early hay harvest this year – the usual complaint, as far as she could determine – and the quality of the food they were given. That was another one she had heard several times along the way.

"Hey, there's not enough room. Can we share your table?"

"Sure." She shifted to the end of the bench, turned away from the three dirty, sweaty men who plunked themselves and their drinks down, immediately taking up most of the table. They continued their carping, but she could tell that their attention was being drawn to her. She glanced around, but there was no way out without brushing much too close to one of them. She could tell by their increasing comments about the rich folks and their treatment of the poor that she was meant to hear. Finally, she decided to make her move.

She shoved back her plate, looked at them, tried to remember how old Dusina had talked. "So you're bein' treated bad, are ya?"

"Aye, we are, Missy."

"I wonder. You." She lifted her chin towards the largest of them. "How much money'd ya make in Snowe last year?"

"I dunno. About two crowns."

"And how many days'd ya work here?"

"I dunno."

"Come on, it was only a year ago. How many feast-days? How many extras?"

Another man frowned. "We was here two feast days, but we stayed two extra days after."

"So that's fourteen days, right?"

They glanced at each other. "No, remember, we come two days late. Twelve days we was here last year."

"Fine." She made a show of counting on her fingers. "So that's twelve days, 'n' you made two crowns. That's one crown for six days...that's twenty pennies, that's about three and...and a half a day, isn't it?"

"I guess so."

"So how many days'd ya work this year, and what'd ya get paid?"

"Ten days, and we got paid one crown and three quarters."

She went through the finger counting again. "Well, that's 35 pennies, for ten days, that's...three 'n' a half a day. You got paid the same this year as last year. There's just less work. Maybe the crops ain't as good or something. You expect the farmer to pay you extra when he's gettin' less crops in? That's hardly fair to him, is it?"

"I guess not."

She shrugged. "Bad times all 'round, I guess. My Dad's in cartage. Farmer's sendin' less grain to the mill, Dad gets less work. I don't get no new dress this year. I don't like it, but I ain't sittin' here bellyachin'."

Another man leaned forward. "Aye, but the food."

"Aye. The food's terrible this year."

"You sure? You sure that's not just you thinkin' it was better before, like you thought with the money?"

The bigger man shook his head. "No, we all agree on that. The food ain't as good and there ain't as much of it. Platters 'r' empty, the end of every meal."

"You tell the farmers?"

"Huh? No, I didn't say nothin'."

She looked around, received several shrugs.

"So the food wasn't as good, but you didn't complain. You didn't tell anyone, you just let it happen for ten days. Then at the end, you come in here, drinkin' and bellyachin', disturbin' my supper, when the guy you should be talkin' to is home, worryin' about whether he'll get through the winter and have enough left to buy seed grain for the spring. Maybe he's wonderin' whether anyone noticed the food, and thinkin' he got away with it so he can feed you-all the same way next year."

There were several mutters around the table.

She nodded. "You're a fine bunch, you are. You remind me of my little brother. Always bitchin' and complainin', but you don't do nothin' about it. You don't have to take it, you know. You get together, real polite and firm, and you go to the farmer, and you tell him. Maybe you let him know that you realize the harvest ain't as good. But you tell him about the food. You're hard workin' men and you need your grub."

There were a series of nods around the table. The big fellow reached out and took a long drink from his mug. She leaned over and pushed his hand down. "And you don't sit here

97

drinkin' up the courage until you're half-potted and snarly. You go up there in a drunken mob and he'll have the proctors on you, they'll run you out of town and you'll never work here again."

The man muttered, but let the mug sit on the table. Then he looked at her. "You got a pretty smart mouth for a young 'un."

"Don't you go worryin' about me. I got my own troubles to deal with. You get out there and solve yours. Or don't come runnin' in here, cryin' that you bin hard done by." She emptied her own mug, slammed it down.

"Now, I gotta get some sleep, 'cause I got a hard day tomorrow. Go on, get outa the way." She made a shooing motion with her hands, and he rose. "Go now while you're on your feet and you got the courage."

"Aye. Maybe I will."

"You do that." She slid over by the bar and stood, watching with interest to see what he would do.

The man looked around, realizing he had the attention of his companions. He finally pointed. "Jerl and Bisk. You come with me. We got a meeting with a farmer."

The two men hauled themselves to their feet. As they left, the others looked at each other, muttered some, and then, in twos and threes, they got up, took last, long swigs from their unfinished ales and left the inn.

"There goes my night of profit. What was that all about?"

She glanced over at the innkeeper. "They're feeling hard done by because it's a bad harvest. They didn't get the same days of work as last year and the farmer didn't manage to feed them as well. I doubt if you'd have sold any more ale. They couldn't afford to buy it."

The innkeeper nodded. "Aye, it ain't gonna be a good year, that's the truth."

"And if they do come back, I'm not going to be anywhere in sight. See you in the morning."

"Good night, Miss. Sleep well."

She doubted that she would, although she had pounded the straw mattress into reasonable shape, chasing out a few of its larger residents in the process. She laid her own blankets on top and slid gratefully inside.

The next morning, she was just finishing her breakfast when the door of the inn slammed open. The big man from the night before stomped in, a grin on his face. "Hey, is that girl here? The one...oh, there you are."

"Hi. What's got you so lit up?"

"You was right, Missy. You was completely, bang-in-the-middle right. We went up there to one of the farmers and we asked, real polite-like, just the three of us, to talk to him. He asked us into the parlour, wouldn't you know, and we sat down. I told him, real polite, like you said, about the food and the days of work. And you know what he said?

"Tell me."

"Well, he said just what you said he would. He said he was sorry, but the crops weren't that good. I was real smart. I popped that in about the seed grain for next year, and he nodded, all serious. But he seemed real happy that we was so understandin', and he invited us all back tonight for what he called a 'real good supper'. He said he may be havin' a rough year, but he wouldn't have the men goin' off sayin' he din't feed 'em right.

"So we're gonna have a real feed tonight. He was goin' out to butcher a pig first thing this mornin'. And all because o' you!"

She grinned. "I'm real glad about that. But I didn't do it because of you."

"You din't?"

"No, I didn't. I did it because I was a lone girl, stuck in a room full of ruffians, set to get themselves plastered and mad, and I figured I'd better get your minds on somethin' else."

He looked down at her, his jaw dropping. "You're serious?"

"You think I'm wanderin' the countryside like some sort of prophet, solvin' people's problems for them?"

He shrugged. "I thought you was maybe one of those that've bin wanderin' the countryside, stirrin' people up with their talkin' 'bout injustice an' rebellion an' a new Galesia."

She laughed. "Don't you go tellin' anyone I'm one of those. My Dad'd have the skin off my back, he thought I was doin' that."

The man laughed as well. "Don't you worry, Missy. Me 'n the boys're right pleased with how things worked out, an' we wouldn't want you comin' to no harm about it."

"That's good, then. I'll be on my way."

"Well, maybe we'll see you around, Missy, if you're on the road again. You have trouble with anyone, you tell them you're a friend of Reynon's crew, an' they better back off."

"Thank you, Reynon. It's kind of you, and I will remember."

She nodded to the innkeeper, who seemed to be trying to hide a smile, and headed for the door. As she opened it, she heard the big farm worker's puzzled voice. "What are you findin' so funny?"

As she paused to hitch her pack straight, she heard the innkeeper's reply. "Reynon, you've been done right and proper. Do you know who that girl was that you was talkin' to?"

She grinned and strode away.

That was the closest she came to real danger, although there were a few lonely nights and rainy days. After that incident, she listened more carefully to what the people were saying and watched their faces as she passed them on the way. It was not a good year, that was certain, and there was an undercurrent of muttering and unease all along the road. Not that she knew if it meant anything. In some people's opinion, the peasants were always complaining. The carters who worked for her father did their share, although she never heard any of it, of course. However, she noted the unrest as something to discuss with her father when she got back.

She stayed her final night in Costend, only half a day from the Citadel. She wasn't in a hurry, and due to her economies over the journey she could afford a decent inn. It wasn't proper to show up too early or too late, and she thought she was probably a bit slower than most, but well within the expected range. What she wanted most was a good bath and clean clothes, so that she looked her best when she arrived.

It piqued her curiosity that she saw no other Questers. Most would be coming in from other directions, but she had thought there might be someone on her schedule. But no one showed up at the pleasant inn she chose, and she wasn't about to go around searching the town.

So she was walking alone when, just before noon, she swung up the long, sweeping avenue that led to the ancient seat of the Andeberg Dynasty, a dark and imposing fortress that she had always considered past its usefulness. It had been constructed to defend the pass through the mountains to the west, when the great Empire of Domada had held sway there. These days the realm of Domaland was more concerned with commercial conquest, and the most dangerous items that came over the pass were the printing presses that produced the daily newspapers in Kingsport and Oudonsford.

The great stone walls looked bright and cheerful on this early summer day, with Galesian royal banners aflutter and ceremonial bunting around the main gate.

Someone must have noted her approach, because there was a fair crowd waiting, her mother and father in the front. She strolled in, grinning, to the cheers of the assembly. Praetor Marmen presented her with her Cumulato scroll and a short speech of congratulation. She regarded him as he spoke, and it seemed that he really was enjoying himself. She wondered what kind of idealism had pushed him into his present position.

Then she chuckled to herself. Maybe the Quest had been good for her. She had certainly never given a second thought to the Praetor's personality, writing him off as a dry old stick, and that was it.

"So, how was it, dear?"

She glanced at her father. "It was more useful than I expected."

"Useful? That's an interesting way to put it."

She shook his arm. "It wasn't any kind of a test, that's certain. So if it isn't going to be just an empty ceremony, it has to have some use, and I think it did. I learned some things, and I met some people, and I have some ideas to discuss with you."

She could see her father's glance across to her mother, who smiled. "I remember having similar thoughts when I finished mine."

"You did?"

"You're not the first to notice that the Quest has become more of a ceremony than a test of ability."

Aleria laughed. "So what are we going to do about it?"

"Nothing, of course. We don't destroy cherished traditions just because they don't suit our personal preferences, my dear."

"Mother, you are so stuffy sometimes."

"Stuffy, is it?" Leniema gave an exaggerated sigh. "Something that comes with maturity, I suppose."

She grasped her mother's arm. "If you don't mind, I'll cling to my immaturity a few more years then."

Her father chuckled. "Don't be so hard on yourself. Most of us call it 'youthful idealism'."

"That has a better ring to it, certainly." She took an arm of each. "What sort of luxurious accommodation have you prepared for me, when I have suffered the rigours of the road for so long?"

Again her parents crossed glances, and it was her father who answered. "Since you ask..."

She laid a dramatic hand against her forehead. "Oh, no! You were unable to find proper accommodation, and we have to camp outside the castle walls?"

"It's not quite that bad. We have a beautiful suite for tonight. It's just that, well, you took a little longer getting here than we expected, and both your mother and I have to scoot back to the Capital tomorrow, first thing."

"And then I'll be moving into the dorms with the rest of the girls."

"It seems a waste to have you in that big suite all alone."

She looked around. "Am I the first? Any word on Mito or the Twins?"

"You're the first, as usual, Aleria."

"But not the first of everyone. Just of my friends."

Her mother regarded her a moment. "No, not at all the first. Quite in the middle, as it happens. Is it that important to you?"

"Not really. Once I got on the road I forgot all that and just travelled the best I could. I'd have been here five days ago if I wanted to. It was just better to do it the way I did."

"Five days? Nobody came in that early. Even the weaker girls who were given the short routes."

She shrugged. "If it was a race I would have been here earlier than that. But it isn't. Once I got out there I decided to have a good time, so I set my own pace, did what I wanted to do."

"And what was that?"

She grinned at her father. "I met people."

"That's it? You took an extra five days meeting people?"

"Something like that. I also came in with three crowns of my original allotment left over. No need to touch my emergency cache."

"Three crowns left? How did you live on so little?"

"I was careful where I stayed and I was treated with a great deal of hospitality by many people along the road. You know, there is a completely different reason for the Quest that I had never considered."

"What is that?"

"Not for the girls on Quest. I had it figured from the beginning that it was pretty well meaningless, as far as challenges go. No, it has to do with the people in the towns we go through. They look for us, you know, and take care of us and tell stories about us. Some of them even dream about what it would be like to be us. It seems to make some kind of important contact between our classes and the people of the realm. I don't know. It just occurred to me."

Her father nodded, looked at her quizzically. "I get the feeling that this Quest has been of more importance to you than you think."

"Of course. It's been a real learning experience. But don't ever let anyone tell you that it's any kind of challenge, any kind of accomplishment. It's a little like going to the Spring Ball. You've never done it before, and it prepares you for similar occasions in the future, but you don't need it, and you don't need to feel you've conquered the world, just because you were there."

Another girl had come in while they were talking, and Aleria swept a hand over the dispersing crowd. "Just watch. They'll all make it. Some because they learned something, some because they cheated, some because of dumb luck, some because the local people helped them all the way. It doesn't matter much, when you look at it that way."

She linked her arms through those of her parents. "But we're here to celebrate and you have to leave tomorrow, so let's go find our luxurious suite and luxuriate in it."

Ignoring their concerned glances, she towed them away.

11. A New Plan

Mito wandered in the next day, looking as if she had just been for a stroll in the garden, a small bouquet of flowers in her hand. Her pack looked half the size of Aleria's and she was dressed plainly, but she looked happy. Aleria rushed over to seize her in a bear hug. "How did it go?"

"It was wonderful. Everyone was so nice to me. It rained a couple of days, but that was all. I met so many wonderful people. I really enjoyed myself."

"What? No trials, no tribulations? No close escapes, near-death experiences?"

Mito grinned. "There was one carter who seemed to be in a hurry, but he slowed down when I asked him to."

"You were riding with a carter?"

Mito looked uncomfortable. "You know, people kept organizing rides for me to the next town, and it seemed so impolite to refuse..."

"People arranged rides for you."

"Wasn't that nice of them? You know, I don't think very many of them knew I was on Quest. What about you?"

Aleria frowned. "It's hard to tell, isn't it? I think more people know us than let on. In fact, I'm sure of it, because someone told me. But many of them are so pleased to have spotted you, they just have to let you know. It's sort of a game they play. But you're good with people. If you don't think you were recognized much, you probably weren't."

Mito giggled. "There was one woman I told. I had to, because she was going so far out of her way to do all these things for me. Finally I had to tell her, so she would let me do it on my own. She was so surprised. Then she wanted to do a whole lot more for me. It was quite difficult at the time, but I laughed about it afterwards."

Aleria nodded. "Sounds about right. I go bashing through, fighting off bandits, wolves and thunderstorms, and you waltz through with everybody helping. Yes, that sounds normal."

"Did you really meet bandits and wolves?"

"No wolves, at any rate. I'll tell you about the bandit. Now, I have a surprise for you. Come this way."

She grabbed Mito's pack from her and led the way up the main street of the Citadel.

"I thought the girls' dorms were over there..."

"That they are, but my parents were here to greet me, and they had a suite in one of the big guest houses. I persuaded them to let me keep it, for when you and the Twins showed up."

"A suite?"

"We're not on Quest any more. We can use all the money we didn't spend for fancy food to make up for our starvation on the road."

Mito looked down at her waistline. "I don't think I starved very much, as I recall."

"I imagine there were all number of people wanting to take you in and pat you on the head and feed you."

Mito's nose lifted. "I did not get patted on the head. Well, only once, and she was old and I didn't want to embarrass her, so I let her."

Aleria laughed. "Once again we prove that this whole Quest is a joke."

"How so?"

"I sounds like you had a nice holiday in the country, meeting the people and getting fat. Some challenge."

Mito smiled. "It really wasn't very hard, was it?"

"No. I can't wait to hear the stories, though. Some of those girls will have been through blizzards and floods and dealt with marauding savages and wild animals, the whole thing. Just wait."

As the girls trickled in over the next three days, Aleria's predictions proved exaggerated, but not by much. Looked at from a cynical point of view, most of the troubles her classmates had experienced occurred through their own stupidity or ignorance, and most of them got out of trouble not by thinking or learning anything, but by a liberal application of money or reliance on their rank. By the time the last awards were given out, Aleria had lost any sense of accomplishment she might have felt.

As she stood at the final ceremony, she looked around at the girls of her class and she saw them for what they were: well-brought-up children of the ruling class, with a full store of knowledge, style and social grace. But few of them with enough guts or talent to get through any sort of real trouble.

She thought of Dusina, back in Dargilan, with her arthritic hands and her weathered face, refusing to give up her sense of humour no matter what old age brought her. Dusina's friends, who took their enjoyment when they could in a dull and lonely life and kept their small dreams stoked with every scrap of wonder they could glean.

She looked around and wondered who would be the slightest bit interested in the lives of those women. Mito would understand. The rest of them wouldn't. To be fair, maybe Gita; she was a deep thinker. The others?

She stared once more at the shining faces around her. She would probably never bring up the topic. It would be too disappointing to find out.

Once the ceremony was over, the girls were all gathered together in the Ladies' Dorms, because there were other lessons and duties to accomplish. Aleria left the suite without a backwards glance. The rooms she stayed in were beginning to be less important to her. No spiders in the bed, no leaks in the roof and she was happy.

Others weren't happy, of course, complaining about the rooms, the beds, the food. Aleria found it possible to ignore them, but when they started to complain about how rude the peasants were, how they had to pay high prices for everything, she had to speak up.

Aleria leaned over closer. "So you learned something, Plendinta. You pay for the privilege of letting people know how much better you are."

The other girl looked up at her. "You certainly do."

For once, Aleria couldn't think of anything to say. She held the other's gaze for a moment, then turned away.

As they were walking down the corridor, she glanced at her friend. "Is it true, Mito? Do I really lord it over the others?"

"Sometimes." Mito walked a few paces, then grinned. "But only when they need it."

* * *

The following day, Aleria was alone in the courtyard. She was bored enough to be practising one of the warm-up routines for barehand when Master Ogima walked by. She stopped, feeling guilty because she knew she had not been putting her best effort into it.

"The third punch in the last block-punch-kick sequence."

She repeated the move, held the position.

"That's it." He walked around her. "You are out of balance at that point. If your opponent applied pressure...here..." A touch of his finger against her shoulder, and she had to shift her footing.

"I see. Thank you. I wasn't trying very hard."

"It is sometimes a good thing to go through the motions and let the mind work elsewhere. When you do that pattern at full speed, you flow through that weak point without noticing. Only when you are working slowly could I see it."

"Thank you, Master Ogima. I was just wondering why we even take these lessons."

"You were wondering that, were you?" He sat on a nearby stone bench and looked up at her. "That is one thought I never heard from you during your schooling. I thought you rather enjoyed our practices."

"I did. I still do. But what use are they?"

He smiled. "That, I have heard before."

She turned to face him. "Master Ogima, how often does anyone have trouble on the Quest?"

He sized her up for a moment. "Not often."

That fitted. "How long is it since anyone had trouble? Serious trouble, I mean."

He seemed reluctant to answer. "Well...I think it was...eleven years ago, one girl broke her leg."

"How did that happen?"

"A cart she hitched a ride in overturned."

Aleria's open hands came down with a slap on her thighs. "That could happen to me on one of my father's freight wagons!"

"True."

So she was right. The whole thing was a farce. "But once this must have been a serious ritual."

"A hundred years ago, participants might be waylaid, robbed, even killed. Nowadays, a girl travelling alone by the main road isn't in much danger. Of course, in those days they were better trained than you are."

"You mean all our training...?"

His raised hand anticipated her thought. "Of course your training is worth something. It keeps you in good physical shape, and the techniques you have learned are real. If applied with enough will, they can injure an opponent." His shoulders rose in a faint shrug. "In my opinion, few of the candidates, unless hysterical, would have enough mental strength to make an attack with enough force to give a fighting man more than a moment's pause."

"What you are telling me is that all my training has been a joke. That the Quest has been a joke."

"I thought that was what you were telling me. I would prefer to look at it more realistically – as a bit of a warning. Don't consider that you are prepared for going it on your own down any lane you might wish to travel. Life isn't quite so pleasant out on the back roads, and some of the people are equally unsavoury."

"You've heard all this before, haven't you?"

He nodded. "Not often enough for my peace of mind. Only a few seem to catch on. Fewer still ask about it."

"What do you do for those who ask?"

Again he shrugged.

She had rarely seen the old instructor less sure of himself, and it fuelled her anger. "Well, I might just have to do something for myself. I might just light out home again without all your fake protection. I might look for some of those back roads I'm supposed to be so afraid of, to see if they're as bad as you say."

"Do not do something rash, Aleria."

"How am I going to find out about myself if I don't? Your precious Quest hasn't told me a thing." She stood over him, willing him to answer her, but no response came. This made her angrier still, and she whirled away from him, slamming the door behind her as she strode inside. Several heads rose towards her in the anteroom, but she was past noticing. She grabbed her cloak strode out of the fortress, glaring down the guards at the gate who looked half inclined to question her.

She returned several hours later, no longer angry, but still unsatisfied. Deep in thought, she sought out Mito. "Can I talk to you?"

"You need to ask?"

Aleria stopped frowning and plopped down on the bed facing her friend. "All right. So what if the Quest is sham? It does teach us something. I learned a lot about travelling, come to think of it. I learned some of the dangers, I learned about finding rides, choosing inns, navigating without proper maps.

"Do you remember how hard it was, the first time you had to go up to a stranger and ask for directions?"

Mito's brow furrowed for a moment. "Not really."

"It was for me. I couldn't decide who to ask. Several times I thought I would talk to people, but at the last moment they didn't look right, so I went on. Finally I realized how many hours of walking I might be wasting, going the wrong direction, so I just got up the nerve and asked an old lady. Of course she was very nice, we had a little chat and on I went. After that it got easier."

"I suppose some people have to have practice at asking for help."

"I suppose. Anyway, you get my point. I have some experience, now. I should be able to do all right on my own."

"Aleria, what do you have in mind?"

"Exactly what I told Master Ogima. I'm going to make my own way back. Just like the Quest, but without help."

Mito raised her eyebrows. "And why are you discussing it with me?"

"I'm not sure. I guess so you'll tell me if I'm doing something really stupid. I'm not angry now, like I was this morning. I might even listen to reason!"

"That would be a change."

"Mito!" She aimed a pillow at her friend's head.

Mito ducked easily, laughing. "There you go, being reasonable again."

Aleria sat down, leaning forward. "But Mito, you understand. You know what I'm like. For most people, the Quest is enough. But not for me. I hoped it would give me a challenge, prove something about my abilities to handle the real world. I know it didn't. So what am I going to do next?"

Mito nodded. "You're going to go out and find some stunt that does prove something."

"Right. And if I don't, I'm going to go home and be miserable."

"And then you'll find something stupid to do, just to prove yourself. And you'll keep on doing more and more stupid things until you get into some real trouble. You're an adult now, and you'll have to take the full responsibility. Need I go on?"

"You know me too well. That's the problem. I've got to do something."

"And you're trying to decide whether this is less stupid than the other alternatives."

"I guess that's it. What do you think?"

"Well, at least if you get into trouble there won't be a scandal. It's not that kind of stunt."

"True."

"Of course, I imagine your family would rather have you in a minor scandal than dead on the road."

"I'm not so sure about that. Oh, of course they would rather have me alive. I know that. But think about it. What good am I to them, if I'm just going to go home and cause trouble? I'm just not cut out to play the 'good little wifey' game like most of the girls. I'll be better off making this trip, proving something to myself, and if I don't come back, maybe we're all better off."

Mito sat staring at her for a long time.

"What's wrong?"

"I never knew you felt that way. You're always the strong one, the confident one. I never thought you'd place such a low value on yourself."

"I'm not placing a low value. I'm just being realistic."

The dark-haired girl shook her head.

"Think of it this way. I'm trying to improve myself. If I succeed at a new Quest, a real one, I'll be a better person. I'll be happier with myself. I need challenge, Mito, you know that. To have real challenge, you have to have risks. Real risks. Besides which, I have every confidence I'm going to come back alive. This isn't some half-used trail through the jungles of Shaeldit. This is through the middle of the kingdom! It's not going to be that bad."

It was her friend's turn to lean forward for emphasis. "It could be that bad. You have to go into this believing that it could be. None of us knows the truth about how dangerous it is out there. It is impossible to tell how much help we got because of the Quest. Maybe there was an agent in every town, even in every inn. Who knows?"

"I agree with you. I'm not going to be stupid about this. The whole idea is to prove I can do it properly. I'm going to be prepared and very careful. Proper clothes, not too pretty, but sensible. Proper equipment. Enough money."

"You can have the rest of mine."

"Mito, I can't take your money."

"Of course you can. I don't need it and you can pay me back when you finish. Don't be stupid. You are going to do this properly, remember?"

"Right. I'll take your money and sew it into the hem of my coat. As emergency funds."

"Good idea. And take this as well." Mito slid up her skirt to reveal a small hideaway dagger strapped just above her knee.

"Mito! Where did you get something like that?"

The girl ducked her head to fumble with the straps, also to hide a blush. "It was a gift."

Aleria waited, but no more information was forthcoming. Her friend seemed to be in real distress, so she decided not to push it. "Thank you. I'll feel much better, having an extra weapon. Now, what road should I take?"

Mito pitched into the new subject with relief. "I don't suppose you'll be taking the straight route."

"What good would that do? They've all just had the Quest class go through. They'd probably recognize one of us coming back. No, I think the best thing is to make it look like I'm going that direction, then duck out to the north through the Duchy of Canah. There's a good road out that way, well maintained and well used. I'm not looking for trouble."

"Aleria." Sudden concern showed on Mito's face. "What do you want me to do? What do I tell them?"

Then Aleria realized what she had done. "I'm sorry, Mito! You are going to be stuck in the middle of this, aren't you? They are going to be questioning you, over and over, to figure out how to find me and bring me back."

"That's all right. I don't mind."

"You don't mind! When my father starts in on you, all concerned for my safety, you won't like it much, believe me."

Mito's back straightened. "Listen, Aleria. You have stood up for me countless times over the past years. This is my turn. You are going out on an uncomfortable, difficult, maybe dangerous journey. The least I can do is stay home and take some of the pressure."

Aleria looked at her friend with new respect. Then she laughed and slapped her shoulder. "That's the attitude!

She leaned forward with new enthusiasm. "I think it's best that you don't tell them anything. Not at first. I don't want you to lie. They'll assume I took the shortest route. You only tell them if I'm late."

"How late is late?"

"What do you think? What about one week longer than the Quest time?"

"That's too long. The route through Canah is only two days longer. I'll give you two more days after that, and then I'll send them on the right road."

"Good enough." She realized again what a good friend she had, so much better than all the bubbleheads in her class. "Mito, just do your best. I trust you to say what you think is right. Whatever you do, I won't be angry. Anything more?"

"Are you going to take a tent?"

"I don't think so. For the first few nights I'll sleep out, but the area is well populated and probably safe. I'll hide out in barns if the weather's bad. Once I know I'm away and clear, I'll stay at inns. I have enough money to do that if I'm careful. I'll tie another blanket across the top, and that will serve."

"Sounds rough to me. Are you sure?"

"I'm not expecting this to be a Sunday stroll."

"I suppose not. Well, rather you than me."

"Thanks."

"You're very welcome. I'll think of you when I'm at home, lounging around the baths, sipping iced wine." She broke off to duck a barrage of pillows.

"I'll go tomorrow, then."

"No, the next day."

"Why?"

"Because you don't want to miss the Reception tomorrow night. And because it will take us time to get the proper gear together, carefully and quietly."

"Granted. No sense rushing it and getting caught. Now, what do I need...?"

12. Much More Like It

Getting out of the Citadel was a bit of a challenge, but they managed it. Hana and Gita were heading home the day after the Reception, as their family tradition was to spend the first week of the holiday floating down the Chanaan river to the Capital on one of anDennal's huge rafts of logs. Aleria slipped out early the same morning, leaving Mito to spread word that she had gone with the Dennals.

For the first few days Aleria was pleased. Her time on the road had hardened her, and the weather was fine. However, sleeping out turned out to be more trouble than she had expected. Most barns were too close to the main buildings, protected by the farm dogs. The storage sheds in the fields were either locked or empty of anything soft to sleep on. The third night, after creeping around two prosperous farms in the rain, she got tired of acting like a criminal and took the next empty shed, spending the night on the hard floor, but at least under a dry roof.

She found, as the days of hiking passed, that she was travelling through rougher territory. The mountains were closing in from the northwest and there were more hills, more forests, less civilization. As the farms got farther apart they also grew more locked and guarded, and sleeping spots became more of a problem. She started to think about using an inn.

The fifth night, cursing her lack of a map, she found herself at sunset on a barren stretch of road with no farm in sight and no idea of how close the next town was. Shrugging mentally, she prepared to sleep out. A huge spruce tree almost out of sight of the road provided protection from the dew, and careful reconnaissance showed her that a small hillock hid her fire as well. Curled in the deep bed of needles at the base of the tree, her economical fire safely set on flat rocks, she was quite proud of herself. She munched her toasted bread and cheese, musing at what a bore camping was. There was a mild pleasure in staring into the ever-changing coals, watching the flickering of tiny flames. It got one to thinking. The warm red light somehow brought back the upstairs rooms at the Sailor's Desire. Her face heated when she thought of Kalmein. Then she tossed her head. What did she owe him? He had a good time...for most of the night anyway. A small voice tried to remind her about going through with promises, but she pushed it aside. She had made no promises. At least not spoken ones. If he had misinterpreted, that was his problem. And a girl had the right to change her mind, didn't she? Soothed by thoughts of this sort, she curled tighter in her blanket and fell asleep.

Her head came up, and she stared around without moving. What had wakened her? There was no sound. She waited a while longer, peering into the darkness. The fire was a mound of ashes, its glow almost gone. Perhaps she should replenish it, but she was so warm, here in her nest.

There it was. A sound. Something was moving through the brush. Something big, by the sound of it. Big, and confident enough not to worry about how much noise it made. Was it a person? The rustling sounds moved across in front of her, then stopped. Then she heard a snuffling sound. Right where she had walked to the tree. Not a person. A bear? For a moment she was frozen with fear. What did bears do? Weren't they supposed to be afraid of people? This one obviously wasn't. The snuffling stopped, and she waited, silent.

Should she light up the fire, or stay quiet and hope it went away? There was a long stillness. Then the sounds began, slowly, cautiously. They were coming towards her! They stopped. Straining her eyes, she realized that there was a darker blot in the darkness outside the skirt of the tree branches. A large blot, and the snuffling noises came again. Then, lit from below by the dim, red glow of the coals, she could make out the short snout, the rounded ears, and the faint glow of two dark eyes, staring at her, edging forward.

Too late to think of the fire. Her hand crept out to her pack and she gently dragged it towards her. Her eyes never leaving the craggy visage in front of her, she fumbled out Mito's dagger, stuffed her blanket into the pack. Then, ever so slowly, she edged to her feet, backing against the trunk of the tree. The branches were close together here, and she groped with her hand behind her until she found one strong enough to bear her weight. It was difficult to start the climb with her back to the tree, knife and pack in her hands, but she somehow felt that, should she take her eyes from the bear's, it would attack. Choking down a hysterical giggle, she took the dagger in her teeth like a bandit from a folk tale. Trying not to hurry, she wormed her way upward, pushing her pack ahead of her, ignoring the twigs that caught and pulled at her clothing, hair and skin. When she thought she was twice her height into the tree she stopped and listened, peering down through the darkness, her hand clutching the hilt of Mito's tiny knife.

She could hear the snuffling again, closer now, and a rank smell wafted up to her. The bear investigated her little camp, stopping several times, and she could picture it peering up at her, deciding. She realized that she could still see the glow of her campfire, but then it was blotted out as the bear investigated that, too. It must not have liked what it smelled, or maybe it burned its nose, because there was a louder "whoof!" a crackling of branches, and she could see the coals again. A few smaller "whoofs" and then she could hear the rustling of the bushes moving away from her tree.

She realized that a cold sweat was running down the centre of her back and that her fingers were clenched to the branch. She made herself relax. Well, it was gone for the moment. What to do now? Go down and make up the fire? No, it would take too long and the bear might come back. Besides which, it would just burn down again and she'd have to stay awake to keep it lit.

No, the only way she would feel safe was up in the tree. Feeling around, she could tell that she was sitting where two large branches joined the trunk. If she put her back against the

117

main stem and leaned her arms on another branch to her left, she just might be able to get comfortable...

It took several long minutes of squirming around, but just as her heartbeat began to slow, she found a position that was semi-comfortable and she finally drifted off.

To be roused by the feeling of falling. She jerked awake, grabbing the branch. She tried to keep the sleepy feeling, but realized it was no good. She was not going to get to sleep if she was afraid of falling off the branch. And she wasn't going back to the ground. Digging around in her pack, she found her long sash. She wound it around her torso, then around the branch. She sagged into it. Yes, it would hold her. Again, she drifted off to a light sleep, vaguely conscious of her uncomfortable position, of the hard branches digging into her, the prickly bark under her hands. But she slept.

* * *

The first light and the loud twittering of birds brought her reluctantly awake: stiff, aching, scratched. She tried to sleep again, but it was no use. The light and the pain had roused her, and the birds finished the job. She looked around and listened for a long time. There seemed to be nothing moving on the forest floor. She untied the sash and climbed down, amazed that she had made it so high through the tight branches in the dark.

Quickly, she stoked up the fire, blowing the faint coals into brightness. At least there was ample dry wood under the tree. Yawning, she toasted the last of the bread and drank a stale swallow from her canteen. Tonight she was going to need an inn.

After carefully extinguishing the fire, she took one last look around her small haven, shouldered her pack and moved back towards the road. She noticed a crushed trail through the undergrowth, proving that her night's adventure had not been a dream. A footprint in a muddy spot was not large, as far as she could tell, but big enough to make her shiver. She moved more quickly towards the open.

But not so quickly that she didn't check both left and right before she stepped onto the road. Sure enough, a figure in the distance was moving towards her. She faded back into the forest, watching.

As the man approached she got a better look at him. He swung along, his head up and his shoulders back. Tall, young, blond hair. Good quality clothing, but not too good. Perhaps chosen, like hers, to attract no attention. The medium-sized pack did not seem to slow him down, and he strode with cheerful purpose. She slipped back further and froze behind a fallen log, only her eyes showing.

To her dismay, as the stranger reached the spot opposite her, he stopped, looked straight at her and smiled.

"You might as well come out."

She almost fell for it. He couldn't know she was there. She stayed still, cursing her carelessness in packing the dagger away.

Sure enough, his eyes moved on, scanning the forest, then the edge of the road. Probably her footprints in the dust. "I know you're there. I can smell your fire. I should tell you, I have nothing worth stealing. I'm nobody worth kidnapping, and if you're afraid of me, I assure you I'm perfectly harmless." He reached out empty hands, stood there a moment.

Again, she almost stepped forward, but a fierce surge of determination held her. If he was so smart, let him figure it out. After a while his hands slowly dropped, he shrugged and moved on.

She waited a long time, moving only enough to keep her eyes on his retreating back. Once, he turned quickly and looked back for a moment before continuing his stride. Maybe she imagined it, but he might be walking a bit faster. She grinned. So he was a bit afraid, was he? Good. Let him stay that way.

She made herself comfortable and waited a bit longer. Let him get far ahead. At his pace, he would leave her behind.

119

Repositioning her dagger closer to hand, she hoisted her pack and moved on with more care, noting the dust at the side of the road, listening to the sounds of the birds and squirrels nearby but trying not to be obvious about it. He hadn't looked like trouble, but she had started a game and he looked like he had a sense of humour.

So she was ready when a voice came from close behind her at the side of the road.

"Ahah! I thought so!"

She spun, slipping out of her pack straps and jumping forward instead of back as he might have expected. She was satisfied to see the man's startled face as he backed against a tree, eyes crossed in a vain attempt to track the point of her dagger.

She smiled coldly. "You should know better than to jump out behind people."

He raised his open hands. "Be careful with that thing, lady. It looks sharp!"

"It is sharp," she flicked the point at his fingers, "Keep your hands down."

He lowered his hands. "All right, all right. What do you want?"

"What do I want? I want to walk down the public road without being hassled. What did you think you were doing?"

She allowed him to edge backwards and away; she didn't want his hands that close to her wrist anyway.

"I was just checking. I knew somebody was in the forest and I didn't know what kind of game you were playing. There could be bandits around here, you know."

"And aren't you lucky I'm not a bandit." Keeping her eye on him, she retrieved her pack. "Who are you, and where are you going?"

He relaxed some more. "My name's Shen Waring and I'm going to Izeu. Carrying some documents for my father's business. No money. I'm not that stupid. We're in the textile business. Woollens, cotton, silk, the whole lot. Who are you?"

"I'm Aleria and I'm travelling...a lot further than that."

He glanced at her with more calculation than she liked. "Aleria. That's a pretty name."

"What do you mean by that?"

Again the empty hands came up. "Nothing, nothing. Can't a man say something nice to a lady?"

He seemed genuine, but there was a hint of a smile that made her wonder. "Let's walk. You go ahead."

"I'm not going to walk ahead of you with that knife at my back. Can't we walk side by side? The road's plenty wide. Then we can talk."

"Who says I want to talk?"

He turned and started off. "Why not? It gets boring, walking by yourself. I'm glad to have a pretty girl to talk to, and you've got to be safer with me along. It's a good idea for both of us."

"Safer?" She slid the knife back into its sheath and hefted her pack. "That remains to be seen." However, she matched him stride for stride, and they moved off.

She soon discovered that Shen Waring was the only son of a textile dealer in Taine, several days' walk to the southwest. He, in turn, asked about her family.

"Oh, my father's in cartage. Half the wagons you see around here are probably his." It was a clever misdirection, she thought, since most people would take it as an exaggeration, while in truth her father's dealings with Lord anCanah meant he probably did own half the heavy cartage that used this road. Her new companion looked impressed but sceptical, just as she hoped.

"Does your business need any carting done?"

He shook his head. "Sorry, we have our work all contracted out, mostly to Lord anDalmyn. He charges top price, but he has only the best animals and equipment. Very reliable, and nobody messes with his wagons, if they know what's good for them. My father says its best to go along with the powerful. You make yourself useful to them, and after a while they realize they need you and they don't mess you around."

"Has Lord anDalmyn ever messed you around?"

121

"Not yet. We do a lot of business with him, and at the prices he charges, that means it's a lot easier for him to keep his big mansion in the capital and his wife and daughter in new gowns for the balls." He glanced at her and grinned. "No, anDalmyn is much better off treating us well. It's worth his while."

She nodded. "I suppose. Still, it's tough trying to compete with that kind of power."

"Tell you what. You get your father to contact Waring Weavers next time he's in Taine. I'll put in a word with my father, and maybe you can pick up some of the smaller, unscheduled runs."

It was a relief to relax and smile prettily at him. *This is such fun!* "Why thank you, Shen. I'm sure my father will appreciate that." She turned a half-pirouette in the road. "Maybe then he can afford another gown for his daughter for her next ball."

He grinned back. "As long as I get to go to the ball with her."

"We'll just have to see, won't we?"

They walked on, laughing.

He was fun to talk with, but she was impressed at his knowledge of the road. When she asked about the danger, he shrugged. "There's not much danger to me. I wasn't lying back there. Nothing I carry has any value, as the papers are no good to anyone else except my father's business." He grinned, "And I can talk my way out of any trouble I meet."

He strode on. "Not much romance in it, but I like getting out, getting free from the business for a while. What about you?"

She grinned. "Not much romance here, either. This is a one-and-only for me, and I didn't choose it. I was visiting relatives, and had to leave because...let's just say I didn't get along with my cousins." She shrugged. "So I'm going home."

"Just like that? You packed up and headed out?"

Her head came up. "That's right. They never thought I would, so they thought they could boss me around. I showed them."

"I suppose. Still, it's dangerous out here, travelling alone."

"Huh! I have less of value than you do."

"Don't be so sure, little girl," He leered at her, his fingers plucking at the front of her blouse. She laughed and slapped his hand away and the incident passed.

"How much farther to Izeu?

"Don't you have a map?"

"No, I just ask people."

"I don't have a map, either. I know the way. Here." He picked up a stick from beside the road. "This road goes through Ocady and on to the east. There's a line of mountains ahead of us, here. The road goes around the end, I cut off here to Izeu, you keep going to Kingsport."

She took the stick, drew a wiggling slash through the dirt. "What are these mountains like? It looks like a long way around them."

"I don't go around them. I go through them. I know a shortcut."

"You do?" She stood, arms akimbo, staring at him.

He mimicked her stance and her tone. "I do. I use it all the time. It would take three days to get around the end, and I can do it in two, going over the mountain. Sure, it's a tough climb, but it's not dangerous or anything and it's much faster."

"I see. What about other dangers? Other than the trail."

"You mean animals and bandits? No bandits in that area. Nobody to rob. Sure, there's bears and wolves and that, but I've never heard of anyone being bothered by them. My father showed me the trail and my family knows I use it, so if anything goes wrong they'll know where to come looking."

She considered. "That's good, because they'll come looking for you before they come looking for me." She looked him over again. Everything she saw told her that he was exactly what he said. If she could have a little adventure, and save a day's walk... "Can I come?"

He shrugged, grinned. "Why not? Two is always safer."

She smiled back. "Great. Where do we cut off the road?"

"Not for a few hours. We'd better stop at a farm soon, to pick up extra bread and cheese, maybe some smoked meat. That's better for you, anyway."

"It is?"

"It's always good to have someone know where you're going. We tell the farmer who we are and what our plans are. If anyone comes looking for us, the farmer will tell them where we went."

"That sounds logical."

"Let's go." They picked up their packs and started out.

Soon they had settled into their travelling pace. Shen was loaded a bit heavier than she was; that made up for her shorter legs and they moved comfortably together. Scattered clouds covered the sun, so the day never got too warm.

True to his plan, Shen stopped at a farm, where the lady seemed to know him and jibed him about his new travelling companion while she made up a package of food. As they left she winked at Aleria. "Now don't you let him fool you into doing all the cooking and the cleaning. I know what men are like in camp. They think they're having a holiday. You make him do his share."

Aleria nodded, grinning. "I knew that already, but I'm glad he heard you say it, too." She reached out and pushed Shen towards the road. "Come, my trusty pack animal. Bear my load to my destination." She could hear the woman's laughter following them down the lane. It was fun to joke, but now she was sure the woman would remember her in detail.

Soon, Shen stopped where a small creek tumbled down the rocks and crossed the road. "See the path, there?"

She looked, dubious. "Yes. I see it."

"That's our trail."

"Is it that small all the way?"

"No, it gets wider and narrower depending on the terrain and the use."

"Why would the use be different?"

He shrugged. "Various reasons. There's one spot where a larger trail joins in. You have to know where to cut off again or you end up going down the mountain chain instead of across it. There's another spot that passes near a salt lick and the trail is well-used along there."

She shrugged. "You're the trusty local guide. Lead on."

It was cooler under the trees, so the climb wasn't too hard. They hiked up a ridge, crossed over the stream and followed its valley, climbing all the way. Soon they were out of the heavy forest of the valley, into the pine groves higher up. They stopped for a rest after a steep pitch and looked back out over their trail, where they could see the faint, light line of the road far below.

"We're making good time. There's a decent campsite a couple of hours up. I think we'll stay there."

"Fine with me. I'm not too tired yet." She looked out at the scenery for a while. "What's a salt lick?"

"That's a place where the ground is salty. The animals love it. Deer, sheep, and mountain goat all come there."

She glanced at him. "The animals come and lick the ground."

"That's right."

"And I'm supposed to believe that."

He held out open hands. "Why would I lie? They do lick the ground. They really like the salt, I guess. It's a great place to hunt, although not very sporting.

"Have you hunted there?"

He shook his head. "I'm a sport hunter. If I really needed the meat, I'd hunt a salt lick. I don't need the meat to live on, so I give the animals a better chance."

"How kind of you."

"Are you against hunting?"

"Not completely. As you say, if a person needs the meat..."

"But if he doesn't?"

She shrugged. "If you enjoy it, I suppose it's a good skill to have. Even in our modern society, it's possible that you might need it some day."

He nodded. "Shall we go on?"

"Might as well. We'll just be tireder later."

He reached out a hand and hauled her to her feet. "All right. On we go."

It was more than two hours later that they reached the campsite, and Aleria was wet up to her armpits.

Shen regarded her. "Once you stop moving you're going to get cold. If you take off your pack and go looking for extra wood, I'll get a fire going."

"Whatever you say. You're right about getting cold."

"Get some big, dry pieces. If they're heavier they'll keep the fire going longer."

"And keep me warmer, hauling them back."

"Exactly. Let's get to it."

When she came back dragging two short but rather thick logs, there was a wisp of smoke drifting up from the twigs and grass between his hands. Soon a tiny flame appeared, and he started to add larger branches. Once the flames rose to waist level she started to feel their warmth, and she held her hands out to take it in.

"You'd better get out of those wet clothes."

"Some good. My other dress was at the bottom of my pack, and it's wet, too."

"You can wear some of mine." He reached into his pack, pulling out items, smelling them, and putting them aside. "I know I've got something clean in here somewhere. I was saving it for a special occasion."

"That's good to hear. I can't think of an occasion more special than a friend freezing to death."

"So get out of your wet dress. Don't worry. I won't peek."

"You better not, if you know what's good for you."

She struggled out of her clinging dress and started on her boots.

"Ah, here we are. Oops."

He had turned to hand her the shirt, and 'forgot' not to look while he did so. She frowned at him. "Put your eyes back in your head and hand me the shirt."

"Uh, sure. I'm sorry, just a slip of the eye, so to speak."

She turned her back and tugged the shirt on. "Well, don't slip again, or you might get that eye blackened."

"It might be worth it. You're very beautiful."

"It sounds like most women are, once we get our clothes off. Do you have any pants?"

126

"Here you go."

She turned, and this time he was holding out the clothing with one hand, the other covering his eyes, his face averted.

"Now he does it right. Thanks, anyway. That feels much better."

"I'm glad. Now. Who's cooking?"

They began a good-natured wrangle about the camp chores, and soon there was meat in the frying pan and the smell of cooking wafted over the camp.

After supper, they sat by the fire staring into the coals in the gathering dark.

"Gotta ask you a question."

"Sure."

"I wasn't supposed to look, I know, but I had another reason."

"Another reason. This is going to be good."

"No, I did. Do you keep your dagger on your leg?"

"Yes."

"Hmm."

"Is that what you needed to know so badly?"

"I was curious. I know it sounds funny, but I have to be careful too, you know."

"Now you know. I'm well-armed and well-trained, so you better watch your step."

"Well-trained?"

"I do barehand and sword as well as dagger."

"I see. Who trained you? Family?"

"I went to lessons."

"What sort of parents send their daughter to fighting lessons?"

"Parents that want her to be able to handle whatever the world throws at her."

He thought about that for a while. "Can I make a suggestion?"

"Sure."

"It's about the dagger on the leg. Who told you to put it there?"

"That was the place the girl who gave it to me wore it."

"Well, I don't know how to say this, but that could be a problem."

"How so?"

"If a guy is going to...well...rape a woman, he throws her down, lifts her skirt, and...there's your hideout in plain sight."

"I see. What do you suggest?"

"Most of the time you wear long sleeves, right? You only changed into that sleeveless top once we got off the main road."

"You mean I should wear it on my arm?"

"Yes, like this." He pulled up his right sleeve, and there, on the inside of his forearm was a small dagger, hilt down. "I have a special sheath. I only have to do this..." he flexed his wrist, and the dagger slid down into his hand. A flick of his fingers and the point was towards her.

"Very neat. Do you think I could do that?"

"You wouldn't be able to do the drop-sheath, but if you hung it hilt-down on your left arm you could get it out with your other hand almost as fast."

She stared at him, daring him to look, as she pulled down her pants to remove the sheath from her leg. He gazed skyward, smiling the whole time. Then they experimented until she had the sheath fixed on her inner forearm: firm, but not tight enough to cut off circulation. With a bit of practice, she knew she could get it out smoothly and quickly. At the moment the weight seemed strange, but she would get used to it.

It was a warm night and they lay on opposite sides of the fire, staring up into the stars, chatting about this and that. Nothing important, just those many small thoughts and minor details that allow one person to get to know the other. Tired from their climb, they soon fell asleep.

13. The Real Thing

Aleria woke feeling damp. A heavy dew had fallen, penetrating her blankets. Shivering, she dressed and checked the fire. There were some coals deep in the ashes, so she blew on them, adding small dead twigs until they burst into flame.

Soon she had a fire going and a pot of water on for coffee.

"You going to get up at all?"

"Probably. It was just so pleasant to watch you doing all the work."

"You're a man with a turn of phrase. Was that supposed to be a compliment?"

"As long as you keep working, you can take it as such."

"Don't worry. You'll do your share."

He watched her some more. "You do know what you're doing."

"I should. My mother's an excellent cook, and some of it must have rubbed off. I don't have the patience to be good at it."

"In that case, I'll get up and watch the biscuits cook. I have plenty of patience for that sort of thing."

She snorted and went on with her preparations. "Just like you had patience to watch me take my swim yesterday."

"You didn't expect me to play the hero, did you? Jump in and save you?"

"I hardly needed saving. I just had the bad luck to step on a loose rock exactly above that hole."

"It was bad luck, all right."

She turned and looked at him. "All right. It was also careless. I need to be wary were I place my feet."

"Lesson learned, no harm done. Tell you what, though. If you like, I'll cut you a walking stick before we set out today. One for me, too. A stick would have saved you."

"Good idea, after it's all over."

"We live and learn. At least some of us learn."

"It's a mistake the first time. If you make it twice, it's stupidity. My grandmother used to say that."

"Smart lady."

Their conversation continued like this all morning. It was a hard path, continuing to climb through several tight passes, and there was a certain amount of clambering over rocks. At first the stick got in her way, but as the day wore on she learned how and when to use it and soon she didn't know how she had managed without.

Shen was a good companion, not overly protective, but wary of spots where she might have trouble. She did her best not to let him down, but some places she had to ask for help.

"How did you get down there?"

"I leaned my stick way down and stepped across to here."

"I can't reach that far. The rest of it is too smooth. Should I jump?"

"It's pretty rough landing. You might turn an ankle. Here. Reach your stick over there, push sort of sideways. Put your hand on my shoulder, and lower yourself. Hey, careful!"

As she swung off the rock, her full weight came against him, and they leaned back against the wall, pressed closely together. They stayed that way for a breathless moment, then she laughed and pushed herself upright. "Thanks. Next time I fall off a mountain, make sure you're underneath, will you?"

"I think I could be persuaded."

She laughed again and continued down the mountain, but she could feel a shaking inside her and warmth spreading up her neck. She hoped he didn't notice. Maybe she hoped he did.

There was a spattering of rain that afternoon, but it came to nothing, only cooling them, and they made good time. They had come out on top of the mountain range above tree line, and the trail led along the top of a ridge: white stones against the green moss.

Shen gazed around for a long time. "This is the other reason I come this way."

The mountains, dappled with sun and cloud, sloped down to flatlands, fading away into the haze. Just below them a small lake ruffled its waters into lively sparkles.

"Beautiful, isn't it?" She laid a hand on his shoulder. It was a simple gesture, meant only to share the moment more closely.

He nodded and did not move.

After a while, they tramped on, walking slower, admiring the beauty. Then they were down off the ridge, the trail grew steeper and the brush closed around them, showering them with leftover raindrops. Soon they were both soaked, but the day was warm enough, so they kept going.

By evening the clouds had not broken and Shen said they were making good time, so they stopped early to give them time to dry their clothing. They were well down the mountain by now and it was easy to find a dense tree to camp under.

Shen looked at the sky. "I think you'd better have the tent tonight. It might rain."

"How about you?"

"I'll borrow your extra blanket if you don't mind, and wrap up under the tree. I'll be fine."

"Are you sure?"

"Sure, I'm sure."

"But that's not fair."

"Let me play the gentleman just this once, will you?"

She grinned. "I can't complain, can I?"

"So don't."

They finished their camp chores and went to bed. Silence descended. Then it was broken by a soft, high-pitched whine.

"Drat!"

"What's wrong?"

"There's a mosquito in here."

"Oh? There aren't any out here."

"Well, there's one in here and it's too dark to find it."

"So go to sleep. Some time it will bite you, and that will be it."

"That's a great consolation."

"You're welcome."

"Say, I bet if there were two of us in here it would halve my chances of getting bit."

"I'd say that's pretty good arithmetic."

"So are you coming? The damsel needs rescuing."

"You don't really mean that."

She paused a moment. "What if I did?"

She could hear him moving outside, and suddenly his head pushed through the flap, his voice serious. "You know what would happen, don't you?"

Serious as well, she gulped. "I guess I do."

Then he was gone. Forgetting the mosquito, she rolled her blanket around her and tried to sleep.

* * *

Aleria had little to say during breakfast, and Shen seemed to be thinking as well. However, once they got moving the mood lightened, and soon they were walking down the trail, making up alternate lines to "His Hand Began Upon Her Knee." It was a song she had sung with great enthusiasm with the other girls, but as the story developed she remembered where the last two verses went. Shen seemed to realize it as well, and both their voices faded. There was a moment of embarrassed silence.

"Not an appropriate song for mixed company, I suppose."

"No." They both walked along, thinking.

Shen stopped so suddenly that Aleria, her mind on other things, almost ran into him.

"What?"

"Look!"

The trail was straight for some distance in front of them, and a bear had appeared, ambling along in their direction.

"The wind's the wrong way. He can't smell us."

"Won't he see us?"

"His eyes aren't that good. If he doesn't know we're here before he gets too close, he might decide it's safer to attack than to turn his back and run. Then we're in trouble."

"What do we do?"

He raised his voice. "We stop whispering, is what we do. We make lots of noise, so that he can hear us."

She spoke louder. "We make lots of noise, do we?"

They continued to call out to each other. The bear stopped, looking puzzled. It was not a large bear, as far as she could tell, black in colour, its shoulder about as high as her waist. Not too big, but big enough to be very frightening. It began to cast its head from side to side, sniffing and staring.

"He still can't smell us. What if he keeps coming?"

"Get off the trail. If he wants it, he can have it. Get up on that log over there and bash your stick against it. I'll go over here.

"No! You come with me, on this side."

"No, we get apart. That way the bear won't want to attack either of us, because he'll have to turn his back on the other one. If he does attack me, you rush in, screaming, to attract his attention. When he comes for you, I'll do the same."

"Will that work?"

He frowned across at her. "We could always just run. Slowest one gets to be lunch."

They continued to shout and bang their sticks. The bear stood on its hind legs and cast around some more. Then it moved forward, weaving from side to side, nose searching to the wind.

Suddenly its head came up. It stood again, weak eyes peering. It made a "whoof" sound and trotted back a few paces. It "whoofed" again and cut to the side of the trail. Then it made up its mind and turned, scuttling away to the east. They watch it go until it was lost in the trees.

"Is it safe to go on?"

"I think so. Once he smelled us properly he left. That's a good sign. Let's go. Don't run, though."

"I won't."

"Keep talking."

"Right. What do I say?"

"I don't know. Sing a song."

"I don't feel so cheerful at the moment."

"Neither do I."

They marched along for a while, shouting nonsense, all their senses straining towards the trail behind them.

All of a sudden she couldn't go any farther. Her knees began to shake, and her pack felt like it was full of lead.

"Aleria, come on, keep walking!" He turned. "Hey, you don't look so good. Here, take your pack off." He slipped out of his own straps to help her.

"I'm all right. Just a bit shaky."

His arms went around her.

"I'm not going to fall down."

"Not if I can help it."

She felt the strength in his arms, and the need to hold someone. She put her arms around him, and then they were kissing. She felt a fire starting to burn in her and held him even closer. After a long, fierce moment, he pulled back and looked straight into her eyes. She tilted her head up, but he disentangled one arm, put a finger to her lips.

"I don't want to be taking advantage."

For a moment, she felt like bursting into tears; she didn't know why. Instead, she laid her head on his shoulder. "Sorry."

"No, it's a common reaction after danger, I've heard."

"Well, I suppose that's all right then." She kissed him again, more carefully. "That's to say thanks for getting me through."

"A pleasure, I'm sure." He looked back along the path. "Do you know how difficult it was to train that bear to walk down the trail like that, at exactly the right time?"

She slapped his chest with the back of her hand, laughing. "I don't think I want the chance to find out. Let's get out of this place."

They walked on down the trail with Shen leading. Aleria watched the muscles of his shoulders roll with the straps of his pack.

"It's getting late, isn't it?"

"If I remember this right, we're almost to the main road. It would be nice to camp where there's water." As they walked on, she was thinking what could happen once they camped.

On down the hill, the forest became thicker, the trees taller. Birch and aspen began to fill in between the evergreens, and their way became more shaded.

Soon they reached the main road and turned east. On the wider path, they could walk side-by-side. It seemed natural to reach out and take his hand.

"Here's a stream."

He nodded. "We can camp anywhere around here."

She dropped her pack and raised her arms, glad to be free of the weight. "I feel like I'm floating." Arms outstretched, she 'flew' around in a circle. As she came past, he grabbed her by the waist, and she put her arms around his neck, kissing him again.

The fire started once more, and she pushed against him, her mouth pressed against his. After a long kiss, she threw her head back and pulled against his restraining arms, looking into his eyes. Very gently, she disengaged his hands. Then, with a smooth motion, she pulled her blouse off over her head and stood in front of him, her arms raised, her bare torso arched back.

It seemed a long time that she stood there, aware of her complete vulnerability. She knew her breasts were good, rather large and firm, although one was slightly higher than the other. What if he didn't like large breasts? Her hands fell to the top of her head.

Then she could stand the tension no longer. "If you don't do something soon this is going to become very embarrassing."

His eyes flew upward to her face. "Oh, Aleria, you are…you are…"

"I know. Beautiful. Kiss me, dammit!"

A gush of molten fire spread through her lower body as he locked his hands behind her back and pulled her forward, to touch her breasts with his lips. It tickled at first, but then his mouth moved more firmly, and she twined her fingers in his hair to guide him.

They sank to the ground together, their hands moving over each other's bodies. Everything was in a whirl, and she was melting in to a frenzy of passion when she realized that he had slowed, even stopped. She opened her eyes, concern bringing her back to reality.

"What's wrong?"

He smiled. "Nothing. But don't you think we should put up the tent?"

"Why? What do you want the tent for?"

"I sort of though it would be nice if we could take a few more clothes off, and there seem to be mosquitoes around here."

She smiled and laid one hand on his chest, absently rubbing an itchy spot on her neck with the other. "I suppose you're right. Let's set up the tent."

She started to get up, then a thought struck her. "You haven't changed your mind, have you, and are going to use this as an excuse to stop?"

He smoothed one hand across and under her breast, lifting it and pulling her forward. He kissed her very lightly on the lips, then along the line of her jaw, up to nibble on her ear lobe. "What do you think?"

Grinning, she slapped his hand away. "You're worse than the mosquitoes. Where are we going to put up the tent?"

He was busy with his pack. "There's a nice clear spot just over there, and there's water right here."

A sudden chill of caution struck through her mood. "I don't know. It's awfully close to the road. Hadn't we better try to get hidden, even a bit?"

They looked around the clearing. Undergrowth was heavy and filled the spaces between the trunks of the young trees, where limbs grew low and twined together.

He grinned. "I don't think you want to push through that stuff too far, especially dressed like you are."

His smile was slightly crooked, in an endearing sort of way. "Look. There's a level spot just behind that tree. It's not too obvious from the road. Once it gets dark, someone could walk right by and not notice us. Let's get this tent organized."

It took quite a while to get the tent set up, since he kept insisting on helping her with everything. Close enough that his hands kept straying to other matters and he had to be chastised frequently, made to pay with contrite kisses wherever she demanded. In the end, it was the mosquitoes that drove them to hurry, and soon their bedrolls were spread. They clambered in, tied the flaps, and sat, quite still, looking at each other in the light of a small candle.

She reached out to undo his shirt, and he shrugged it off. Soon the rest of their clothes followed, and they stretched out naked together. She moved closer to him, then raised her head to look down into his face.

"Shen, can I tell you something?"

His brow wrinkled at her serious tone, but he smiled softly. "Of course."

"I...I haven't done this before."

He nodded. "I see. Do you still want to?" He raised himself up on one elbow to look across at her in the dimness. "Because you don't have to, you know. I mean, it won't be great, you understand, but you don't have to. I can...well, I'll survive, I guess."

Touched by his concern, she pushed him back down and laid her head on his chest. "Of course I still want to. It's just that I haven't ever tried it before, and I though maybe you could...well, I don't know. That's the problem. I don't know what you can do."

Again she raised her head to look at him. "Have you ever? I mean, I can ask that, can't I? Have you?"

His head moved back and forth. "Well, yes and no."

"What?" She put both hands against his chest, raised herself up to look down on him. "I didn't think there was any doubt about that sort of thing. Have you or haven't you?"

He grinned, and reached out to lift her breast with his hand. "You have beautiful breasts, you know."

"Answer the question. Yes or no?"

"Well, the answer is yes, a few times. But never with someone who has never tried before, no. Yes and no."

She raised her nose. "You play with me, my good fellow," she twitched her shoulder, removing her breast from his hand, "in more ways than one. Demonstrate your vaunted experience!"

She lowered herself upon him, and soon all thought was lost in a whirl of fire.

Much later, they lay nested together, his drowsy hand stroking her stomach, the tip of his tongue tracing the line of her ear. It was a perfect moment, just as she had always dreamed. She reached up and smoothed his hair, ran her hand down his cheek. He kissed her fingers, and her hand dropped. He reached over and snuffed out the candle.

Then the great, silent stillness of the forest descended upon them, and they slept.

14. Wake Up!

She was startled out of her dreams by a sudden stiffening of his body, his hand grasping her arm.

"What?" She struggled to move, but he clamped her other arm.

"Listen!"

She was frightened by his intensity. After a long pause, she heard it, too. The mutter of voices borne on the breeze. Then it was gone. They waited a moment longer, then the noise came again, and the click of metal on metal.

"Men. Coming."

His head, silhouette against the light canvas, nodded. "Any group of men travelling at this time of night, you don't want to be seen by."

"I've got to hide." She started grabbing her things in the dark, stuffing them into her pack. "Help me."

He unlaced the tent flap, and she slid out.

"You don't have your clothes on."

She knew her grin was unseen in the dark. "I'll be back when they've gone. Then we'll see if I need my clothes." She jammed her feet into her boots.

She stood upright in the bright moonlight, a twinge of fear going through her as she regarded the impenetrable darkness under the trees, remembering the bear.

Then a louder voice called something, and she could hear the thud of feet, many feet, on the hard ground of the road. She slid into the forest as quickly as possible, glad of her boots, trying to ignore the branches scoring her naked skin. She blundered along for a few more steps then stopped to catch her breath, listening.

The voices were louder, but the marching had stopped, and she realized the men had reached the stream. To her dismay, she heard orders being called out, and then a light sprang up. They were making camp! If someone came collecting firewood...

She started to move again, slowly this time, circling away from the camp towards the road further along. It would do no good to get lost in this forest at night. When she felt she was a safe distance, she fumbled in her bundle for something to wear, cursing to herself as the tangled clothing and bedding refused to cooperate. Hopefully she wasn't leaving anything important on the forest floor in the dark.

Dressed, she stumbled on, stopping frequently to listen to the sounds of the camp. Soon they faded behind her and she cut more to the left, angling for the road. She had been forcing her way through the clinging undergrowth for what seemed hours and she was still in the forest. She should have been at the road long ago. She stopped to think. If she was lost she should bundle herself up in her blanket and wait for dawn. That would be better than blundering around in the dark, maybe getting more disoriented or hurting herself. Worse still, she might be heard by one of the men. She listened again. Louder voices arose behind her, and she realized that she had got her directions switched and was walking directly away from the camp again. Turning left, she started out once more.

Then her reaching hand felt an opening and she stepped out onto the road. Realizing her mistake, she leaned back into the bushes and froze, but no sound disturbed the night. She stood a moment to consider. What should she do now? There was enough moonlight that she could travel slowly. She would be better not to be seen by those men. But what of Shen? Surely they would find him. What would they do to him?

Another thought struck her. What if they were friends, people he knew, and she spent the night crawling around in the forest for nothing? Was it worth the risk to go back and find out? She though longingly of Shen's smooth body against hers, his lips soft on her skin. It was probably stupid, but she had to know.

Stashing her pack behind the white trunk of a large paper birch she was sure she would recognize again, she crept back up the road. She tried to keep out of the direct light of the moon, but the shadows were so dark she couldn't see where to put her feet. She had gone farther than she thought, and with her slow pace it took her a long while to approach the camp. The voices continued to sound loud and free, with the occasional deep laugh ringing out. No alarm had been raised.

Wary of a sentry, she stopped when she could see the fire, a large blaze that got in her eyes and made it difficult to see anything in the darkness in front of her. She waited, shielding her eyes from the light, and soon she was rewarded by movement. A man stumbled down the trail towards her, calling another man's name. Closer to her than she would have liked, a figure rose from a log at the trail's edge.

"Right here, you fool. What have ya bin doin'? Starin' inta th' fire?"

The new sentry muttered something and the other man laughed. "Well, thanks for comin'. I was thinkin' maybe ya fergot it was yer turn, and me so hungry an' all. If it wasn't for I knew Melask would skin me alive for leavin' my post, I woulda come in ta see what was happenin'.

"Nothin' happenin' except that kid."

"What kid?"

"There was a kid camped behind a tree, right by the crick."

"What'd they do to him?"

The shoulders of the man on the road gave a hunching motion. "Nothin', I guess. He's pretty harmless. Some kind o' courier. Melask checked his stuff over and he ain't carryin' nothin' of value. Whataya think we oughta' do to him?

The other man stepped onto the road. "Prob'ly keep him with us in the mornin' just to make sure he don't go tellin' no tales. Once we get to Izeu it won't matter 'n' he can go his way."

"Just let him go?"

"Listen, you ape. We may not be the King's Guard, but we ain't the kind of guys go around knockin' off innocent people just for fun. We gotta make a livin' in this area. Some merchant's messenger goes missin', there's a passle o' sojers beatin' the bushes for days. They find out we did him, nobody'll hire us."

"I thought we was hirin' out to that Slathe for his rebellion."

"Hah! Don't never count on revolutions to make your livin'. Half the time they lose and then you never get paid. The other half they win and then they want to get ridda you 'cause you're a danger to 'em." He slapped his companion on the shoulder. "Don't worry. When there's someone needs messin' up, I'll call on you first. Now I'm gonna stop jawin' here and put my mouth to work on summa that shoeleather the cook calls steak. You keep watch out here for a while. I'll make sure someone remembers to come after you." His feet crunched gravel as he turned. "And don't look back at the fire." With a guffaw, the larger man strolled towards camp, and the new sentry settled himself on the log.

Aleria took advantage of their noise to cover her own departure and stole back down the road. Well, that was that. Shen was in no danger that she could see, and there was no use her trying to make contact while he was travelling with his captors. Her best chance was to get some distance away from them then hide out, sleep, and let them go by in the morning.

As she picked up her pack her water bottle sloshed and she realized that she had not eaten that evening. Remembering why brought a smile to her lips and her whole body tingled.

Chewing on the piece of bread, she squared her shoulders and leaned into the pack straps. This was only a setback. She would be seeing Shen again. That was certain.

She stumbled on until she was so tired she couldn't walk farther. Finding an animal trail that showed a faint trace in the moonlight, she followed it until it turned and disappeared in the darkness. A large spruce tree stood among a scattering of young aspens, its shadow a pool of invisibility against the white trunks. Hoping it would be as good a shelter from prying eyes come daylight, she crawled under the long, drooping branches, wrapped herself in her blanket, dropped her head on her bundle and slipped into a restless slumber. With the first greying of the sky she awoke and looked around. She was well hidden from the road, she was sure.

She waited, slept again, waited again. The men did not come. Did she sleep through their passing? She rolled up her belongings and crept back to the road. Surely she could recognize the footprints of that many men. The road looked unused.

Shouldering her pack, she set out. Either they were sleeping late or they had taken some other path that she had missed in the dark. She knew where Shen was going. She would find him.

As she walked, she began to remember the conversation she had overheard the night before. Mercenaries, hiring out to someone called Slathe for a rebellion. As she thought about it, that sounded serious. She wondered what she should do. At least she should tell someone. Maybe the authorities in Izeu.

But would they believe her? Well, she could always pull rank on them, forget her little game, tell them who she was. With renewed vigour she tramped on, her eyes scanning the forest on either side for any sign of trouble.

As she walked, she began to think about her situation. Her little game suddenly wasn't a game any more. She was alone. She knew no one in this area of the realm. Her father's teamsters came this way, but not on a schedule, and he had no agents here. If this was a revolution, she would be terribly vulnerable, having no safe place to stay and no one to identify her. Fear began to creep its fingers through her mind.

* * *

By the time she reached the next small village she was ready to forget her precautions and talk to anyone. She was far enough along now that here was no point in continuing to hide her trail, and if there was a revolution coming she wanted people to know where she was.

She went straight to the only inn on the main street, ordered food and ate ravenously. She sized up the woman who served her: older, better dressed, confident; she must be the innkeeper's wife. She mentioned avoiding mercenaries on the trail and having overheard something about a revolution.

The woman was immediately concerned. The moment Aleria was finished eating, she found herself rushed over to the mayor's cottage to repeat her story. She was unable to give them much detail, but they were appreciative.

"You must go on to Furane. There is a military post there. They will know what to do."

"How far is that?"

"It is only three hours walk. If you will go and take the news, we can keep all our people here. We will need them if there are rebels around."

She could hear the basic selfishness behind their words, but understood it. She agreed, took their gifts of food and water, and headed out, leaving them preparing for the worst.

Once again the forest seemed frightening, but she found that it helped to have something to do, a sense of purpose. She must get to Furane to warn the commandant there. She hoped he would believe her. The people at the last little town certainly had. She upped her pace, although her sides were heaving and her heart thudded.

She had no need to worry. The moment she mentioned the name of Slathe, the commandant, an older lieutenant, was all ears. "Slathe? Are you sure you heard that right?"

"I'm sure. 'Hiring out to Slathe for his rebellion,' were the exact words."

"And these mercenaries were coming in from Layesse?"

"I assumed they were. We took a shortcut over the mountain and hit the main road just where it crosses a creek. They were coming from that direction." She cursed herself for saying 'we', but the commandant seemed to miss her slip, and continued his interrogation.

"How many of them?"

"I have no idea. I just heard a lot of marching feet and I thought it was no place for a girl."

"You're right there, young lady. So as far as you know, there is a band of mercenaries half a day's march back along the road to Layesse, who are meeting up with a revolutionary called Slathe?"

"That's all, sir, I'm sorry, but I didn't want to risk staying around for more."

"I'm sure you didn't. Now, I have a problem. What to do with you."

"With me?"

"Yes. If there's a revolt going on, this is no place for you. This is the first spot they'll attack. But wandering alone is no place, either. Can you ride a horse?"

She bit back the indignant response. "Yes. I can ride."

"Good. I'm going to send a messenger to Piche-Frenne to warn them. You can go with him. You'll be safer, there. There's far less chance of an attack and it's a much bigger town. If they're warned they'll be harder to overcome."

"Thank you, sir. I'll do whatever you say."

"Fine." His attention left her as a problem solved, and she could see him begin to think of a thousand other things.

Soon she was on the road again, this time on a fast horse. The messenger, a slim young soldier with dark hair, galloped beside her.

"You ride well."

She glanced over at his grinning face. "I'd better be able to."

He nodded and turned his attention to the road.

It was, fortunately, not too long a ride, as she found that she was hardened to walking but not to the saddle. However, it was mid-afternoon when they rounded a corner in the road and thundered into a town, very small in her eyes. It was not completely walled, but the houses were built together so that they could be easily defended. Once inside, she saw that the streets were narrow and the windows small and high, the houses joined together there as well. Each house could be defended against invaders inside the gates. She had never looked at architecture from a military point of view before, but this town seemed much safer than the little village where the garrison was stationed.

The soldier swung from his blowing horse in front of a three-story half-timbered building, shouting for the mayor. Soon a crowd had formed and some official-looking men gathered around him. Aleria decided that this was her opportunity, dismounted and faded back out through the crowd. There were several larger buildings on this central square, including one that looked like a prosperous inn. She hitched her pack to her shoulder and strode over, stumbling a bit as the blood rushed back into her legs. If there was ever a time to spend her money well, this was it.

There was no one around, so she rang the small bronze bell that sat on the bar. It was a long time before there was a response. Then a stooped older woman shuffled through the door.

"What's going on? Where's that dratted girl who's supposed to answer the bell?"

Aleria couldn't help but grin. "Out listening to the hubbub in the square, I would guess."

Dark eyes peered up at her. "And what's going on in the square, since you seem to know so much?"

That sobered her. "There is a report of a rebellion in the area. The messenger just came in from the military post at Furane, warning everyone."

"Another dratted rebellion. Why can't they settle that lot? Why do they keep on making trouble?"

"I don't know. Who is making the trouble?"

"Ah, it's always the same bunch. A lot of no-goods and lay-abouts, too lazy to find a trade and nothing better to do than cause trouble. Oh, they say wonderful things about freedom and their rights, but when it comes down to it, all they want is a free ride so they don't have to work. It all comes over the mountains from Ferboden, you know. Bunch of anarchists over there. Got no government at all, so I hear."

"How do their ideas get here?"

"Agitators. They send 'em in, tryin' to mess up our government so they can come and take over. All those awful ideas."

Aleria felt her interest rise. "You have heard what they say?"

"Oh, sure. There was a young fellow through here a few months back, speaking to anybody who would listen."

"What did he say?"

"I didn't pay much attention. Just the usual stuff about oppression by the Ranking classes and freedom to work. Hah! Freedom to work. I looked at his hands. Not a callous to be seen. He's never worked for his bread, I'll tell you that."

Aleria dropped her hands from the counter.

The sharp eyes turned to her. "And what about you, young lady? What brings you to our town in the middle of a rebellion?"

"I didn't plan the rebellion part, Ma'am. I'm looking for a safe place to stay the night."

"Ah. A room, then. We've got plenty of rooms. More than usual. Might have known."

She caught Aleria's puzzled look. "The pedlars have a sense for trouble and stay clear when they feel it coming. Usually we have three or four here, any normal night. Only one last night, none today. So we have rooms." She shot Aleria a calculating look. "Three-quarters."

Aleria stared her down. "You just raised the price because you know I'm worried about safety. There are other inns."

"All right. A half-crown, and two extra pennies for food."

Aleria considered that; if they were attacked her money would be worth nothing to her anyway. "Done. Will you show me the room?"

The old woman looked around. "Doesn't seem to be anyone else to do it, does there?"

Aleria followed the woman upstairs, accepted a room much better than most she had been using, and was soon unpacked. She rested until suppertime, ate early, and in spite of the rushing around on the street, was asleep before it got dark.

15. Captured

She was startled from restless dreams by a crash that seemed to shake the whole building. As her befuddled senses straightened, she heard loud yells from the common room beneath her. A wrenching scream tore through her, cut off in a gurgle, followed by a thump, as if a body had hit the floor.

A hoarse voice laughed. "This is it. We'll set down here for the moment, have a drink or two. But we're not gonna get much service, you lot keep killin' the servants."

Shaking, Aleria crouched on her bed, the blankets clutched around her. How could they be already inside? There was no sound of attack. Someone must have let them in. A red flickering brought her attention to the window. A fire had started somewhere, and now the screams were coming from farther away. Several loud bangs told her that someone had guns.

Only the Royal Army was supposed to have guns. Was it a rescue? The gunshots were not repeated, and her hopes fell.

She heard the tramp of booted feet on the stairway.

Her stomach knotted in fright. She crammed her feet into her shoes, wrapped her cloak around her body and scrabbled for her pack. The boots were coming down the hallway, and she rushed to check the door was locked, her fingers trembling. Then she darted to the window. By the light of the fires, she could see a mass of men in the courtyard. No escape there. Maybe she could get out on the roof, hide behind a chimney...

She tried to stifle a scream as the door behind her splintered inward. A tall man with a big moustache and a fierce snarl strode into the room, glanced around. There was nowhere for her to hide. He cursed and grabbed her. He yanked her over to the window, held her face to the light and cursed again. Sheathing his bloody sword, he jerked her pack off, tossed through it, shaking his head. Then he looked at her again, reached out and tore her cloak away, stuffed it in her pack, and threw it in the corner. Once again he hauled her into the light from the burning town beyond the window. Then he shoved her onto the bed. She lay there shivering, staring up at him, barely able to breathe. He yanked her shoes off, jammed them under the bed as well.

Then he reached out and roughed up her hair, grabbed her by the arm and hauled her out of the room.

Her mind could make no sense of his actions, and she could hardly keep her feet under her as he dragged her down the stairs. Just outside the common room door, he stopped and hauled her face up to his. She could smell his rotten breath in the darkness, and shrank away. "When we get out there, you say nothing. Got it? Nothing!"

Her lips tried to form a sound.

"Say it. Nothing."

"N...nothing."

"Good girl. Just don't say anything. Keep your face down."

Then she was propelled violently through the door and into the common room. Arms windmilling, she regained her balance and stood, head down, breath coming in gasps.

"Hey, Slathe. Look what I found in the attic. Can I keep it?"

A roar of laughter greeted this. "Whattaya want it for? It don't look big enough to be worth messin' with." A stocky man, his belly held in by a wide leather belt, strolled over, grabbed her hair, and lifted her head up. "Not a bad face, for a slut. Maybe I do her a favour and take her myself, the first time."

"I tell ya, Slathe. I sorta took a likin' to this one. Reminds me of my first one, back when I was a kid. I tell ya what..." Her captor leaned over and whispered in the leader's dirty ear.

The fat man burst out laughing. "Why, Raif, you sentimental old lecher. If the skinny slut means that much to you, have her. I like 'em a bit more padded, myself." He waved a thick, grimy hand in her direction and she ducked, stumbled, and fell to the floor. Her gorge rose as she came face to face with the body of one of the serving men, his throat a torn mass of blood.

The man with the moustache was suddenly standing astride her, his face close to the leader's. "And she's all mine, right? That's the deal?"

The leader's laugh cut off. He looked at his subordinate with cold appraisal. "That's the deal, unless I decide to change it. No one else."

Her captor grinned, slapped the other man on the shoulder. "That's good enough for me, Slathe, any day." He reached down, hauled her to her feet. "Now, if you don't mind, I think the fightin's done for a while. I may just go and enjoy the rewards of the day. I suspect there might be some nice, comfy beds upstairs. Come on, Sweetheart, and just see what a surprise I have for you!" To the claps and jeers of the other men in the room, he dragged her up the stairs. Unable to resist his cruel grasp, she stumbled after him, terror freezing her muscles. He kicked a few doors open, glanced inside each, then continued down the hall. When he reached the door to her room, he thrust it open, exclaiming loudly.

"Just the right spot. Come to papa, dearie!" He shoved her in, slammed the door and spun her across the room to the bed. She lay where she had fallen, trying desperately to think, to force her mind to deal with this huge, dark man leaning over her, his fist lashing out. Pain exploded across her face, and she could feel tears streaming from a blurry eye.

His face loomed into her line of vision, and his voice grated in her ears. "This is going to hurt, but a whole lot less than it might have." He looked at her a moment, shook her shoulders. "Listen to me, and listen well. You are about to be raped, and it's going to be noisy and violent. Got it?" He shook her again, and she felt her head flop.

"Dammit, girl, don't pass out on me now. You've got to pay attention. You've got to put on a show. They're all listening down there, and if they don't hear the right stuff, we're both done for. Do you understand?"

She whimpered, shook her head.

"Oh, Gods, don't tell me I picked a dumb one. Put on a show. Scream a bit. Can you scream?"

She managed a nod.

"Then scream, dammit. Scream like I just twisted your arm."

She tried to scream, and a weak sound dribbled from her lips.

"I mean scream!" He grabbed her wrist, twisted it up behind her. Her arm was on fire, the shoulder socket strained past endurance. Pain tore a shriek from her lips, her voice rising until his hard, dirty hand crushed down across her mouth.

Above her, his rough laugh rang. "Oh, my. Isn't she frightened!"

Then his face came close again. "You've got to show some spunk, girl. Scratch my face."

"What?"

"If you don't show some spunk, every lout in this army is going to have a go at you. Now scratch my face. At least two nails, a nice, long, scratch."

In a daze, she reached up. As she saw her nails dig into the flesh of his cheek, a sudden surge of anger threaded up from inside her, and she dug in, watching the blood trail behind her fingers.

His shout of fury rang in her ear, followed by a slap that slammed her breath out against the wall. He raised a hand to his cheek, considered his bloody fingers. "Well, well, well! So she has some spirit after all." He grinned. "I didn't mean you to scar me for life. Sorry if I over-reacted."

He reached out to take her chin, tilting her head from side to side while he considered her face. "Not too bad, though. The lip is swelling already, and that slap will show up for days. Now it's acting time. Can you moan a bit?"

"What...? I don't...acting?"

His cruel hands gripped her arms, and he jerked her upright, his face so close that she could feel the spittle on her cheeks. Her chest strained as she held her breath. "I will explain this one more time. Do you know what is happening out there? All over this town?" He paused, and a scream echoed up from the streets. A sudden flare of fire outside lit the room. She shuddered at the realization.

He nodded. "That's right. Put on a good act up here, or I really will rape you. I will rape you down there on the floor in front of all of them if I have to. At least that would be better than having them all take their turn. You are in a tough situation here and you have got to rally around. Can you do that?"

She didn't know whether he could see her nodding, he was shaking her so hard. "If you stop that, maybe I could think."

He grinned again, yellow teeth behind the drooping moustache. "That's better. You're catching on. Now moan in fear. It shouldn't be too hard; you're scared to death anyway, and you know what'll happen if you don't."

He was right. It wasn't hard at all. Her moans were real as he dropped her on the bed, reached down to tear at her clothes. Then his weight was on her, crushing her, the rough cloth of his coat blocking her mouth. She could hear the bed banging over and over against the wall. She gasped for breath, but could not get enough air. Then he shouted, a long cry of triumph, and the weight was gone.

She opened her eyes, moaned again when she saw him standing over her, straightening his clothing, grinning from ear to ear. Then he glanced behind him as if checking for an audience, and his face became serious.

He leaned down to whisper to her. "There you are, girl. That's the easiest rape you'll ever have, I guarantee it. Now keep moaning a bit while I fix things up. Whatever you do, don't leave that bed."

Whistling, he stomped out of the room, and she could hear him banging doors open down the hall. Once he stopped for a loud jest with someone in another room. Then her door opened. There was a moment of silence.

She raised her head. A huge, fat man, slobber running down one side of his face and blood smearing the other, was standing in the doorway regarding her. Never in her worst dreams had she seen such a monster. With no counterfeit, she whimpered and burrowed back under the quilt, but there was no safety there. The thought of those hands on her body, the blood and filth…then loud bootsteps marched closer, and she heard a familiar voice.

"Hey, Balek. Not in there. That one's mine. You go find yerself a sweetheart of yer own. Go on, now. Why don't ya try the street down by th' gate where we come in? Good luck, there, friend."

She peeked again, to see her captor slap the huge man on the shoulder and steer him away. Then he turned back, coming in and closing the door. He was carrying a bundle of cloth in his hand. He reached under the bed, pulled out her pack.

"Now get your boots on, and put this blanket in your pack. Ditch the fancy shoes and jacket. We'll be pulling out immediately, and I don't dare leave you behind. You think this army's bad. If the king's soldiers don't get here by tomorrow, the sewer rats who follow this poor excuse for an army would change your mind."

He stopped, then sat down beside her on the bed, looking into her eyes. Then he spoke, very softly. "Look, young lady, I know I haven't handled this too well, but you have to understand I was in the middle of a battle when I found you. I could tell by your clothes and the cut of your hair that you didn't belong here, so I did the best I could on the spur of the moment. In case you haven't figured it out, I'm your only chance to get out of this town in one piece. I'm sorry I had to hit you, but you can't fake the kind of bruises you'll need to make them believe I really worked you over. Now, I paid a great deal to get you to myself, and I'm going to have to play it very carefully to make sure Slathe has no reason to change his mind. Don't mess this up for me, and you'll be all right. Do you understand?"

As he talked, certain things began to filter through the fog that was enveloping her brain. *His accent is different. He didn't rape me, just pretended. He's…in as much danger as I am and…I have to go along.*

"What do you want me to do?"

"Act like I just raped you. Act like you're afraid that I'll do it again, at any moment. I'm the master. Completely. If I say lick my boot, you do it."

He leaned close. "But if anyone else touches you, crosses you, even looks at you wrong, you fly at him. You tear a strip off him as wide as you can. And do a good job of it, because if you can't scare him off, I'll have to come and kill him. Understand?"

She understood. "What about the big one, Slathe?"

His face looked grim. "Stay out of his way. I can't do much about him if he takes a liking to you. Oh, yes, and Balek. The fat one. Don't yell at him. Just say my name, over and over again. He likes me, but it might take him a while to remember."

A shout rang out below.

"There we are. We're leaving. Put on a good show; our lives depend on it." His voice rose. "Come on Sweetheart. Pick up yer pack, and let's go downstairs and meet yer new family!" His hoarse laugh preceded him as he strolled down the stairway, his scabbard thumping on the steps behind him. Ducking her head, she followed him down.

It occurred to her that he hadn't told her his name, but there was no time to ask. She simply followed, hoping Balek was otherwise occupied. And all the others like him.

Fortunately, the rebel camp was only a half-hour's stumble along the dark, crowded road. The army swaggered through, some of them already drunk on the proceeds of their night's work. They reeled into her, clutched at her, stepped on her feet. Her protector did his best to shield her without seeming to, shouting equally at her and at anyone who touched her.

When they reached the camp, he dragged her to a little tent set at the end of a row of shelters of varying sizes and shapes. He twitched open the flap and made a mock-gracious bow. "Home, sweet home, Sweetheart."

She stood, uncertain what to do, which gave him an excuse to shove her down and through the low doorway. It was pitch dark in the tent and it smelled of sweat and dirt. She crouched to one side while he struck a match and lit a tiny oil lamp. The only furnishings were a canvas cot and a folding stool. He hung the lamp from the ridgepole and smiled at her. "It's not much, but it's home." He gestured, and she sat on the cot, staring up at him.

"What happens now?"

"Well, Sweetheart, I'm sorry to disappoint you, but I've had a rough day, what with the battle and all, so I'm not going to entertain you as you might have expected. We'll be moving early in the morning, so I suggest you get whatever sleep you can. Not on the bed."

She looked up at him, puzzled.

He moved to the cot beside her, spoke softly in her ear. "If someone was to stick his head in, and find me on the floor and you on the bed, they'd be suspicious. You're going to have to sleep on the floor. Use the blankets from your pack."

"I also have my cloak."

"You can lie on it, too. Cover yourself with my coat."

"I'm warm enough, thank you."

"This isn't time for pride, little girl. Take the coat. It's not too clean, but it's good wool. Once the excitement dies down, you'll be cold."

"Excitement!"

"I'm surprised you haven't gone into shock already. It's been a pretty rough night for you."

"Kind of you to notice."

"Look, my name is Raif. What's yours?"

"Aleria."

"Aleria. Ranking class. What's a girl like you doing out here alone?" He continued without waiting for her answer. "I won't be using your name when anyone can hear me. I'll call you 'Sweetheart,' since I started it already. Maybe you should think up a name for the other women to call you. The other men shouldn't be talking to you. If they do, let me know and I'll deal with them. Keep yourself small and inconspicuous as you can. Cringe and keep your head forward so your hair covers your face. Don't look at anybody. You're way prettier than is safe."

"Was that a compliment?"

He grinned, fingered the two scratches on his cheek. "You do have a bit of spunk, don't you?"

"A lot of good that's done me so far."

"Don't fool yourself, Aleria. If you hadn't been able to keep up your part of the act tonight, either I would have lost you, or I'd have ditched you in the dark to make your own way home. I'm on too important a mission to risk it on someone who can't hold up her end."

"Mission? What kind of a mission?"

"Keep your voice down. Don't worry about my mission. You think I'm hanging around with this bunch of scum so I can rescue any young ladies I come across?"

"I hadn't given it a thought."

"I'm sure that when you do, you'll realize how lucky you were it was me that kicked your door in and not one of the others."

She shuddered, but refused to let him see. "I can't say I'm terribly impressed at your chivalry, so far."

He shrugged. "Sorry about the first slap. You already paid for the second one." He touched the scratches again, checking his fingertips for blood. "I'm never going to hear the end of it."

"What do you mean?"

"It's their kind of humour. They love to see anybody brought down to their level. Given the chance, they'd be joking about it for months. I'll try to see they don't get the chance."

He turned to his pack, propped against one end of the tent. "Here, I've got a spare blanket. With three folded under you, and my coat on top, you'll be comfortable enough." As he spoke, he was arranging a bed for her on the ground. "I was serious about leaving early. Get some sleep if you can, just rest at least."

She lay down, and he stepped over her and stretched out on the cot. Then his head came up, and he stared down at her. "You wouldn't be stupid enough to try to escape, would you? Slathe is very careful about sentries, and there are always people moving about in the camp."

She shook her head. He regarded her a moment, then nodded, leaned over and blew out the light.

She lay back on the hard ground in the smothering darkness, the rank scent of an unwashed man in her nostrils. She felt a shudder start, deep in her chest, but she suppressed it. She would not give him the satisfaction of hearing her cry. Clenching her fists, she lay in the blackness until her fatigue overtook her, and, half-dreaming and half-waking, she slept.

* * *

A scream, sharply cut off, awakened her, and she started up, gazing around the little tent as if coming out of a nightmare. A stab of pain shot through her as she realized that the horror would continue with the coming day.

In the dim, early, dawn, Raif didn't look much better than he had in the flickering light of torches and burning houses. His hair was shaggy, his moustache too long, dragging into the corners of his mouth. His fingernails were filthy, and as he lay on his back, the foul sound and smell of his snoring denied her the chance to get back to sleep. Finally, he opened his eyes. He seemed to come instantly awake.

He stretched and yawned, showing yellowed teeth. "Another day of the ongoing struggle for the freedom of the common man."

She glanced at him, suspicious of the irony in his tone. He jumped from the cot, fully clothed, and looked down at her, head and shoulders bowed under the canvas roof.

"I was doing some thinking. I want to show you a trick I learned from some actors who visited while I was at school." He reached down, enclosed her neck with his grimy hand. "When I grab your throat, like this, you grab my wrist with both hands. Yes. Like that. Now if you throw yourself around, it will look like I'm shaking you, but you're the one making the movements, so you can control them."

He lifted her up with surprising strength, and she found that she could support her weight on his wrist, with no

157

pressure on her throat at all. "A pleasant way to wake a lady up in the morning. Why am I learning this?"

"Because most of the men here treat their women like that sometimes, and I'm going to have to act normal."

"Don't overdo it on my account."

"I'll try not to, but you realize that if I don't treat you normally, people will begin to get suspicious, or jealous, or see a chance for an advantage."

"So we'll just act normal, will we?"

"I thought you'd agree."

What he called 'normal' seemed to involve a lot of work. He set her to taking the tent down while he went to the common fire to get breakfast, which was a huge bowl of porridge.

"Don't eat it all. We only have one bowl, so I'll have what you leave."

She stuck the big iron spoon into the gluey mixture, withdrew it with difficulty, then jammed it back in and passed him the bowl.

He shoved it back. "Eat. You're going to need it."

She met his eyes, realized that he was in deadly earnest. She took the bowl back, forced herself to eat. After she had crammed down a few mouthfuls, it was impossible to tell whether she was full or her stomach had reached the end of its endurance. But she really felt she could eat no more, so she handed 'breakfast' to him. He nodded, dug in himself, seeming to relish the glutinous mass. The bowl was soon empty, and he shoved it at her.

"Washup's over there." He motioned with his chin.

She was about to ask what she was supposed to do when he abruptly rose and walked away, tossing a comment over his shoulder about having the tent packed in double-quick time.

She looked around, realized that most of the camp was disappearing into packs and decided she had better hurry. Remembering to keep her shoulders rounded and her head down, she scurried over, jammed the bowl and spoon into the greasy, lukewarm water in the big metal pot and wiped the remaining porridge off with her fingers. She looked around, found nothing to dry them with, so she wiped them on the hem of her dress as she had seen another woman do.

Then she went back to fight with the stiff canvas. No matter how she made the folds, it seemed to end up twice as big as would fit in her pack. She was just about to quit and was sitting on it thinking what to do next, when Raif came striding up, shouting before he even reached her.

"What are you doing, sitting around? Can't you see everyone else is packed? Do you want to be left on the road?"

Her instant response – that she would be quite happy to be left behind – was cut off by a slap that, while it used most of its power on her shoulder, caught the top of her ear painfully. She toppled to the ground, then scrambled up, ready to give him a piece of her mind, but the look in his eye and his raised hand gave her pause. She stood there, chest heaving for a moment, then remembered where she was. They had an audience. She dropped her shoulders.

"I can't get it in my pack."

He tossed the tent open. "Of course not. You've done it all wrong. I'll show you once." He folded the tent and she paid attention, even though her mind was seething. When he was finished the tent was a neat package that slid straight to the bottom of her pack, landing with an ominous thump.

"I expect it done properly from now on. Get the rest of my stuff in there, and let's get moving."

"The rest...?" But he was already handing her a frying pan, various kitchen utensils and the folded cot.

She stowed the cooking materials without comment, but paused at the cot. "You sleep on it, you carry it."

He picked up the cot and shoved it into her chest, knocking the wind out of her. As she lay on the ground gasping, she could hear laughter and looked up to see several of the soldiers and camp followers, all with their packs ready, entertained by her problems. With a vicious look at Raif she slammed the cot on the top of her pack and tied the flap over it. The time this took allowed her to regain her senses and she stood, her hair hiding her burning face, refusing to look at any of them.

Then orders were called, and they all slung their packs and started out. Hers was abominably heavy. She knew that she would not be able to bear it all day. Raif, carrying only a smaller pack and his weapons, walked beside her for a while. As the 'army' strung out along the road he adjusted their pace so that there was no one close enough to overhear.

"You have to learn different reactions, Aleria. Here, your pride is going to get you into trouble."

"My pride is all that's keeping me going."

"Then turn it inside. Don't let it show. Every time you show a spark of life, there's a chance that someone else will take an interest. I won't be here to guard you all the time. Your best safety is invisibility."

"Sort of hard when you make me the laughing stock of the whole camp."

"I had to do something, Aleria. I can't allow you to stand up to me. Having you here puts me at a higher risk, you realize."

"I realize that. Whatever you're doing here."

"Something important. That's all you need to know. I don't dare tell you anything you might be forced to reveal. That's safer for you, as well."

"Safety seems a relative term, the way you use it."

"Aleria, even back in your father's mansion in the Capital, your safety was only a relative thing."

"I suppose."

"I think that was one of the things your little Quest was supposed to teach you. It obviously failed in your case."

The weight of her pack helped her restrain the urge to whirl on him. "Nobody knew this was going to happen. The Dukedom of anCanah is supposed to be one of the safer areas of the kingdom."

"Which goes again to prove that safety is only relative. At home, your safety goes up or down a percentage point or two, it means nothing. Here it might mean your life. Think about that before you let your temper get the better of you." He glanced around. "We're pretty well set in our marching order now and it will look strange if I stay back with the camp followers when I should be out scouting. I'll see you at noon if I'm around, otherwise in camp tonight."

"But...but wait!"

"What?"

"What do I do?"

"Stay invisible. Watch what the others do and act like them. I've never taken any interest in the followers, so you'll have to figure it out for yourself."

Before she could protest further he was gone, striding ahead at a much faster pace, leaving her with her aching shoulders and her nightmare imagination.

16. Dance!

Slathe's army moved slowly, at least. There were few draught animals, and most of the materiel was carried on the backs of the soldiers and their women. By gritting her teeth and enduring, Aleria was able to keep up. She watched the other women, noted how they acted, what they did, how they talked to the men.

When the noon halt was called she was dismayed to realize that no food was being provided. The women around her dug into their packs and pulled out an assortment of supplies, eating where they sat. She remembered a soft sack that Raif had given her, and pawed through it. A hunk of smelly, hard cheese and a likewise-stale crust of bread was all that she could find, but she wolfed them down. She realized that the others were filling their canteens at a nearby stream. It seemed that it was safe enough to leave her pack while she did so. Once that task was done she huddled down and rested. She had chosen her spot well, just far enough from the others to discourage talking, but she hoped not so far as to be singled out for any reason.

Soon enough the order to march was relayed down the line, and she groaned aloud as the pack straps cut into her sore shoulders. As she rose, all the stiffened muscles of her legs and back complained. Her eyes grimly focused on the pack of the woman in front of her, she trudged through the heat of the afternoon.

In the end, what saved her was the indecision of the leadership. After about two hours the line slowed, and soon those in front of her stopped. Everyone took advantage of the break to down packs, although no one left the line of march.

After a while, shouts were relayed along the line and they were off again, but only for a few minutes. Now it was an actual order, delivered by a mounted rider, that set them on a break. Aleria had figured it out by this time and scrambled for a shady spot under a small tree. She was forced to share it with a large older woman who pushed in without ceremony and proceeded to take up as much space as she could. Aleria used her stubborn obstinacy and the weight of her pack to keep her position. The woman sat mopping her brow, not the least put out.

"Hot day."

Aleria considered that no response would be worse than answering. "It is."

"You're new."

"I am."

"Picked you up in town last night, did they?"

"One of them did."

The woman turned with new interest. "Only one?"

"His name's Raif."

"Oh. Him. Aye, I can understand that. Thinks a lot of himself, that one. What's he like in bed?"

"What's he like?" It was easy to let the heat rise to her face. "He raped me! What do you think that was like?"

The woman laughed. "Don't worry, dearie. It's better the second time. Soon you'll get to like it."

Aleria glared and shut her lips tight. The woman laughed again and leaned back against the trunk of the tree, stretching her legs out and wriggling her toes in her sandals. "Don't look like we're goin' too far today."

"You don't think so?"

"Naw, you can tell. When they can't make up their minds and the troops start complainin' they always stop early. Keeps everybody happy."

"I don't understand. Aren't we going somewhere?"

The huge shoulders heaved once. "I don't know. Probably. Ask your friend Raif. He's one of the scouts."

"I guess I'll do that."

The woman glanced over at her. "You watch that one, missy."

"What do you mean?"

"I dunno. There's somethin' about him. He's holdin' back. I think he's a lot tougher than he looks."

"Oh, great. Just what I wanted to hear. What can I do about it?"

Again the mountainous shrug. "Sorry. Just don't rile him. He could be a mean one. Some of them are. Oh, I know, they're all rough. They try to slap you around, show how manly they are. Don't work with me, of course, 'cause I slap back, but a little, young thing like you, you can't do that. No, you take my advice, missy, and play it real small with that Raif. Whatever he says, you do it, and quick-like. Otherwise, I wouldn't be surprised if you don't just disappear some night, and nobody the wiser in the mornin'."

"You think he'd..."

"Who's to stop him?"

"But, isn't there some kind of rule, some law?"

"You need to catch on quick, girlie. You're in the middle of a rebel army. The laws don't apply. Whatever Slathe wants, he takes. Him and his friends. He decides you're better dead, then you're dead. We may not like it, but that's the way it works."

"But...but...why are you here, then?"

The woman's eyes took on a flat stare, as if she was seeing something far away. "Because it's better than where I was."

"Oh." There didn't seem to be any fitting response, and the two sat, sharing the shade of the tiny tree, while the sun beat down on the rocks around them. After a mercifully long time, the order to move came again, and they descended from the mountain trail to a campsite in a grove of trees. She found a spot for their tent, in that halfway area that put her at the edge of camp but not too far out, and got it to stand without assistance. She was staring at the tent with a certain amount of pride when his voice startled her.

"Don't just stand there. Where's my supper?"

She turned. He slung his pack to the ground, winked at her, and flopped against the nearest tree. "I need some beer."

"Where do I get that?"

He waved a hand negligently. "They're doling it out at the supply tent. Go get me some."

She was about to retort when she noticed his posture. When she looked closer, it was obvious that he was spent. His body moulded to the shape of the tree root and the ground and his hand, splayed on the pine needles beside him, shook. His eyes were half-closed already and his head sagged.

Changing her mind, she hastened to dig the big mug out of her pack and rushed to the supply tent before the beer was all gone. A stern glare made sure the cook's flunky filled her cup to the brim, and she stopped a few paces away to drink enough that it wouldn't spill. It was sour and warm, but it cut the dust in her throat, and she stopped twice more on the way back to sample it.

There was still plenty left for him, although he roused enough when she approached to glance down into the mug before he drank. "Had your share, did you?"

"I did."

"Hot day." He swilled the beer in huge gulps, emptying half the mug before he set it down. A long sigh eased from his lips, and he smiled, the first real smile she had seen. "Now, that feels good." He sipped again, slower, looking up at her over the rim of the mug. "You do all right today?"

"I'm here."

"That you are. All that counts."

She could see that his eyes were drooping again. "There's someone coming."

His eyes flew open, registering the two figures approaching. Then he relaxed again. Or seemed to. She could see an alert glint under his lashes. The two men approached and stood for a moment, looking down on him.

He yawned and stretched before he seemed to open his eyes. "Whataya say, boys? Want I should get Sweetheart to bring you some beer?"

The two glanced at each other and moved back half a step. "No, Raif, that's fine. We was just sent to get you. Slathe's havin' a meetin'."

Raif opened his eyes. "Well, that's right polite of you, comin' and givin' me the word." He seemed to glide to his feet, towering over the two. "Let's drop by the supply tent and make sure they send some of this beer to the meetin'. And you," he turned to Aleria, "make sure there's some food for me when I get back. Put a fire there."

He turned away, a hand on each man's shoulder. Aleria noted with appreciation that he had left the mug. She cradled it a moment, checking to see if anyone was watching, then drank, enjoying the liquid as it swirled down her throat. Then she looked around again, thinking. If he said to light a fire, she was probably supposed to cook. If she was supposed to cook, that meant that someone was giving out food. She stowed the rest of the mug of beer in the tent, grabbed the pot, and headed back towards the supply tent.

She returned with a despairingly small amount of rice and beef in the bottom of the pot. She was so busy wondering how she was going to make this into a meal for two people that at first she didn't realize that there was someone near her tent. It was a small man, about her height, and he had his hand inside the tent flap. She stepped forward, anger surging.

"What the hell do you think you're doing?"

He jumped as if she had struck him and turned. It was one of the soldiers, smaller and younger than most. "You got beer in there."

"Raif has beer in there."

"He'll be gettin' more. I didn't get any."

"I don't give a damn what you got. That beer's Raif's, and you steal from him, you know what you're gettin' into?"

The little man stumbled back, tripped on a tent peg, then recovered himself, his hands held up. "No, no, I wouldn't steal Raif's beer. I just thought..."

"You just thought Raif was busy and you could sneak some, and he wouldn't notice. Well, now he's gonna notice."

"No, no, don't tell him! I'm sorry! I wasn't really gonna..."

"Yes, you were. You were gonna steal his beer, an' the only reason you're sorry is because you got caught." She stared down at the poor wretch, realizing how pitiful he was. She dropped her hands in disgust. "Aw, get outa here."

He scuttled sideways, his eyes never leaving her face. "Yeah. Yeah. I'm goin'. Don't tell Raif, will ya?"

"Don't tell Raif? You want me to lie to Raif to protect you? You got dreams, boy. Your best hope is to stay away from our part of the camp for the next few days. You got that?"

"Yeah. Yeah. Thanks, thanks..." He turned and scurried off, glancing back over his shoulder as he ran.

She stood there, watching him out of sight. Then she glanced around to see if she had any audience. There were soldiers and women within hearing, but they all seemed busy with their own affairs. She opened the tent flap and took out the beer. She drank the rest down, but the pleasure was gone. Setting the mug aside, she began to gather wood for the fire.

Despite her fatigue and fear she worked hard, and by the time Raif returned, her campsite looked as good as any of the others nearby.

He grinned. "Well, isn't this nice. What's for supper?"

"What they gave me."

"That's all?"

"Was I supposed to get something else?"

He sniffed at the plate in front of him. "Would have been nice." Then he snickered. "Might have been some left for you."

He dug into his meal, ignoring her.

She glanced around, saw that there was no one near, spoke quietly. "Is there any way I can get more food?"

"Some do, but maybe you shouldn't. We don't want you getting noticed." He passed her the half-full plate. "I'll see what I can pick up tomorrow. You did fine, tonight. How are you?"

"Tired, sore, afraid."

He nodded. "That sounds pretty normal."

"What do you mean?"

"These people, especially the women, spend most of their lives that way."

"Well, let's not try too hard to keep things normal, then."

"Sorry, the more normal you act and look, the less likely you'll be to attract attention."

"Great."

"Normal" also seemed to be a steady stream of orders, jokes, and lewd suggestions. Whenever any of the other soldiers were listening, he abused her to their great entertainment. Sometimes he would find the chance to give her a wink to tell her it was all pretending, but usually he couldn't. Or didn't. Aleria gritted her teeth and bore it all, cramming her fear and humiliation off into a corner of her soul where they didn't interfere with the simple necessities of survival.

The fourth night she collapsed on Raif's cot, aching in every limb. There was a certain grim satisfaction in the fact that she had survived the day. Neither the heat of the trail, the weight of her pack nor the constant fear and bullying had beaten her down. She lay back, idly watching the flickering shadows on the tent wall, allowing her fatigue to wash over her, listening to the sound of a fiddle and drums. She felt a vague respect for the woman who, after all that work all day, still had the energy to entertain the men by dancing.

As her mind ranged away from her pain and fatigue, she realized that someone was walking towards her tent. A rasping voice laughed. "Say, Raif, can she dance?"

Raif's chuckle chilled her. "I don't know. Let's find out."

She couldn't believe it. After all he had drilled into her about staying invisible! A level of quiet of anticipation fell among those around the fire. She could hear his footsteps approach, and her anger grew. When she saw him framed in the light, she hissed out. "What are you doing?"

He winced, shrugged. "No choice, Aleria. If I ducked, they might get suspicious. Now listen. Whatever you do, don't dance."

"What?"

"Don't dance. Whatever I do, whatever I say out there, don't dance. We don't want any of them lusting after you." His voice rose. "Come on, Sweetheart. Dance time."

He grabbed her by the arm, and his voice hissed in her ear. "Think of something, but don't dance if you value your life."

She began to resist, making him drag her, but not too much. It was a relief to be able to fight.

The ring of outcasts laughed as they approached, throwing catcalls and lewd comments.

"What's wrong, Raif? Is she modest?"

"I hear she dances nice enough in your tent at night."

"Hey, girl, show us your stuff."

He tossed her into the firelight, a hateful grin on his face. "All right, Sweetheart. Show us what you can do." He motioned with his hand, and the musicians struck up a tune.

She stood, her head bowed, shoulders slumped, trying to make herself as unalluring as possible. Watching him through the fringe of her hair, she could see his expression change.

"Come on, girl. Dance!"

Still she refused to move, her pleasure in the defiance drowning her fears as to where this scene might lead.

The crowd waited, chuckles and soft jibes circulating.

"You heard them, girl. Entertain us."

Again, she did not move, partly because it seemed easiest. His face changed again, anger pulling his brow down. He strode to her, grabbed her arm, and pushed his bristling moustache in her face. "Dance, girl, or you'll regret it."

"He's sure got a way with the women, ain't he?" The voice cut through the murmurs. The crowd laughed.

"Dance, you slut!" He shoved her, spinning her around. She stumbled and sank to the ground, cowering before him. As the crowd laughed again, he hauled her up. She hung, limp, in his hands, ignoring the way his fingers dug into her arms.

As the jeering increased, she could see his breath come faster, his colour rise. He held her up to his face and shouted curses and insults. Still she refused to respond, cringing, trying to remind herself that he really didn't mean this, he was only trying to save her life.

With a final curse, he flung her again. Again, she collapsed, this time huddling in a ball, her head protected. He rained blows on her arms and knees, missing her head most of the time. Finally he calmed and stopped, looking around him at the crowd. She peered up and realized with a shock that he was grinning.

"Well, I guess she can't dance!"

They roared with approval. She was disgusted to see that the women were as loud as the men in condemning her.

He entwined his fingers in her hair. She shrieked and grabbed his hand as he had shown her, allowing him to drag her to her feet, her weight supported by her own arms. Spinning her to face his tent, he booted her, none too gently, through the door. The force of the blow propelled her accurately so that she landed on her blankets, cushioning her fall somewhat. Another jest, this one that she couldn't hear, brought another cheer from the crowd. He slapped the tent flaps closed and strode back to the fire.

She lay in the smelly blankets, her head spinning, her face hot, sobbing in anger, humiliation and fear. The music rose again, and the noise of the camp swarmed over her like greasy fingers.

It was some time later and the ruckus of the party had died down when she heard footsteps approaching. She almost hoped it wasn't him. She would love the chance to tear into someone, anyone, and she didn't think any of this scum would hold out long against her anger. When the tent opened she was ready, but it was Raif. She couldn't hold it back, and all her tortured feelings burst through.

"You enjoyed that!" She curbed her voice to a whisper, but it hissed through her teeth.

He seemed taken aback. "What?"

"You enjoyed that. You made me look a fool, you hit me and insulted me in front of an audience, and you loved every minute of it. What kind of a pervert are you? At least Slathe is honest. If he wants a girl, he takes her. He doesn't pretend to be a friend and then torture her, mind and body."

His face blanked, and he stared at her. She held his gaze, but he continued to stare, until his breath steadied and he had control of himself. She was surprised at how calm his voice was.

"Are you alive?"

She stared at him.

His voice dropped to a harsh whisper. "Is your precious maidenhood still with you? At least as far as I am concerned."

She had understood him. She just couldn't believe what he was saying.

"So don't complain."

"Don't complain?" She was just getting started. "After the way you have been treating me? You hit me, you abuse me, you make them all laugh…"

Her voice was cut short by a calloused hand over her mouth. His whisper came, hot and angry with his foul breath on her face. "Shut up, you little fool. You'll give us both away!"

She bit down, not too hard, on his palm. She found herself flying across the tent, her head ringing from his open-handed slap.

In a leap he was on her, his fierce scowl a warning. "There is something you had better remember. There are three factors that are important here: your life, my life, and my report to Colonel anTetrono. Think very carefully which of the three is most important. Notice that your comfort, your good opinion, and your doubtful virtue are not even mentioned."

"What do you mean?"

His voice dropped again but lost none of its intensity. "I'm not just out here playing games, girl. I have endured this lot of barbarians for months, working my way into their confidence, learning their plans, watching their contacts, predicting their moves. Soon I must get that information to the King's army. Slathe has allies spread throughout this area, and he is trying to gather them together. This whole operation is coming to a head, and Colonel AnTetrono needs my report.

"I will tell you one thing. It is absolutely imperative that we keep this army out in the west. Think what could happen if they got as far east as the Chanaan River and grabbed a bunch of anDennal's coal barges. They could be down at Kingsport in a week."

She nodded dumbly, thinking of the Twins, on an innocent holiday drift down the same river on their father's log booms.

"Now, if by some lucky chance I decide that you are the best way to get that report through, then your existence jumps up the list a bit. But think again. You're not stupid; I know that. Think what chances there are of that happening. All that information is in my head. To give it to you, I'd have to write it down, and there doesn't seem to be much in the way of stationery available in this mob. None of them can read. And what if we got caught with it? Solid proof that I'm not who I say I am. So what are your chances of moving up the list? Not great, are they?

He stared into her face for a moment, then, satisfied, released her with a nod. "Think of all the lives that might be saved if the Colonel has accurate knowledge of the numbers, armament, and deployment of his enemy. The number of guns they have scrounged up really bothers me, and it's going to bother my superiors as well. That information must reach the Colonel, and soon. I cannot allow anything to deter me from that objective. You do understand, don't you?"

Faced with this earnest plea, the rigidity drained from her shoulders, and she gave herself up to the support of the hands crushing her arms. "I know. I understand that I'm just an impediment."

He waited a moment, then released her. "Good. I'm glad you understand. Most girls wouldn't. I will do my best to get you out of here. You must realise that. After all, I've taken a lot of risks to get you this far, with small thanks in return. I'm the type of man who sees a project through to the end, no matter how difficult."

"But I'm a minor project right now. I see." She looked up at him, gauging his mood. "But do you really have to be so mean? Oh, I know, in front of the others, I can take that. But here, where no one can see?"

He shook his head. "I'm sorry. You have no idea the atmosphere in this mob. No one trusts anyone who isn't in his sight, and preferably within the reach of his sword. There are spies everywhere. The only way to gain power here is to step on someone who has what you want. Can I tell you something?"

He leaned in closer, spoke even softer. "I'm afraid too. All the time."

"You are?"

He nodded. "You think what they would do to you would be bad. Think what they would do to a traitor."

"Oh." She shuddered, looking into his face with new sympathy.

"There are twenty men within the sound of my voice right now who would like to take my position. One of them hearing one wrong word, seeing one kindness, is all it would take. He would go straight to Slathe to curry favour. Slathe would be suspicious. He would find a way to punish me and test me at the same time. Can you imagine what that would be?"

She shuddered. She could imagine all too well what her role would be in that scenario. She nodded, mutely.

He was silent for a moment, listening. Then he leaned closer to her. "I'm sorry. I know it's rough on you. But I can't just switch it off and on like that. I'm still new with this lot, and I have risen rapidly in their ranks. There is suspicion, jealousy. I have to be on edge every minute of the day. If I relax with, you, I might not react properly a few minutes later, when it counted. You understand; I can see that."

She repressed a shudder at his touch. "I suppose. Do what you have to do. Count on me to do my best to get us and your precious report out of here. I don't know if my best will be good enough, but I'll try."

He laughed, realized that it had been too loud, then laughed again, more coarsely. "That's my little Sweetheart. I knew you'd come round!" He winked at her, patted her hand, and swaggered out of the tent.

She sat for a moment, numbed. Had she made any impression? Had she straightened anything out? He seemed to think so. She would just have to wait and see. She thought back over their conversation, winced at his doubts of her virtue. She knew that she had handled that wrong. Instant indignation would have been the only correct response, and her honesty, and perhaps a bit of guilt, had held her back for that quick moment, and then it was too late. She wondered if he had noticed. Of course he had. He wasn't stupid either. He wouldn't be here as a spy if he was. She grinned to herself. On the other hand, maybe he was stupid. What intelligent person would put himself into such a position? Oh, well. Lucky for her that he had. As he so bluntly put it, she was alive and as intact as possible. What did she have to complain about?

Pressing her arm against her stinging cheek, Aleria curled on her hard bed, fading into a vague sleep where she was chased around and up and over the rocks by a band of grinning, jeering men while Raif stood above her, stony faced, and watched.

17. Battle

For the next few days the nightmare continued. Slathe seemed to be in a hurry to get somewhere, so they marched for long hours. However, he wasn't in such a rush that they didn't stop to destroy two small villages and several isolated farms, killing everyone they found. At least the lucky ones. Aleria endured it all, kept her head down, her eyes looking nowhere but where her next step would take her.

Raif seemed to be rising in the leader's esteem. He knew the roads and paths, and several times he pulled them away on some obscure trail while the king's army apparently went haring off in the opposite direction. She could never figure out where he got this information, but she didn't like it. It meant that Raif was often out scouting, and that left her alone. As long as they were travelling it was not a problem, but if he hadn't returned by the time camp was set up, there were always a few men with nothing to do who would wander by too often. She would have stayed in the tent, but with the coming summer weather it was too hot to endure. Added to this was the worry that between the dangers that he faced and the fact that his report was due, one day Raif might not come back at all.

Finally, one of the men got so persistent that she had to mention it. He was a short, stocky man, as many of them were. He had stopped to speak to her twice, and when she had refused to answer had made several obscene suggestions.

The third time, her stomach clenched the moment she saw him approaching. "Hey, there, Sweetheart. Raif givin' you enough?"

She turned away, but he moved in front of her. "You lookin' for some from a real man? Bet I could make that skinny body of yours hum!"

He reached for her, but she ducked around him and scrambled into her tent, slapping the flap shut in spite of the heat. Then she crouched, sweat pouring down, sobbing into the rough, smelly wool of the blanket so no one would hear.

When Raif returned that night she waited until he had eaten, then reluctantly told him.

Raif sat there for a moment, then sighed. "Is it that blonde-haired one with the torn leather vest?"

"Yes. That's him. Fancies himself handsome."

Raif sighed again.

"What should I do, Raif? If he touches me, I'll tear his face off. But then…"

Raif nodded. "Then he'll either kill you, or I'll have to kill him." He heaved to his feet, and she saw the fatigue in his movements. "I'll deal with him now."

"No, Raif! You're too tired! Wait till you've rested."

His face was set in hard lines, and she realized that he was angry, like she had never seen him before. "No time like the present." He strode over to where some of the soldiers were seated.

It was too far away for her to see the details, and for that she was thankful. There was no preliminary, no warning. Raif simply walked up to the man, grabbed him by the hair, and lifted him to his feet. There was a flurry of movement and several meaty smacks. Then Raif was striding away, leaving a huddled, unmoving bundle on the ground.

Raif approached, the fury still on his face. His voice rose. "Now it's your turn, slut!" She huddled back in real fear. What was he going to do?

His hand shot out, taking her by the throat. Her scream of surprise was choked off by the pressure. He pulled her face close to his. His breath was heavy, but he forced a whisper. "That's good. Now grab my wrist, and hold on tight." She locked both hands around his wrist to support her weight, and he relaxed his own grip just enough that she could breathe. His voice rose again, and he lifted her feet from the ground, shaking her violently. "Keep your eyes off the rest of them, and they'll leave you alone!" His other hand swept open the tent flap, and he tossed her inside, slapping the canvas closed behind her.

She lay on the bed where she had fallen, her breath escaping in huge sobs. Why had he done that? Why had he shaken her like that? It wasn't her fault the fools were slobbering over her! She felt her neck. His little trick had saved her from injury, but she was sure there would still be bruises. Of course there would. He would be sure of that. It had to look good. She knew that. She shuddered to think what he had done to the man who had insulted her.

By the time he returned to the tent, her anger had subsided somewhat. He kicked aside the flap, but she could see the concern in his eyes. "How are you?"

"I can still breathe, if that matters!"

"How's your throat?"

"Oh there will be some nice, showy bruises, I'm sure. Are you happy?"

"I'm not happy. Mind you, I wasn't loath to do the first part of that little job. He's a nasty piece of work, and he deserved it. The other part..."

She cut him off. "Oh, you don't have to explain. I know how these men think. If he was interested in me, it must have been my fault. So you had to punish me, or they would have."

He sighed. "Aleria, I'm so glad I saved you in that inn. You pick up so quickly. I don't know of any other woman who could go through what you just did, and explain in so clearly afterward."

"Oh, I can explain it, all right. But I don't have to like it. I think you went way overboard." Her voice dropped to hissing intensity as her anger rose. "You just admitted you enjoyed injuring that other man. I bet you enjoyed throwing me around, too, didn't you? Admit it! You got carried away, and you liked it!"

He turned away, shaking his head. "No I didn't. It was necessary, and I did it. I hope I didn't hurt you badly." He turned back to her. "Look, I know these things are painful, but I try to be careful. Admit it, none of the times I've hurt you

177

have been any worse than you've done to yourself, in training or falling off your horse. If it wasn't me doing them to you, you would just shrug them off, wouldn't you, and go on with your day? Isn't that true?"

She had to nod. "It's the fact that I'm terrified half the time."

"I know. There's not much I can do about that. At least we're both still alive, and I don't think anybody suspects anything."

"Raif, when are we going to get out of this?"

"Soon, I hope."

"You're not just saying that?"

"I don't dare say any more, but things are going very well."

"I noticed that you spend a lot of time with Slathe, and he listens to you."

"He doesn't know this area at all, and he's pretty well depending on me to guide him. The other scouts are getting slack because I'm doing all the work. I keep them looking good by letting them bring in the good news, like when a regiment of the king's soldiers misses us and heads up a mountain." His voice dropped even further, his lips by her ear. "So this army is going exactly where I want them. Do you understand?"

He pulled back, and his look of triumph stilled any fears that he was lying to her.

"How soon?"

"I'm sorry, I shouldn't tell you even if I knew for sure. But soon. Count on it." He faced her, as if sizing up her mood. "Aleria, you are going to have to stop moving around so much."

"Moving around?"

"Yes, stay closer to the tent. Stay in the tent. Don't let them see you so much."

"Raif, it's summer! That tent is like a furnace. I can't stay in there all the time." The thought of the sweltering tent walls closing in on her was more frightening than all her other imaginings.

"Nonetheless. Keep out of sight. It's only for a few more days." He grinned at her. "Shame to get killed at the last, after all the trouble we've gone to keeping you alive."

There didn't seem to be any answer she could give to that without getting angry again, so she threw herself down on her blankets, her back to him. He brushed out through the tent flap, and the heat descended on her again. She rolled over, trying not to look at the canvas so close above her face. The heat increased.

Raif was away more and more in the next two days, leaving earlier and returning later than before. The army moved in shorter spurts, hurrying in one direction, waiting for Raif's word, then rushing somewhere else. She had the feeling that Raif was playing some gigantic chess match, moving the players from both sides, carefully arranging them for some great endgame. When he did return he was always tired and he often thrashed around for hours after he should have been asleep. Since his one concession to her comfort had been to get rid of the heavy cot, he slept beside her and it made her nights difficult as well.

While she saw less of him, she also noticed that the other men were careful to avoid her, turning their backs if she passed them, giving her tent a wide berth when they were camped. In turn, she stayed out of sight as much as possible.

The third night he did not return until long after dark. She had worried herself into a fine state when he finally slipped into the tent. He didn't say a word until he had removed his outer clothing and slipped under the blankets beside her.

"Are you awake?"

"Am I awake? I've been lying here for hours, thinking you're dead or gone off for good. Not much chance I'd be asleep, is there?"

He chuckled, a friendly sound she had heard rarely from him. He turned so his lips were close to her ear. "It's all set up. Tomorrow."

His hand on her head stopped her reaction, held her down.

"Listen carefully. Tomorrow I'm going to make the army move fast. I want everybody good and tired. We're getting close to Disda, and Slathe's plan is to take the town and hold it. He thinks the king will negotiate with him at that point. The other scouts have confirmed that a large part of the garrison has been pulled out to chase after us. Only I know that they haven't gone very far, and the rest of the army is nearby. When we camp tomorrow night, I want you to set up the tent as far to the north of the trail as you can. To the north. Do you have that?"

"To the north of the trail. That's the side away from Disda, isn't it? I heard somebody say we were going north of the town."

"Good girl. You have it perfectly. Now, everyone will be attracted to the south side of camp, because there's a spot where we can overlook the town. I'm going to make a big fuss over there, hold a meeting, celebrate the victory in advance. When everyone is busy, you slip out of camp. Start for the creek and take a water bag in case anyone stops you. I'll post the sentry farther down the trail. When you're sure no one is following, go up the creek. Keep going, no matter what you hear behind you. Wait until dawn, then go down to the town. Circle around to the east so you don't run into anyone hiding out from the fight. The King's men will be in the town, and you can just walk in. I suggest you stay away from the soldiers while you're coming in. They might not believe you in time."

She shuddered at the thought of escaping the rebels, only to be raped by the king's soldiers. "What are you going to do?"

"I'll slip away when the fighting starts. I'll hide out myself and come in when it's light, just like you."

She thought for a moment, then reached over and pulled his head close to hers. "I don't like it."

"What don't you like?"

"For one thing, I suspect the attack will be just about dusk, right? There will be several hundred bandits running in all directions, with the king's soldiers hunting them down. How are the king's soldiers going to know who you are? I doubt if your precious Colonel has told his whole army to look out for you. He must assume Slathe has spies of his own. No, your chances of getting killed by your own men are too great."

"I thought of that. I know the country better than they do. I'll make out all right."

"Of course."

"I will!"

"Listen. Why don't you just come after me?"

"Come after you?"

"Don't echo me like a dummy. Think! I assume you know when the attack is going to be. Just before then, you find out that I'm missing. Make a big fuss and take out after me. They all know how you treat me. They'll think it's a big joke, right?"

He was silent a long time.

"Well, what do you think?"

"I'm trying to think reasons why it won't work."

"Someone might try to help you look for me."

"I'll wait until we're far enough away, then kill him."

"What if someone follows me?"

"Even better. That way I'll be there to protect you."

"I must admit I would prefer that. Do you have a weapon I can carry?"

"You have your dagger."

"The hideaway? I mean something useful against a man with a sword. That little thing hasn't been good for much except giving me a rash."

"I'll leave a big dagger in the bedroll in the morning. The black-handled one. Keep it well hidden."

A thought struck her. "What about the march tomorrow? I'll get tired, carrying all the camping stuff, and I'll need all my energy later. Can we leave some behind?"

"We don't dare. Couldn't explain it if anyone noticed. I'll sneak the heavy fry pan out with me when I go on patrol, and ditch it somewhere."

That was all the preparation they could think of, but she lay awake for a long time, torn between relief and anxiety.

The next day was a scorcher. Slathe marched them at unmerciful speed despite the weather, urged on by Raif. Aleria was beginning to think she was not going to make it when she had an inspiration. She began to fall back and tried to look

181

sick, especially when Raif was near. He shouted at her to keep moving. She moaned and began to limp.

At this moment Slathe strode by, clouted her, sending her spinning into the dust. "If she can't keep up, throw some of that junk away." He grinned, an evil stretch of fat lips across rotten fangs. "There'll be plenty more, and better, by tomorrow night."

Raif hauled her to her feet, hiding a grin, and proceeded to toss all the cooking utensils and heavier gear out of her bundle. Soon she was left with nothing but the tent, the blankets, and some food. He shoved her forward, and she stumbled on, her head down but her feet light.

Raif was off scouting when she reached the campsite, a wide ledge on the side of the mountain overlooking the town. She found a secluded spot between two boulders to pitch the tent. The ground was rocky, but since she didn't plan to sleep here tonight, she only made a show of leveling it off, and set up the tent. There were no fires this close to the town, so she didn't need to cook.

When they finished their cold supper there was a small package left over, and she wrapped it with the heavy dagger in an over-the-shoulder bundle made with a blanket. She tucked it inside the tent flap and tried to wait. It was difficult to act as if all was normal, when the tension was wound so tight in her that her stomach hurt. She wanted to walk around to do something but she had to sit still. She kept herself going with the thought that by dark she would be out of here, by tomorrow it would be all over.

The sun had set when Raif got up from where he was sitting, swaggered over to her, hauled her head up to look at him. Several soldiers and a few of the women were watching, so she steeled herself for something 'effective.'

He leaned down, kissed her hard, and grabbed her breast. He had never done anything like this in public before, and she squirmed away, snarling.

He laughed and grabbed her again, hauling her to her feet and crushing her body against his. "Don't complain,

Sweetheart. There'll be plenty of that for you tonight. A little victory celebration in advance, maybe."

Coarse laughter and obscene comments greeted this wit. She ducked her head, covering her face with her hair.

"Better get it while you can, Sweetheart. I might find something I like better tomorrow."

"Hey, Raif, you get tired of her, you can give her to me."

There was a sudden silence, as Raif's head swung to face the soldier, who immediately sat down. "Just jokin', Raif. Just jokin', really."

Raif held his eyes a moment, then grinned. "A good joke, Mellas. A real good joke, but I wouldn't do that to a friend. She's not worth it. When I find another one, we'll just leave her behind on the dung heap!" The soldiers roared at this, but Aleria could see, peering out through her hair, that the other women's laughter was forced.

Raif clouted her, the usual blow that seemed to hit her ear, but spent most of its force on her shoulder. Laughing, he shoved her into the tent. "Get in there, slut."

He pushed through the canvas after her. "We've got a problem."

"What?"

"Slathe has left the camp. He's going to meet with another group, and it means he won't be here when the attack happens."

"Isn't that better? They'll be disorganized."

"Yes, but he won't get caught." He sat and pondered a moment. "Maybe I should stay."

"Raif, this attack is going to destroy your credibility. If you stay, you're not going to get out alive."

"I'll worry about that. You go as planned."

"What about your precious report? Sooner or later you've got to deliver it."

"I know."

"Then don't be a fool. You're so caught up in this spying role you don't even know when it's time to quit." She grabbed him by the lapels. "It's time to quit, Raif. Now. Today!"

He shook his head. "Yes, I suppose you're right."

Then he squared his shoulders. "Yes, you are right. Let's get out of here."

He thought a moment, then raised his hand. "Scream."

She did not question, complying with a short, sharp, yell, cut off as he slapped the back of his left hand violently with the palm of his right, giving off a meaty smack. Then he grinned, winked at her, and raised his voice. "And there's more where that came from. Don't you forget it."

He shoved his way out of the tent, but then turned back. "There's no fresh water. You can get me that, but then stay in the tent. You hear me?"

She mumbled a reply, relieved that she had come off so lightly.

"Come on, lads. Let's go look at the orchard we'll be pickin' tomorrow!"

The group outside straggled after him. She waited as their footsteps faded, then peeked out of the tent. No one. Slinging her blanket pack over her shoulder, she headed up the trail towards the creek. If anyone stopped her now it would be hard to explain the food. She would just have to hope her shawl hid enough. It took an iron clamp on her will to walk with her usual slow slouch through the other tents and onto the trail

Trying to act naturally meant she couldn't look around until she reached the creek and was bending over to fill the water skin. Again, all was still. The camp was just out of sight around the bend, so she slipped her bundle behind a big rock and waited as if resting, staring off through the trees into the valley below, her eyes alert for any movement around her.

When she was satisfied that no one was following she got up, stretched, and looked around one more time. There was no sign of the sentry. Raif must have been successful in that part of the plan. She leaned against the rock, then edged around it until she was hidden from the camp. The moment she was out of sight she moved fast, slinging on her bundle, jumping from rock to rock up the streambed, careful to leave a few obvious footprints in the mud for Raif to 'discover.'

She stopped several times to look back, but it seemed as if no one had noticed her escape. If they had seen her, surely they would have stopped her by now. Unless they thought she was a spy and were following to see where she went. That was all right; she wasn't going anywhere important. By the time Raif caught up to her, secrecy wouldn't matter any more, and he could deal with the problem.

More confident now, she clambered up the steepening streambed, still watching her back trail, careful not to reveal herself to the camp, which showed through the thinning trees below her. After a while the excitement wore off and the day's walk began to take its toll. Finally she had to stop, lying on a slab of rock, her head screened by a bush that clung to a crevice.

From her vantage point she could see the camp far below and indistinct in the dusk. There were only a few figures at the lookout spot so she assumed the planning was over. She hoped Raif had made his escape and that he wasn't followed.

A flash of movement off to her left caught her eye. A column of soldiers was marching in plain sight up the trail from the east. She could see that if they did not stop soon they would reach the crest and be in sight of the sentry. She looked to the west, and sure enough, there was another column coming from that direction. Down the hill, she could see a ragged line of men creeping up towards the camp. She pictured the form of the battle. The army would attack from three directions, overwhelming the camp. Those who escaped would be forced up the mountain, out into the open on the rocks above tree line.

A good plan, but it sent all the escaping rebels right on her trail. *Great tactics, Raif. I'd better get moving.* She pushed her aching body back up the rocks.

The second time she found a viewpoint she knew she would have to stop for a proper rest. She was starting to stumble, and a broken ankle would be a fine thing in the middle of a battle. She peered down at the rebel camp again, now indistinct in the gathering darkness. The soldiers to left and right were massed now, and the line climbing below the camp was very close. As she watched, there was a sudden movement among the tiny figures in the camp, and she knew the soldiers had been discovered. The troops along the trail moved forward, and the rebels rushed to meet them. The climbers pushed upwards, but were met with stiff resistance at the edge and were thrown back down the hill.

Just about that time the troops from the west broke through into the campsite. It was all a swirl of figures, like a battle in an ant's nest, too far away and dark to see who was winning or to hear the awful sounds. Only the faint pop of rifles assured her that she really was watching a battle. She had little doubt as to the outcome. There had been too many soldiers. All she had to worry about was getting higher.

She forced herself on, relieved that the streambed swung away from the higher slopes and climbed up over steps and ledges through a narrow valley hanging between the peaks. It leveled off for a few paces and she hiked on with renewed vigor.

As she moved ahead she could hear a low shuddering sound that seemed to come from the rocks beneath her feet. It got stronger as she climbed and she wondered what happened to the stream ahead. Rounding a corner, she found out. The creek fell over a sharp ledge a good hundred feet above her. The sheer cliff plugged the valley and the rocky walls formed a canyon out of which she could never climb, especially in the coming dark. The mist blowing in her face made every surface slippery and moss grew everywhere.

So this was the end. She could go no farther. Had Raif known about this? Probably. It seemed he knew this area well. So what did he expect her to do? First thing, there was no sense staying near the falls. She would never hear anyone, friend or foe, in the dark and the noise. The best thing to do was to hole up somewhere close enough to the stream to hear him when he came, far enough away that any enemy would not notice her.

With this in mind, she started back down, thankful that she did not have to climb any more. She found what she was looking for just at the top of the steepest pitch: a ledge that overlooked the stream but was not obvious from below. It had the added advantage of an escape route along the eastern end out onto the rock face above the town. A small overhang would shelter her from any rain, although she didn't want to think about what it would be like in a full storm.

Topping up her water skin at the stream, she climbed onto her ledge and settled in to wait for Raif, gnawing on a piece of dried meat from her pack. It was good to be resting, but the anxious tension refused to leave her, growing as the darkness deepened and he did not show. She wondered if she was still too high. Should she climb down farther? *Don't be stupid, girl. Sit till he comes or daylight. Doesn't matter which.*

A rock clicked.

She held her breath, listening, but that was all. She peered down through the darkness. There was no movement. Then a figure materialized, moving silently up the streambed. A tall figure, if she could judge. Was it him? A sudden wariness held her back. Not knowing what to do, she let him continue past. Well, if it was Raif, he would get to the falls and turn back, knowing he had missed her. If it was anyone else, then hopefully he would strike out in another direction.

Sure enough, soon the figure returned downstream, moving even more slowly as if searching for something. He stopped, his head up, seeming to look straight at her. Then he sat on a nearby boulder, a soft curse rising up to her ears. Now she was almost sure. Her fingers scrabbled for a pebble, and she tossed it to land on the other side of the stream. He was on his feet in an instant and his whisper startled her.

"Aleria!"

She tossed another pebble, this one hitting him. He spun to face her.

"Aleria! This is no time to play games. Come on down. We have to get moving."

"How did you know I was up here?"

187

"I hunted this valley years ago." He caught her arm, peered at her. "Are you all right?"

"I'm fine, but tired. How did it go?"

"Smooth as silk. It worked just like you said it would. They thought it was oh, so funny that you had run out on me. When we discovered you had gone up the mountain, not down to the town, they were quite happy at the thought of me stumbling around in the darkness looking for you. Did you leave the tracks on purpose? I thought so."

"So no one followed?"

"Not a chance. I moved too fast and I watched. The attack went well, too."

"And now the defeated rebels are headed up the mountain after us."

"Well, that's a small problem. It's too bad you moved so fast. I hoped you wouldn't get this far. We have to go down a ways to catch the trail that goes east along the mountain."

"Can't we go off the end of this ledge?"

"It's too hard a climb in the dark."

"Don't you know of some place we could just hide out?"

"Yes, but this is too close to where the rebels will be running. A frightened man can go a long way, even in the mountains in the dark."

"All right, then. Let's get moving."

18. Army

Dawn found them high on the slope of the mountain, far to the east of the battle site. They woke, wrapped together in her blanket for warmth, in a small half-cave protected from the damp breath of the ice fields hanging above them.

She knew he was awake from his breathing, but it was too chilly out to move. "Raif? You know your original plan?"

He grunted. "The one you said would get me killed?"

"Yes. Did you plan to go back and fight, once you were recognized as a king's soldier?"

"No."

"Not even after all the atrocious things you had seen the rebels do. After the things you were forced to do? Why not?"

"Well, I'm not so happy about killing a lot of those men back there. Sure, they're a rough lot, and Slathe and his bunch are real monsters. But most of them are just soldiers. I could take a third of them, drop them in the middle of my regiment, and in two months you couldn't tell them from the regulars. And Balek, well, he's too stupid to take care of himself wherever he is. Heaven knows how he got mixed in with this lot, but he's so strong that he makes a good fighter, so they put up with him.

"That's one reason."

He nodded. "Another reason is that I wouldn't like to look in the faces of men I've betrayed. I don't enjoy this spying business. It was necessary, but I hope they never find out."

"That worked out well, then. They will believe you got out of the trap because you were chasing me. That way, if you have to go back again, no one will know you betrayed them."

He smiled crookedly at her. "Good thinking, but I don't plan to go back."

"I've got a better idea. When it's all over, why don't you let them see you captured, so that they know you're still on their side? I could even drag you around for a while as my captive, tables turned and all that."

He barked a short laugh. "And beating me around whenever you liked as well, I suspect. That would be a good revenge, wouldn't it?"

"Well, can you blame me? You hit me, you ordered me around, you treated me like dirt."

"It was necessary! Can you get it through your head what I saved you from?"

She pulled away, preferring the chill of the morning air as it rushed between them. "I know. I have little doubt that I owe you more than my life. It's just that it was a horrible experience, and you're the only one around that I can complain to."

He rested his hand lightly on her shoulder. "Complain all you like. I know it was bad, and you held up well. You should be proud of yourself."

She suppressed a shudder at his touch. "Come on, let's find the Army."

He gathered up the blanket and led the way down the mountain. She watched his broad back in front of her, wondering if she would ever lose the churning she felt in her stomach whenever she looked at his face.

They were a long way down the mountain when Raif stopped, motioning silence. She froze, peering around for danger. He motioned ahead, leaned down to whisper. "Army scout."

She looked where he pointed, and after a moment saw movement. A man was climbing towards them, making use of what cover he could, his head up, eyes scanning the forest. He was dressed in nondescript clothing, but it was in better condition than anything the rebels wore and he carried a rifle that looked shiny and well kept.

"How do we approach him?"

"Just step out and say hello, I suppose."

"And get shot. You're a rebel, remember. Better if I do it."

"I suppose you're right."

"You stay here. I'll just slip out on that rock. He'll see me."

She moved cautiously and made it to a comfortable position before the man noticed her. He stopped, stared at her a moment, then disappeared into the bush. She waited a while, but there was no movement.

"What do I do now?" She spoke without turning her head.

"Nothing. He's just checking you out. He'll get here."

Sure enough, a long while later the man's head appeared over a boulder along the mountain from her, his rifle barrel pointed at her.

"Hi." She tried a friendly smile, despite the gun.

He looked at her for a moment, then again scanned the area. "What do you want?"

"I want to be taken to Colonel anTetrono, please."

"Are you alone?"

"No."

"Who is with you?"

"One of your officers. He just doesn't look like one at the moment."

"Who?"

"Raif." Only then did she realize that she didn't know his family name.

"Tell him to show himself."

Raif rose slowly and stood beside her.

"I don't know him."

Raif grinned. "But Colonel anTetrono does, and the password for today is 'Dagger'."

The soldier considered a moment. "That's the password, all right. Just the two of you?"

They nodded.

"Would you just continue on down the mountain a ways?"

They complied, and he disappeared behind the rock. After they had gone a hundred paces or so, she heard his voice behind her. "You can stop now."

They turned and he was closer, but still had his rifle ready. "Were you in the fight last night?"

"No, we escaped from the camp earlier. I have a report to make to the Colonel: information he needs immediately."

The man nodded. "And you want her to come, too?"

Raif grinned. "She's not exactly what she looks like."

"Your choice. Go down this trail until you hit the main path, then turn right. I'll follow."

"You're a careful man."

"I'm a live man, and I intend to stay that way."

"I approve."

"Thank you."

It was still a fair distance down the mountain, and Aleria noticed that both her escorts were very watchful. She kept her own eyes open, but the stress of the night was beginning to tell, and she had to watch her footing to keep from stumbling. Finally, they reached smoother ground and a better trail. Soon after that they were stopped by another soldier, this one in uniform. The scout took care of the formalities and they passed through. Around the next bend in the trail she could see canvas through the trees and she started to believe that they had made it.

A final sentry stopped them at the edge of the camp.

"Two to see the Colonel."

"Who are they?"

"Say's his name's Raif. Don't know who she is."

"You didn't ask?"

"They had the password. You don't stop to chat out in the forest. There's a battle going on, in case you didn't notice."

"I thought it was over."

"Just about."

The sentry turned to them. "So who are you?"

"My name's Aleria Dalmyn. I got caught up in all this by mistake."

Raif stepped forward. "I'm Raif Canah, with His Majesty's Fusiliers. Could you do me a favour, soldier? Send for Kendrin anTahl. He'll be around the Colonel's tent somewhere, if I know him."

The sentry took another look at the ragged man in front of him, raised his eyebrows, then straightened. "Yes, sir." He turned to the scout. "I think you'd better take them to the Officer of the Watch."

Their guide nodded. "Who's on?"

"Magro."

A significant look passed between the two. She glanced at Raif, but he shrugged.

They were ushered into large tent near the centre of the camp. It was almost empty, with only a few canvas chairs and odd bits of equipment scattered around. The scout was just starting to unfold a chair for her when the door slapped open and an officer strutted through.

The scout squared his shoulders, saluted and stood at attention. As they joined him in a ragged line, Aleria was amused to realize that she knew the officer who was looking her over with such a supercilious air. Maltuen anMagro, determined rake and self-proclaimed hero of the class two years her senior. Finally, tired of waiting, the scout glanced at Raif, then spoke.

"These two should be escorted to the Colonel immediately, sir. They just came in..."

He was cut short by a huge sigh from anMagro. "My dear man. In whose opinion should these two be escorted anywhere but to the detention area in chains with the rest of their rag-tag lot? When are you common soldiers going to learn proper procedures?"

The scout cleared his throat, earning a glare. "Begging your pardon, sir, but this lady is Aleria..."

"Lady? Soldier, this is no...Aleria? Great Gods, man, are you sure? Aleria, by the Gods it is you! We all thought you must be dead, caught up in all this. My Lord, girl, you look rough. What a bruise. Who gave you that?"

She glanced over at Raif, standing silently, watching. She could tell what he thought of this pompous young man.

"Him? This lout dared to raise a hand to you?" Before she could speak, he strode to Raif and struck him an open-handed blow to the side of the head that sent him reeling against the tent wall. In his surprise, he slipped and fell to the ground. Maltuen stood over him.

"If you were a gentleman, I would demand satisfaction for this atrocity! Since you're obviously not, I'll give you more of the same!"

Anger surged through her. She leaped at the officer, fingers clawed in the gold braid of his uniform. "You touch him again, you impudent twerp, I'll take both your eyes out! If you had any idea what we've been through out there..." She glared into his startled face, took in the fear, the lack of comprehension. "But of course you have no idea, do you?" She looked down in disgust at the beautiful cloth in her hands, pushed him away from her. "You better get a little dirt on this pretty uniform if you want to go home with stories to tell."

She turned to see Raif getting up from the ground. He grinned, looked like he was about to approach her, but stopped and stared at her instead. She realized that her hands were still tense, and made an effort to relax. Raif turned his smile on the startled officer. "I guess you've figured out she doesn't need anyone to stand up for her. Come on, take me to the Colonel. We have business." He turned in the doorway of the tent. "You'll be all right, won't you? If you need anything, just call and someone will come."

She was about to snap a reply when she realized that she was about to be left alone in this big, empty tent. "No, I'm fine. Um..."

"What is it?"

"Well... If there is someone assigned to look after me, do you think it would be all right if he stayed here? Inside...? I mean..."

"You mean you've just spent several days in a situation where being alone was very frightening, and the same bunch of bandits are still out there somewhere?"

She nodded, relieved and a bit surprised at his understanding.

"That's not difficult at all. I'll be back in a moment." As he left, she heard a quick patter of feet approaching. There was an exclamation, a friendly greeting, and a quick conversation. Immediately he returned with a junior officer, a very young man with a pleased smile. "Aleria, this is Kendrin anTahl, my aide. He will stay as long as you like. He's a good lad; I'll vouch for him. His father plays polo with my father."

He slapped the boy on the shoulder. "We'll talk later." Then he turned and left, ignoring Maltuen, who stumbled after him.

She stood for a moment, staring at the swinging canvas flap. His father. It had never occurred to her to ask where he came from. Polo? Aide? This was interesting. She turned to the young man.

"So, Kendrin anTahl, who is his father, that he can afford polo?"

The young soldier smiled. "You don't know? From the look of it, I thought you two had a pretty good chance to get acquainted."

The warmth faded from her. Perhaps she was safe, but it seemed she was still going to have to deal with the crude jokes of soldiers. She was about to start in on him when the smile disappeared from the boy's face.

"I'm sorry, Miss Aleria. I didn't mean to speak out of line. I just thought the way Lord Canah talked about you, like you were a good friend of his, you wouldn't mind the joke. He always jokes with me, you see, and I thought, well...well, I'm sorry."

Half her mind was realizing that she shouldn't be too hard on the boy, but the other half was dealing with the new information.

"Lord Canah?"

"Yes. Raif anCanah. You mean you didn't know?"

She felt herself gaping, snapped her mouth shut. "What the hell is the heir to the dukedom of Canah doing sneaking around with a bunch of rebels? He could have got himself killed!"

Kendrin shrugged. "I don't know what he was doing, Miss. You were with him, I though you might know."

"I knew what he was doing, but I didn't know that's who he was. Why would he do a thing like that...? Don't answer. It's because he's pig-headed and won't listen to anybody."

The boy blushed. "Well, Miss, also because a lot of his father's lands are here in the North. He can speak with the right accent, knows the area well. He was a marvelous choice, if I might say so. Just risky."

"Risky! That's an understatement. What did his father say? From what I hear of the old Duke, he's not the kind of man to allow his heir to take chances like that."

"I don't think Duke Canah knows anything about it. I saw my father last week, and he was talking about the two of us, that's Raif and me, getting glory on the field of battle and all that. He said the Duke was pleased that I got to be Raif's aide-de-camp. Of course I couldn't say anything. Didn't dare."

"Good for you. Mind you, the duke would have found out sooner or later." She grinned at the idea. "And it's not as if he could have gone chasing off after the rebel army to get Raif to quit. Can you just see it? 'Please, Mister Slathe, could you just stop your rebellion for a minute or so? You see, my son has to come home or he'll be late for his court etiquette lesson.' No, not too likely."

Kendrin laughed. "I don't think that would go over too well." Then his face became serious. "Slathe is one of the leaders, isn't he? What's he like?"

She shuddered. "He's a horrible, dirty man. He's big and heavy and strong, and he takes what he likes. He hits his own people if they don't do what he wants fast enough, and he...he takes any woman he puts his eye on..." She stopped, thinking about what might have happened to her.

"Here, Miss Aleria. I think you'd better sit down." He led her to a canvas-backed chair. "I'm sorry I asked. You've had a pretty rough time of it, these past few days. Would you like anything? Are you cold? Would you like a blanket?"

She was about to deny it when she realized that she was shaking, and she accepted the blanket gratefully. She sat, her thoughts muddled, as he bustled around making sure she was comfortable.

"Would you like a hot drink? I could get you one. I wouldn't be long." Something on her face stopped him. "I'll call for someone. I won't go away."

He went to the tent doorway and shouted for an orderly. In a short time she was sitting with her fingers laced around a cup of hot, sweet tea. As she eyed the plate of biscuits and meat that he set on a folding table in front of her, she remembered how long it had been since she ate good food, even rough soldier's fare such as this. With an apologetic glance at Kendrin, she dug in.

When she had eaten half the plateful she felt better, remembering her manners enough to slow down and make polite conversation. "So this is your Field Experience?"

He nodded eagerly. "What luck, hey? I was halfway through my term when this all came up. They said that since I was here I might as well stay. I should have gone home weeks ago, but here I am."

Thinking about her own supposed Field Experience, where the girls weren't allowed within a horse-length of a common soldier, she had to agree. "If you get home in one piece it will be good luck, all right."

"Oh, I don't expect to see any actual fighting. There aren't enough rebels to make a real attack on this camp," he shot her a sudden glance, "are there? I guess you would know."

She thought of the size of this camp, the long picket lines of cavalry they had passed on their way in. "No, there aren't. I would almost feel sorry for them if they weren't such awful men. And women. You can consider yourself lucky that you aren't fighting. I've seen it, and I didn't like it."

"But you're ..."

"Just a girl. I know. Not meaning to offend, Kendrin, but you're just a boy, and I suspect there's not a whole lot of difference in the way we were brought up. Believe me, when you've seen people being killed, heard the screams..." She felt herself start to shiver again.

"Say, I don't think you had better talk about things like that. You'd best forget about them."

"I'm sorry. I know I shouldn't, but my mind just keeps getting drawn back to it."

"Maybe you need to talk about it, then. It's just that whenever you do, you go all white and your hands clench up. If Raif comes in and sees you like that, well, let's just say I'll be seeing a whole lot of horses' coats, close up, in the next few days."

She laughed, happy to be able to joke. "Well, we'll just have to save you from curry-comb duty and talk about other things. I guess you must be in next year's class?"

They chatted on a while. He was two years behind her on the Young Gentlemen's side of the Academy, and they discovered several mutual friends and one mutually detested instructor. After a while she found herself getting sleepy. Kendrin unfolded a canvas cot, apologizing for its roughness.

She sank down onto it. "I have been sleeping on the ground lately. This feels great."

"You just sleep. I'll sit in the doorway, so I can keep an eye on what's happening in the camp and be here at the same time."

She looked around the tent. It didn't seem so large, now, and the morning sun left a bright splash against one wall. She smiled sleepily up at him. "That's all right. If you need to go find out what's going on, I'll be fine."

"I'll be right outside, then. If you need me, just call."

She didn't even remember him going out the door.

19. Aftermath

For the next two days, everything outside her tent became a blur of uniforms, neighing horses and clattering equipment. Once her fear had subsided enough, Kendrin left her alone most of the time because of his duties. Raif had immediately been sent off on some new mission, for which she was thankful. She retreated into the warm cleanliness of the tent and the safety of the camp, steering her thoughts away whenever they circled towards her recent ordeal.

She was just beginning to take an interest in what was happening with the rebellion when a carriage arrived to take her home. Her last view of the camp was Kendrin waving in the dust of her transport and the troop of lancers who were being transferred back to Kingsport with her. She had no illusions that she was important enough to warrant all that protection. All she could think about was going home.

Where she soon realized that her ordeal was not complete. Her story had spread before her, and she found that her various social circles were almost as difficult to face as a mob of grinning soldiers. The other girls at school were only the beginning.

At one point, Mito came to her rescue, taking her by the arm and towing her out of the Seniors' Common Room.

"You're quite the hero, now."

Aleria closed the door on the mass of fluttering girls. She strode to a nearby meeting room, flopped into a chair and shook her head. "They have no idea."

Mito sat nearby in a more dignified pose. "I think they can figure it out."

"No, Mito. Unless you've been there, felt what it's like, you just can't tell. They don't know. I can hear it in the stupid things they say."

"Aleria, you've always thought that the things they said were stupid."

"Maybe I'm just different. I've always wondered, tried not to be, tried to hide it, but I guess I am."

"You are."

"You can tell?"

"It's always been there. I've always known."

"It's that obvious?"

"Everyone always knew, even if they couldn't put it into words. You were always doing things differently, and if you did things the same, it was always better, or worse, or something. After all, who's your best friend?"

"You are. What's that got to do with it?"

"Come on. Am I a typical friend for someone like you?"

"I don't choose my friends by who everyone else thinks I should. I chose you because I like you."

"You chose me before you knew what I was like. You chose me the moment you decided I was different from the rest. I believe you really do like me, now. But don't you see how what you just said proves my point?"

She grinned. "I suppose you're right. You always see things as so complicated. But you're usually right, I guess."

"I have my talents."

"And getting along with me is one of them."

"It hasn't always been easy."

"But it's always been fun."

The other girl stopped smiling.

"Mito, were they very hard on you? You finally told them, didn't you? I don't mind. Really I don't. It was one of the things that kept me going, when I was with the rebel army, knowing that you would send them looking for me."

"I'm glad you aren't angry. It wasn't that bad, I guess. It was difficult to pretend that I didn't know. I kept thinking that they would see how nervous I was. You know what a bad liar I am. But I suppose they just thought I was worried. Which, of course, I was. As soon as I heard where the rebellion was I realized that you were in danger, so I told Master Ogima right away. He was upset then, asking why I didn't tell him sooner, and I said that I only just found out about the rebellion. After that he was too busy organizing the rescue party to bother about me. I was surprised at how easy it was. I think I was just so worried about you, I forgot to be afraid for myself."

"Typical. Always thinking of the other person."

"Well, it was an advantage, this time."

"I suppose so. And I appreciate it. You know, Mito, I think that if I had been killed, you are the only one of this bunch that would have been truly sad."

"Aleria, that's not true!"

"Oh, the others would have been horrified, I'm sure. But they're too caught up in their own lives to care much about what I do with mine. You're different. You're a true friend, and I will endeavour to be more like you in the future.

Mito took her hand. "I never thought I would hear you say that. I promise you, if you ever die, I will be truly sorry, and I will mourn for ages. I mean it. Why are you laughing?

"I'm sure you do mean it. It's just such a funny way of saying it."

Mito began to laugh as well. "I suppose so. Too bad you have to die to find out how much I love you."

They were laughing too hard to notice a man standing in the doorway. He cleared his throat, and they had controlled themselves enough to make a polite response when they realized it was Master Ogima. He invited them into his office, and Aleria waited in trepidation. He was probably here to tell her what a little fool she'd been, and she prepared to accept his judgement with no reserve. He said nothing as he sat, and she looked more closely at him. His stern face seemed very relaxed, even friendly. He put his closed fist on the table, then looked at her.

She looked at the fist, then his face. He was almost smiling. Then he opened his hand.

Her necklace.

"Where did you get that?" She reached out.

He grinned, opened his hand further. "I bought it."

"Who from?" She looked at the chain as if it might hold an answer.

"A lad I met in Relaz."

"Shen Waring?"

"That name sounds familiar. A rather sad specimen. Seemed depressed."

"But why would he sell it? What did you pay him?"

"I paid him a name. He seemed quite happy with the deal."

"A name?"

"Yes. Your last name. It seems you neglected to leave that little detail with him."

"Oh! Of course. I was trying to hide my trail, so I didn't give out any information to anyone." She looked for an angry reaction, but he was grinning.

"Oh, yes, there was one more thing. I also paid him a promise. That I would bring it to you, along with a message."

"A message?" She could feel the heat rising in her face.

Ogima looked slyly at her. "He seemed quite in earnest. He just said that he would like to hear from you."

Relief swept through her. "Oh."

"That's all? 'Oh'?"

She raised her head. "Yes, that's all. Thank you for delivering my message and my necklace." Then she realized how that sounded.

"I am so sorry you went through all that danger looking for me. I acted like a spoiled brat, and it was only luck that we both got out of it in good shape."

His smile widened. "I'm not sorry. What you said back in the Fortress was true. You youngsters are not very well prepared these days, and the Quest is a joke. Your little adventure has been a real test of your abilities. In fact, I would say you have passed with flying colours."

A dark suspicion formed. "You mean this was another test?"

He laughed. "No, no, this was real. It was just bad luck that Slathe's rebellion spilled into the area just as we were passing through. Until recently, he had half the men and was much farther south. Good thing Lord Canah had a handle on him."

She nodded. "And good luck that it was Raif who found me in that inn, instead of one of the others."

"Some of it was luck. But he was on the lookout for anyone he could save, so he tried to be the first into the better rooms at the inn because he knew that was where any travellers would be. He's a good man, Raif."

She shuddered. "I just can't bear to see his face."

He rose and put an arm around her shoulders. "He understands, I'm sure."

"I don't understand. I know he saved me and now I can't even talk to him. I have dreams at night, horrible dreams, and he's always in them. It's not fair to him."

"If that's the worst that happens to him because of his little adventure, he can consider himself lucky. His father was quite upset when he found out."

"I wondered how His Grace would feel about it."

"The duke wants his son in the army, all right, but out on the battlefield reaping glory, not mucking about in the mud playing spy."

"I suppose."

"The old man also doesn't want him skewered in a minor brawl out in the back country, as you might guess."

"I suppose." Then she shrugged. "I certainly didn't see the polished side of him."

"Tell me, Aleria. Once Mito let us know what route you took we started out right away. I thought we would have caught up with you. Did you get a ride?"

"No, I took a short-cut over the Naskawene Mountains."

"Ah, that explains it. We went the long way and lost track of you until it was too late and we had to pull out. How did you find out about the shortcut?"

"Um...Shen..."

"You went off into the mountains with a man you had just met?"

"I know it seems stupid. I travelled with him for a whole day, and I liked him. He seemed...nice. And trustworthy. That doesn't explain it, but..."

"So either you're a shrewd judge of character or else it was just stupid luck."

She raised her chin in mock hauteur. "I prefer to believe the former." She looked frankly at the two sitting with her. "But I also know I had a hearty dollop of the latter."

Ogima surprised her by reaching out and slapping her shoulder. "Don't worry about it. Of course you had some good luck. Every soldier who comes out of a battle has had his share of luck. But that doesn't take away from how you handled yourself. You demonstrated your courage, a fact that would not change, whether you lived or died."

"Courage? It seems to me I allowed myself to be dragged and battered around like a piece of useless luggage. I don't see where the courage comes into it."

"According to Raif you held up your end of the game very well. He told me that when he calmed down and realized what had happened in the inn he was weak in the knees at the risk he took, and will be forever thankful that you didn't let him down."

"I suppose I should be forever thankful to him, but it was a rough two weeks and he didn't treat me very well. Oh, I know he had to make it look good. Maybe some day I'll get to the point where I can be civil to him."

* * *

Her best friends actually caused her more trouble than all the mindless gossips.

"I think he was horrible to you." Gita hugged a pillow in front of her, as if for protection. "Surely he didn't beat you in his tent, where no one could see."

Aleria passed a weary hand across her brow. She had no joy in telling this part of the story, first to Mito, now all over again to the Twins. "Yes he did. He said everyone could hear. He also said I needed a fresh bruise. So, on the seventh day, he hit me again. He said it wouldn't hurt too much, but it did."

"And he made you do all his camp chores for him?"

"All of them. All the women did camp work. His clothes were filthy and he made me clean them. He made me cook and set up the tent and carry everything when we moved camp. And if I did anything wrong, he cuffed me and swore at me and threatened me with all sorts of things. Then he would laugh, and all those horrible men around would laugh, too."

"That was terrible. Did he really have to treat you that badly?"

"He said he did. He said the others wouldn't suspect him and they would leave me alone. Well, at least he was right about that. No one spoke to me at all. One man bothered me, and he beat him."

"Beat him?"

"Yes. He was absolutely cold and deadly, and he hit him again and again. He was just a little, ragged fellow and he didn't have a chance. I saw him the next day and his eyes were so swollen he could hardly see."

"He sounds like a terrible man."

Mito shook her head. "I don't know. He's a duke's son. He can't be that bad."

Aleria's head came up. "Maybe at court he's smooth as silk. I've only seen him at his worst, and believe me, he was pretty bad."

"But it was all pretend, you said."

She shook her head. "That's what he told me. But how could it have been? He lived with those men for weeks. He ate with them, hunted with them, fought with them, raided towns. He might have even killed people. I wonder how much he was different from them, deep down inside."

Hana leaned forward. "So all the time he was treating you so badly, do you think he was enjoying it?"

"I don't know. Maybe."

"I bet he was. I bet deep down inside he has a mean streak and this was just an excuse to let it out."

"I don't know. It could be. I tell you he certainly blended in with that bunch of renegades."

"Some duke's son!"

"Some gentleman."

Mito looked worried. "But he saved you."

205

"Huh! He did. And I have to be grateful for that. But you would think if he had any sensitivity he could have protected me a bit better."

Mito seemed unconvinced. "I suppose so."

Hana turned away. "You know Mito. Always seeing the good in everybody. I think he's just a pervert who gets his kicks by being mean to women."

"Hana! I hope you won't go around saying that in public!" Mito paused in dismay as the other three stared at her, surprised by this unusual outburst. "Well, it would be a poor way for Aleria to pay him back for saving her. Spreading horrible stories about him."

Hana was unrepentant. "But look how he treated her. He deserves it."

Aleria had a moment's qualm. "Mito is right. We shouldn't spread it around. That would just be vicious gossip."

Gita came to her sister's defence. "But what about some poor girl who is going to marry him, not knowing about his perversion?"

"Gita, we don't know he has a perversion."

"Well, I don't know. If someone gave me nightmares, I can't see I'd owe him too much. Except maybe a knife between the ribs if he got anywhere near me."

The others burst in to laughter. "Gita, you bloodthirsty little thing!"

The smaller girl grinned. "Oh, I'm dangerous, all right. Don't cross me!"

The conversation dissolved into laughter and lighter topics, but it left Aleria with something to think about. Now that she considered, Raif had been very rough with her right from the start. He had hit her several times and made fun of her, made her life miserable. Taken advantage of the fact that she was scared stiff to bully her. But he was a Duke's son and a hero. She would have to be very careful what she said or did about him in the future.

20. And of Course, Her Parents

She had another conversation that she was sort of looking forward to, but with some trepidation. It was difficult to raise the subject, but her mother solved it for her one day as they were working together in the kitchen. Aleria thought that Leniema was concentrating on rolling out pastry, but then her mother spoke without looking up.

"Your father thinks you're no longer a virgin."

Aleria could only stare. "Mother, I never told him that! I couldn't!"

"Quite right. There are certain things best left unsaid between a father and daughter, no matter how close they are. But that doesn't mean he's naive. In fact, he's one of the most intelligent men in the realm."

"I know that, mother. I just didn't want to hurt his feelings."

Leniema nodded. "So he was right. Are you happy?"

Aleria thought back to the tent, and the feel of Shen's body against hers. "Oh yes, mother. It was wonderful!"

Her mother's eyebrows rose. "Wonderful, was it? You've been a lucky girl, I suspect. Are you going to tell me about the young man?"

She dropped her eyes. "You're going to think I'm horrible, but I don't know that much. We met on the road, travelled together for two days. He was carrying messages for his father, something to do with his business."

"So his family are merchants?"

She shrugged. "I guess so. It didn't seem important at the time."

Her mother laughed and reached out to Aleria. "I don't imagine it did." Taking her daughter by the shoulders, she held her at arms length. "Tell me about him. What is he like?"

"Well, he's quite tall, and very slim and handsome. No, he's not handsome. His face is too craggy, and he has a crooked smile. A beautiful crooked smile." She looked up at her mother.

"He was wonderful to me, Mother. He took care of me and was considerate. He gave me plenty of chances to back out. At the very end when he found out it was my first time, he still said we could stop."

"When he knew very well you wouldn't."

"I suppose so, but it was sweet of him to offer, wasn't it?"

"Very. Now, I won't pry for all the details. I think there are some things that should be kept to ourselves. The important thing to consider is what are you going to do about him?"

Aleria looked at her mother. "I don't know, Mama. When we were out in the forest together everything was so simple and right. Now, back in the city with everyone around, it all seems so complicated. I have to see him again. That's certain. But how? I can't very well invite him here for a little visit, can I? You know, if he's a merchant's son, everyone will laugh at us and be mean to him. I'm a little young to be keeping a lover, don't you think?"

Her mother looked horrified. "I should think so! You know I don't approve of people of our class carrying on like that, no matter how old they are."

"I know, Mother. I was just joking. But you see the difficulties."

"I probably see more difficulties than you do. Especially your father. I think you are going to have to keep this young man at arm's length for the moment, much though you might want to do otherwise."

She paused to look her daughter straight in the eye. "You do believe that don't you? You won't go running off and do something silly?"

Aleria reached out and smoothed the tiny wrinkles that she had just noticed beside her mother's eye. "I think you can safely stop worrying about me doing something silly. I know what almost happened because of that. I was a headstrong, spoilt brat, and I hope I have learned something."

Her mother's face softened. "Aleria, you were never a brat. Headstrong, you will always be. Just remember to think first, then go ahead and be as stubborn as you like. Most people will mistake it for strength of character."

"Mother! What a horrible thing to say about your only child! Even if it happens to be true. Come on, stop being mean and help me figure out what to do about Shen. He's so sweet, Mother. You'll love him."

"If I ever get to meet him."

"You mean…?"

"I don't mean anything. It's up to you. Sometimes these romantic interludes are best left alone, never repeated. That way they always keep the glow of a beautiful dream. Something to tell your own daughter about. Or granddaughter. On the other hand, if you are well suited, who knows what may come of it?"

"But Mother, he's a merchant's son."

"And what's wrong with that?"

She looked at her mother for a moment, stunned. "But I thought you…"

"I doubt if you thought at all. When have I ever said there was anything wrong with being a merchant? Where do you think your father gets the money to run his estates? He does business, just like any other merchant. He runs one of the largest cartage companies in the realm, as you very well know. Besides which, what do you know about this young man? There are plenty of merchant families with good blood. You say he was gentle and considerate. Sounds like a good upbringing to me, no matter what his background. I'm sure his parents are fine people, if he was that nice."

Aleria smiled in relief. "I'm so happy to hear you say that. Come to think of it, I never did hear you speak of merchants with disrespect. I just assumed, because of your family and all…"

Her mother smiled. "You just assumed that I would have the same prejudices that your classmates have, because some of them come from Exalted families."

She shrugged. "You know I never went around spouting egalitarian principles to you. Heaven knows, a marriage of

209

social unequals will have its share of extra problems, and a marriage is a difficult enough task on its own. I had always hoped you would marry someone of your own class. It would make things easier. But that doesn't mean I'm set on it. No, my daughter, you consider this young man of yours carefully and make your own decision. After all, you have passed your Quest. Passed it twice over. You are an adult, now."

Aleria sighed. "You know, I thought my troubles would be over when I finished with that Quest. I thought I would be an adult and I would get to make my own decisions. Now I don't want to have to make them."

Her mother smiled. "And what about your other conquest on the journey?"

For a moment, she didn't understand. "What other conquest? You don't mean Rheetie, do you?"

"No I didn't. Who is Rheetie? Don't tell me you had another one?"

She laughed. "No, mother. Rheetie was a boy I met on the Quest. A footpad, I believe, and not too experienced. I think he was going to rob me, but then someone clued him in to who I was. He was disgusted at his bad luck but very nice about it. That was when I first began to realize what a joke the Quest was."

"I see. But what about young Lord Canah?"

"What about him? I don't see why people keep bringing him up. He was part of a very nasty experience and I'd just like to forget him."

"But you owe him a lot. And he had some nice things to say about you, it seems."

"It seems he did. And I do owe him a lot. But he and that bunch treated me abominably. I can tell myself that his was all pretending, but it was still horrible. I was frightened stiff the whole time. I still can't forget it. Even when I'm happy, there's a small cold spot inside of me that remembers it. When someone steps too close behind me my heart goes to my throat, and then I feel like a fool for starting. But I can't help it.

I thought I was going to die, Mother. I thought they were going to beat me, and rape me, and torture me and then kill me!"

All the fear came rushing back to her and she fell sobbing into her mother's arms, clutching for the warm security she had always found there.

Her mother said nothing, only soothed her and held her close. After a while, she gently lifted her daughter's head. "It will pass, you know. These things are always the worst when they are fresh. It is good to talk about them, because that seems to make them less important. I want you to come to me any time you need to. After a while the fear will get less and less, and soon you won't think about it any more."

Aleria sniffled. "I hope so. I don't want to be like this. I don't want to be afraid of everything."

Leniema gave her a little shake. "Might be good for you in the long run. I never thought you had quite enough respect for danger."

"I have now, believe me!"

"Don't worry, daughter. People go through this all the time and come out the other side just fine. It's a natural part of having an experience like that. After all, do you think you're unique? Every soldier who goes through a battle has to deal with it afterwards. The first one is usually the worst, I suppose."

"Have you ever gone through and experience like this?"

"Not as powerful as yours. But then, I never was quite the adventurer you are."

"I think you can count on me to be a bit less adventurous in the future."

Her mother smiled. "I won't be counting on it, Aleria. You are much stronger than that. After all, there are times when it is necessary to take risks like young Lord Canah did. From now on, perhaps you will choose your risks more carefully."

"Oh, I most certainly will. And one risk I can avoid is Lord Raif anCanah. In future, I will stay as far away from him as possible."

With this resolution, she was dismayed the very next day when a messenger arrived, a mounted courier in the full formal livery of the Duke of Canah. She hurried out to meet her father as he returned from the front door.

"Well, my dear! It seems you have an admirer."

"What?"

He flourished a paper. Very expensive paper, complete with a seal. "I can see no other reason for this invitation."

"Who has invited us and where?"

"The duke, my dear. The Duke of Canah. He has invited you to visit his city residence."

"Me?"

"Well, the invitation is addressed to me, but there is no doubt, the way it is phrased, that you are to be there. My inclusion seems incidental."

"What does the duke want of me?"

"I was about to ask you the same question."

"How should I know? I've never met him!"

Her father smiled. "But I gather you have more than a passing acquaintance with his son."

"No doubt about that. I told you, Father. I don't really want to see him again."

He winced. "That creates a bit of a problem, dear."

She felt a sinking in her breast. "Why? Have you already accepted?"

"I don't see an other choice, Aleria. An invitation to visit the Duke is hardly a casual suggestion. One needs a very good reason to refuse."

"And my feelings aren't good enough reason?"

"Not for me. You don't have to go, but I do. And since you are obviously the reason for the invitation, I will feel a bit awkward showing up alone."

She thought furiously. "Is Mother coming?"

"The invitation is not specific on that point, and unfortunately she has an engagement that day. She won't even be in the city. I'm afraid it's just the two of us, my dear. Can you handle it?"

She looked at her father; he was deadly serious. She was knowledgeable enough about his concerns to realize that if she didn't go it could affect his business or his position at court in some way. She also knew that he would never force her.

"I suppose so."

He regarded her. "Is this going to be a real problem? He knows what you went through. You can plead indisposition."

She shook her head. "That will just postpone it. I suppose I had better face it now."

He grinned and slapped her shoulder, "That's my girl," but his look was worried as he left.

* * *

That week her dreams increased. She woke several times every night, sweating and shaking. She had no appetite, and her hands quivered at the slightest provocation. The Twins were visiting out of the city, but Mito spent almost all her time with Aleria.

"Are you up to this visit?"

"I might not be, Mito, but I don't see that I have much choice. Sooner or later I have to deal with the situation. Some day I am going to have to meet him again. I'm sure that the reality won't be half as bad as the dreams, and maybe that will stop the dreams. I don't know, but I have to try."

"But are you up to it? What if you have a breakdown?"

She managed to smile. "I got through the real situation without one. I think I should be able to handle the after-effects. You know what I think happened? I let down too soon."

"Explain." Mito smoothed her dress and sat, hands folded, looking attentive.

"When I was in real danger I was challenged to survive. That kept me going. The moment I was rescued, I thought it was all over. I let down my guard and relaxed. That's when the dreams hit me. I think if I had known how it was going to be I wouldn't have relaxed. I would have kept my guard up. I wouldn't have got into this 'poor little me, poor victim,' attitude. So now I just have to take hold of myself and get back on track, get aggressive again, and I can solve this. It's a matter of will power."

Mito shook her head. "If you think so, you're probably right. After all, when were you ever wrong?"

"All the time, Mito, all the time. It's just taken me a while to realize it."

'What do you mean?"

"I mean that I was so smug, so satisfied at my superiority. I knew I was the best of the class and I thought that qualified me to be a success for the rest of my life. Do you realize what the reality of life is?" She looked at her friend a moment. "Yes, I'm sure you do. More than I do. I'm no more qualified to get along in the real world than a barmaid at a country inn. Considerably less qualified, when I think of what some of those inns are like."

"But no one expects you to handle that part of the world! No lady should have to go anywhere near a place like that."

"Why not? Why should we be different from anyone else? Why shouldn't we be able to deal with the same situations a barmaid has to?"

Mito was speechless.

"See? The only answer you can give is that our class protects us. But what if we get into a situation where our class doesn't protect us? Do we just fall apart? That's what I've been doing. Well, let me tell you, I'm not going to fall apart like some dainty, pampered lady. I'm going to get through this. You just watch me!...what are you laughing at?"

Mito covered her smile. "I'm not laughing at you, Aleria. I'm just happy. This is the first time since you got back that you've sounded like the old you. I even think you might beat this problem."

"Well, I'd better beat it in the next three days or I'm going to make a pretty big fool of myself. Can you imagine the scandal? I'm introduced at the Duke's palace, I look at his son and immediately run screaming from the room? Not the best politics, I think."

Mito giggled. "Not likely to guarantee success in the Most Eligible Graduate contest."

"Most Eligible Graduate? Mito! You didn't!" She stared at her friend in real horror.

"No, of course I didn't. But there's no reason someone else wouldn't have."

"If anyone has put my name in for that stupid award I am going to start remembering the things I saw on my little misadventure and I'm going to perpetrate some of them!"

"I can just imagine. You know what would be worse than having your name put forward?"

"Having it put forward and losing."

"And even worse than that?"

"Winning!"

The two girls were convulsed by laughter, and when they started to compose Aleria's acceptance speech they were unable to speak clearly enough to finish.

21. A Visit With the Duke

Aleria slept better the next few nights, determined not to be bothered by the dreams. Every time she awoke, she dragged out of bed and ran through one of her fighting drills until she was sweating. Then she would towel off, hop back into bed, and drop back to sleep. During the daytime she took the same solution, with training, riding and other physical activity, until she was so tired she would have to sleep, so hungry she wolfed down her food.

By the time the day of reckoning arrived, she was feeling better. She stepped into her father's carriage with a carefully maintained aggressive anticipation, as if she was going into a competition or examination. Her father, observing her at first with concern, seemed relieved at her attitude.

The duke's residence in the city was imposing, a palace rather than a mansion. She had been assured that his county seat, out in the North Country, was much more impressive. Apparently it was all made of huge logs: soaring pillars and spreading beams as thick as wine casks, all varnished and shiny. Looking up at the ranks of gargoyles on the carved stone facade, she wondered.

There were several other carriages in the process of delivering their charges at the foot of the great curving staircase.

"Looks like we aren't the only guests."

"I doubt if the duke has time to devote a whole afternoon to just us. This way he can pay off several obligations and make several connections, all at once. Good planning."

She looked up at her father, thinking how dignified he looked, tall and grey-haired, firm in his stride, strong in his convictions. "Don't you think he might just want to have some friends in to visit?"

He laughed. "There might possibly be a few of those as well."

Gordon A. Long

They entered the ornately carved doors, held open by two small liveried boys who were trying hard to stand perfectly still. She winked at one of them and he almost burst trying not to smile.

They were greeted by a major-domo who somehow knew who they were. He invited them through an echoing hallway to a reception room large enough to dwarf the group of people sitting or standing around looking comfortable. Aleria searched the faces, relaxed when she recognized no one. A polite throat-clearing at her elbow drew her attention to the fact that the major-domo didn't seem to be leaving.

"If you don't mind, Miss Dalmyn…"

"Yes?"

'His Grace would like to speak to you." He noticed her glance up at her father. "Alone. If you please, this way."

"Thank you." Holding herself in control, she followed the man across the room, aware of everyone's regard. She hoped she carried it off. *At least I didn't trip on the hem of my gown.* This thought brought a grim smile to her lips as she entered the anteroom, and by the time the duke was rising to greet her, it wasn't hard to make the smile genuine. Especially since his son was nowhere to be seen. He seated her on a brocade settee, then took a comfortable armchair opposite.

"Ah, Lady Aleria. So nice to finally meet you." He sounded like he meant it. "My son speaks well of you, especially your beauty. It is so agreeable to find that he has not exaggerated."

"Your Grace, I suppose I should be doubly flattered, but I sincerely doubt that your son has ever seen me in any condition to judge my beauty."

He sized her up for a moment. Had she spoken too sharply? Did he expect her to simper and accept empty compliments?

"I hope his appreciation of beauty extends, as mine does, a bit past a pretty face and a slim figure. Character shows, I always say."

"In that case, perhaps I am quadruply flattered."

"A mathematical mind as well! I wonder if Raif discovered that, or am I ahead of him?"

"I don't recall discussing mathematics with him, your Grace. Am I likely to get the chance today?" *There. That should be subtle enough, carried off without a quaver.*

"He'll be around in a while. I wanted to get my own impressions first. You know how young men are when they describe a girl." He winked at her, and she couldn't help but like him.

With that decision, her restraints dropped more, and she let the asperity creep into her voice. "And how did he describe me? Besides my questionable beauty, I mean. Better than he seemed to appreciate me at the time, I hope!"

The Duke laughed. "Oh, he was very complimentary. He said you were a stroke of fortune. He had never been fully accepted by the other men, you know, because he didn't treat the women like they did. Once he had you to help him with his charade, they liked him better. When you wouldn't dance, they loved it for some reason. I think he was too perfect, and they were glad to see him fail."

"Too perfect! That sounds like a father talking."

She liked his laugh. It was friendly and free of restraint. "I suppose it might, but you have to realize who he is, his blood, his upbringing. He is worth twice any man in that rag-tag bunch, in brains, confidence and training. The one thing he acted poorly was humility, and that made them jealous. They probably couldn't even figure out why, they just didn't like him. Very dangerous. So you saved him from that. You also got him away from the camp in time, I gather."

She felt herself blushing. "It was an easy plan. Especially since escape was rather high on my priorities at the time."

He slapped his knee. "I suppose it was." Then his smile disappeared. "It must have been very difficult for you. Raif told me how sorry he was. I hope he told you."

She grimaced. "Often. I'm just not so sure I always believed him."

A frown of concern crossed his high brow. "What do you mean?"

Then she realized that she had stepped over the line. "Oh, I didn't mean anything." He wasn't accepting it, and she retreated into maidenly confusion. "I...I just found it so hard, it was all so terrible..."

He was serious now and his eye held her. "Yes you did. You meant that he took the play-acting too seriously, especially the part about treating you badly. You meant that he might have even enjoyed it."

She squirmed, but only inside. Outwardly she dropped the act and held herself still. "I felt that at the time, yes. I have no idea what the reality was. I don't think I was in any condition to be a proper judge."

He nodded. "Well spoken. It is important that he knows how you felt. A duke must play many roles, and he must not allow himself to get carried away with any of them. I know my son. Sometimes he does get enthused..." He turned back to her, his gaze holding her again.

"You realize that he will be duke after me."

She was nonplussed for a moment. "I suppose..."

"Just so you understand."

Her mind was working again. *I'm beginning to see the light. Was that why...? No!* She summoned up her courage.

"Your Grace, why did you want to see me?"

"What do you mean?"

He didn't seem indignant at her temerity, so she forged on. "Why did you call for me? You never knew me before, had no reason for interest. I didn't save your son's life, or do anything terribly important. So why did you want to meet me?"

He laughed. "For the usual reasons, of course. If any eligible young lady comes in close contact with my son it is necessary that I investigate. I could hire someone to do it, but I find I get better information myself."

She caught herself gaping at him, closed her mouth. "Eligible? You mean that you thought he and I..."

He smiled, shrugged. "It does happen, you know. Your mother is of an ancient Exalted family and your father is a man to be reckoned with in the modern world. Should I be speaking with them? Do I have reason?"

She faltered back, then recovered herself and sat straight. "No! No, not at all!"

The duke, in his turn, seemed taken aback. "I am sorry. I didn't mean to offend you. I thought surely you would realize…"

Aleria took control of herself with difficulty, "I am the one who should apologize, your Grace. I have been so involved in my own worries that I did not consider the obvious. I assure you, any of the other girls my age would have understood immediately."

"But not you."

She glanced at him. *Is he smiling?* "No, your Grace. I suppose my mind doesn't follow those paths yet. I'm too young, I think. There will be plenty of time for that…sort of thing later."

He was certainly smiling, now. "I must say, that is a refreshing attitude. I thought all you young ladies considered little else other than whom you would wed." He paused a moment, looked at her thoughtfully. "But your reaction was stronger than that. Is there some reason why you would not consider an alliance with my family?"

Aleria's mouth went dry. This was an important question, and she knew, when it was stated in that fashion, that more than her own future might be at stake here. She took a moment to marshal her thoughts, then spoke more formally.

"Your Grace, I assure you, I have no reason to slight your family. I would be honoured. The problem is…well, completely personal."

"Aha. So it is my son."

"I'm…I'm sure he is a marvellous person, brave and honourable, and all that."

"But he treated you abominably and he might have enjoyed it."

She was relieved that he understood. "I might eventually be able to understand even that, your Grace. The problem is, I think, even worse. I still have nightmares, sometimes, and, well…" She stopped, unsure of how to go on.

"Raif is in them?"

The gentleness in his voice surprised her, and she looked up at him, catching concern in his eyes. She dropped her own, realized her voice was barely above a whisper, but could not force it louder. "In every one, your Grace." It came to her that this was his son she was talking about, and she leaned forward to persuade him. "I know it wasn't his fault, your Grace. I just can't shake them. They keep coming, almost every night, and…and…no matter what I tell myself, he is always there. I can't think of him without…well…" She did not dare go on.

He nodded. "I understand. You have him tied so closely to your horrible experience that you cannot separate the two."

There was a moment of silence. Then he sat up straighter, and his voice came more quickly. "That is too bad. I must say, I wish it were otherwise."

What?

He smiled at her and gestured with an open hand. "Well…you know. If you were one of those other girls, worrying if you passed the test. You would have passed. With colours flying, if you must know. I think you are a very strong-minded young lady, with plenty of pluck. I would have been pleased to consider you as a member of my family, and I hope this unfortunate situation will not keep you from becoming at least a friend. Tell me now. Is the aversion so bad that you cannot bear to see him? To stand in the same room?"

She considered. "I hope not. It is only in my dreams that I am frightened. It is only in my thoughts that it bothers me. In reality, I ought to be able to face him. I probably should, in fact. My father tells me that the best way to fight fears is to meet them face-to-face. It might even do me good."

He rose to his feet. "He has been waiting in a bit of trepidation, himself, regarding what you would say. He is aware of what he owes you and very concerned as to your welfare."

"Your Grace!" She shot up. "He owes me nothing. He saved my life. More."

"Of course. Come, my Lady. Let us go and speak to the others. I thought that perhaps it would be easier for you in a group…"

She looked up as she took his arm. *This is a very thoughtful man. If I ever thought of choosing a father-in-law, he would do very well.* She smiled at the thought of going out shopping for a father-in-law.

"And what thought brings that mischievous smile to your lips?"

She covered her momentary dismay with a larger smile and a coquettish batting of her eyes. "Why, your Grace! Surely a lady has at least the privacy of her own thoughts."

A servant opened the door, and the Duke was laughing as they passed into to the crowded salon. "I have definitely been put in my place, my Lady. I do apologize!" His eyes scanned the "few guests", now twenty at least, who had all turned at their entry. "Aha! Here are some young ladies with whom I am sure you would like to speak."

To her surprise, he brought her to the Twins, who curtseyed prettily before he bowed and turned away. She clasped their hands, delighted.

"I never expected to find you here. Do you visit the Duke often?"

Hana slapped her hand. "Come on, Aleria. Of course we don't. Father knows him, of course, but we've never been here before. He probably has some business or other brewing with Father, and he invited us because of you."

Gita's eyes sparkled. "How did it go? Are you," her nose went up in impish snobbery, "deemed acceptable?"

"What are you talking about?"

"Oh, come on."

"Of course you know."

"We know why you're here."

"Tell us!"

"Is he nice?"

Aleria was too confused to commit herself. "I think he's handsome, in an older sort of way."

"Does Raif look like that?"

She laughed, louder than she should, then realized that many faces were turned her way. *To hell with it.* She tossed her head and laughed again, but dropped her voice to a polite level.

"Come on, you two, slow down. I can't answer both of you at once. We just had a nice chat. He wanted to meet the girl who had such an adventure with his son. After I assured him that I had no 'intentions,' we got along famously."

"You told him what?"

"I told him the truth, Hana. You know I have trouble being in the same room as young Lord Canah. I doubt if I'm going to marry him."

"Where is he, anyway? I thought he was going to be here."

She had a sudden thrill of terror, which she crushed. "I think he'll be here any moment." She pushed her fear away and scanned the room. To her relief, there was no sign of him.

"What does he look like?"

She looked at her friends in surprise. "You don't know?"

"We don't exactly move in his social circle. What is he like?"

"Well, he's tall, but he's got a bit of a stoop. He has black hair and a long, shaggy moustache. A loud laugh, sort of bossy. Big hands, I don't know. Sort of like that."

She saw the concern in their eyes. "You're upset about this, aren't you?"

She looked down at her hands, clamped them together to stop the shaking. "I suppose so. It will be the first time I've met him since… you know, and then, with all the dreams…I guess I am a bit scared."

Two sets of hands gripped hers.

"Don't worry."

"We won't let him near you!"

"We'll repel him with our combined ferocity!"

"Our lance-like wit will pierce him."

"Our rapier eyes will drive him from the field."

"Who is that?"

She repressed a start and made herself turn casually. A tall, blond young man stood in the doorway, looking uncertain. She turned away, shrugged, then turned back. There was something familiar about his eyes...

The young man glanced around again, then strode to the duke, who greeted him affably. She could not hear what was said, but the duke turned him by the shoulder and pointed in their direction. As he started towards her she was struck by a sudden panic and her knees weakened. Her friends, one on either side, stared as well.

"Is that him?"

"I thought he was dark?"

"Stooped?"

"Is he handsome!"

The force of her hands clutching theirs persuaded them.

"Don't worry, Aleria. We'll protect you!"

"Here he comes. Get ready, Gita, this is going to be rough."

Aleria shook her hands free. "Don't be silly, you two. This is going to be fine." She shot them warning glances. "Don't do anything stupid."

They returned her looks, and she could see a glance full of secret communication flash between the two. Then all she was aware of was the fierce, light-blue eyes approaching.

"Aleria, so good to see you again. I hope you are well?" There was a brief pause. *He looks as uncomfortable as I feel.* "...please introduce me to your friends."

She somehow kept her voice steady as she made the introductions. They curtseyed and chatted something about the fact that they were twins but didn't look alike, giving her time to recover her balance. This was in some ways more surprising than she had feared. The old, ferocious image she was prepared to handle. The handsome, uncertain young man, coming so quickly after such a pleasant meeting with his father, had completely thrown her. She realized that the twins were carrying the brunt of the amenities and tried to toss in her own comments, she knew not what. Soon the conversation ran down and he bowed, took her hand a moment and returned to his father. For a long while they stood, silent, until they realized they were staring and turned away, the Twins giggling to each other.

She had nothing to say, and they mercifully left her alone. That was one thing about the Twins; they were good friends. After a while, they let out a collective sigh.

"Thank you, girls. I admit I was thrown for a moment. He was nothing like I remembered."

Hana shook her head. "We were ready to protect you."

Gita grinned. "Ready to fight tooth and nail. We had no idea we would have to back you with small talk."

Aleria smiled as well. "Neither did I. Thanks for filling in."

"Oh, it was worth it."

"For certain. Imagine, finally seeing Aleria with nothing to say."

"The only problem is, we can't tell anyone."

Hana considered. "I suppose that would be taking unfair advantage."

"Plus Father would have us shot at sunrise."

They all laughed, but Aleria was relieved that these two could draw the line where fun stopped and family loyalties took precedence. They liked gossip as much as the other girls, but no breath of what happened at the palace of the Duke of Canah would escape their lips. Fortunately, that included her own discomfiture.

The talk turned to safer topics and they scanned the room for anyone they recognized.

22. An Unexpected Partner

Soon, "Tea in the garden," was announced, and they all filed out into the sunlight. It was an impressive spread: white tablecloths and silver dishes backed by immaculate, dark-green hedges. Cushions were spread on the grass in the shade of towering oak trees, with lounges and chairs for the more dignified guests. The three girls allowed the servants to bring their plates to a nook somewhat removed from the rest. They giggled again when extra cushions had to be found.

"Now, why would this little hideaway have only cushions for two?"

"For obvious reasons, my dear sister."

Aleria looked around. "I don't see any courting couples. I wonder if it was left for anyone in particular?"

Then she realized that they were both looking at her as if she were stupid.

"Oh, no. I don't think...."

Hana shrugged. "His Grace doesn't seem like the kind of man to leave anything to chance."

"You don't think he thought..."

"I don't think he thought anything specific. I think he just prepares for anything, sort of as a habit."

"Sort of as a way of life. I bet he's the kind of person who thinks ahead all the time."

"Well, he thought wrong this time."

"Looks like it."

"Really!"

"We're agreeing with you!"

"I saw that look!"

"What look?"

She gave up in mock disgust, and they laughed at her, then concentrated on the excellent food.

When everyone had eaten, the party was invited to walk in the garden. Since the duke had a reputation for the quality of his walks and the talent of his gardeners, they all accepted with enthusiasm. Soon the girls were lost in the paths, admiring the sculptured shrubs, the huge trees, and the geometrical symmetry of the beds. As they strolled, Gita nudged Aleria. She looked ahead and realized that someone was walking towards them. Someone tall, blond, and broad-shouldered.

"What do you want us to do?"

"Shall we turn down this path?"

"Shall we ignore him?"

"Don't be silly, you two. Just act normally."

They grinned at her. "Easily said, girl."

"Don't..." and then he was too close for more talk.

He strolled up to them, appearing casual. "Are you enjoying the walk, ladies?"

The twins again filled in for her, enthusing about the garden, and Aleria found it easier to join in. After a moment Raif paused, cleared his throat, and seemed about to speak. Hana nudged Gita, and without seeming to move, they faded back a step.

"I was wondering...uh...Aleria, if your friends wouldn't mind, I mean..." He bowed to them.

The twins looked at her. She knew they would stay if she needed them. Suppressing a shiver, she nodded, although her smile felt tight. "Of course. If they don't mind?"

After a close look at her face, they curtseyed and made their way down a side path, looking back over their shoulders as they left. There was a long pause.

"Is this difficult for you?"

She looked up at him. He seemed concerned. "A bit."

"I know. I've been told. The dreams?"

She could only nod.

"I just wanted to thank you. I didn't get the chance when we were rescued."

"I know. Your report."

"Yes. I had to give it. You really helped me, you know."

'Your father told me."

"Do you understand how?"

227

"I think so."

"Good."

"I..."

"Yes?"

"I want to thank you, too. I know you saved me. I don't want to seem ungrateful. These dreams, I mean, I don't have any control over them. They just happen."

"I know. I have them, too."

"You?"

"What did you think?"

She looked up at him, noted the lines around his mouth. "I suppose. And am I in them?"

"Sometimes."

"Do you get to beat me up in your dreams, too?"

The lines tightened. "No. Not me."

"What do you mean?"

His face softened. "There are some things I don't think you want to know, Aleria."

"Why not?"

"Because you don't. Trust me."

His eyes became hard again, and she shrugged. "All right. I don't want to know." She glanced up for his response, but it wasn't what she had expected. "I don't! I believe you."

"Good. I don't like killing people, you know."

She had a moment's sympathy for him, then all the terror rushed back. The greenery closed in on her, and her head spun. She saw his hand reaching for her arm, and she jumped away. He retreated, watching her.

She stood for a moment, clamping an icy control over her emotions. This was no way to act. This was her host, the man who had saved her life. *Manners, Aleria. Manners.* In a while her breathing calmed, and she could again hear the birds, feel the wind lifting her hair.

"If you don't mind, I think we'd best not talk about that sort of thing."

"No, no, quite right. I didn't want to frighten you. I just...I wanted to thank you."

"Yes."

"I think we should go back now."

"Yes." She looked around. "Which way is back?"

"This way." He was about to offer his arm, then hesitated.

Steeling herself, she laid her hand on his arm. He walked stiffly at her side a few paces, then turned her onto a wider path. To her relief, she could see white linen through the hedge ahead.

As they walked something in her head looked down at the two of them. *This is just stupid.* She glanced up at him, staring straight ahead, his arm and shoulder rigid. She took her hand away, pushed his arm down to his side.

"This is silly. We don't have to be all formal. Only cowards hide behind that sort of thing. We have a problem. It's no one's fault, and it's up to us to solve it."

He nodded with relief, looked down at her. It gave her a lift, realizing that he was waiting for her instructions.

"I need to talk to you face to face. I need to see you in non-threatening situations. I've been told that is the best way to get rid of the dreams. I'm glad you shaved. I hated that moustache!"

He brushed his lip, grinned for just a moment. "So did I. Always getting in my food."

"And some of the food often stayed there."

"You're joking!"

"I am not. You used to have bits sticking to it, hanging there."

"Ugh! I must have looked awful. I know my teeth were terrible, and sometimes I couldn't stand the taste of my own mouth. Can you imagine two months without a toothbrush? I guess it was worth it. Obviously it worked."

"You were not pretty. Definitely not pretty at all. I like you much better blond."

"Why, thank you. I don't know how women stand it. Always worrying the new growth will start to show!"

She was able to laugh a bit at that. Then they were at the front, and everyone was gathering to take their leave.

229

He bowed over her hand. "Thank you for being so understanding."

She curtseyed a bit deeper than custom required. "Thank you for the same."

"If we meet again...?"

"I would be pleased."

"Be honest."

She considered. "It seems our fathers have business together. Do not avoid me, should the opportunity arise. It has been good for me to meet you again."

"You don't need to say it was a pleasure. I wish you freedom from dreams."

Why does he have to say the right thing first? "I wish you the same."

"I think my father would like to say good-bye." He bowed over her hand, led her to the duke, and faded away. When she had finished with her host, his son was nowhere to be seen.

Back at the carriages, the twins were full of a plan to get their fathers to ride in one so they could be together for the trip, but she refused to throw her weight behind it.

"I'm sorry, girls. This has been a hard afternoon. Besides, I'm sure Father wants to speak to me."

"He has all the time he wants when he gets you home."

"No, he hasn't. There will be all sorts of business to take his attention. This is a good time for us to talk things out."

The duke was escorting their fathers to the carriages, a sign of respect that she could see did not go unnoticed by the other guests.

As her father approached, she could see he was hesitant. "I know you girls would like to ride together, but..."

"It's already settled, Father." She led him to their carriage. "You have me all to yourself for the whole way."

He smiled down at her as she allowed him to hand her in. "You seem to be full of surprises today." He seated himself beside her, gave her a sidelong glance. "And not only for me."

She pondered this while they waved their good-byes and set out down the long gravel drive towards the street.

"So whom did I surprise, and was it pleasant?"

"I think you could say His Grace was pleasantly surprised. He said he found you a 'forthright young lady'. I think that was a compliment."

She grinned up at him. "He seems to be the kind of man to like straight talk."

He chuckled. "So I gather your little interview went well."

"As well as could be expected, I suppose."

"By which you mean?"

"You surely had it figured out that he was checking me over as a potential daughter-in-law."

"It could hardly have escaped me."

She smiled ruefully. "Well, I guess I'm not quite so smart. I figured it out quickly enough, though."

"But I gather we aren't making any wedding announcements soon."

"Father! It's not something I want to be teased about. I have just got to the stage where I can speak to Raif without shaking. In fact, I had an attack of fright once, just because he mentioned killing people."

"That was rather stupid of him."

"I guess he learned something, then."

"Other than that, are you glad you came?"

"Oh, yes. It was good for me. I like the Duke."

"Do you?"

"Yes. He talks straight, and he isn't afraid to have you talk straight back to him."

Her father raised his eyebrows. "I don't know many people who would say that. Or who would dare to try to find out."

"Oh. Did I overdo it? He seemed to like me. He even said so!"

"Oh, yes, he liked you. He told me that, too."

"Good." She was getting tired of this. "Did he like you?"

"Pardon?"

She grinned. She had hit a soft spot, she could tell. "Come on, Father. His Grace didn't invite twenty people just for an excuse to meet me. You and the Twins' father had a lot of time to chat with him. What was he sizing you up for?"

"Very good, Aleria. The Duke and I have similar...political concerns. If you don't mind, it's a bit sensitive, so I won't tell you the details.

"But I wouldn't be telling you anything new if I mentioned that this rebellion has shaken the King's confidence a great deal. Now, we know, thanks to Raif's report and your story, that it didn't have the support of the general population. Still, it is worrisome."

"That and the rifles."

"Yes, the fact that someone is bringing guns into Galesia matters very much. So we have to take steps to make sure it doesn't happen again."

"What kind of steps?"

"You have had your Strategy and Statesmanship lessons. You did rather well in those, as I remember. What do you think?"

"I wonder about the men in the rebellion. There were Slathe's nasty lot, of course, but there were all those other ones. Raif says many of them were not really bad men. We have to find out why so many men are unpleasant, angry, and have no better way to support themselves. Then we fix it. Then we have nobody left to rebel."

Her father nodded. "Sounds good. So how do we go about fixing it?"

"Father, I'm just turned eighteen. I just passed my Quest, and as we are all agreed, it was a farce. I have no idea what to do. I don't have any information to make up an idea, even if I wanted to."

"That's very good."

"What do you mean?"

"You have put your finger on the problem. We don't have enough information. Something is wrong in the Northwest and in Shaeldit, maybe in the whole of Galesia, and we don't know what. Oh, we have some idea, of course. There have been major changes in the agriculture system over the past fifty years. Easing the bans on Mechanicals in farming and lumbering was very successful in making our exports more competitive. The new techniques need less labourers, so there are men who need to change occupations, and that is very hard for them."

"And the ones who are stupidest and the worst workers find it hardest to change."

"Very true. We have access to all sorts of information about conditions in the realm, but we think we need to do a better job of analysing it."

"That sounds good." She thought about that for a moment. "But what do you and Duke anCanah have to do with it?"

"Nothing. But Raif does. He's going to be involved in running the new system."

"I don't know if he'll like that. He didn't like spying."

"He doesn't have to spy. He only has to collect and analyse the information gathered by the gatherers. His experience over the last few months is invaluable."

"And what does this have to do with us?"

"Ah. Well, I suppose you would have to know." He leaned closer and spoke softly in spite of the rattling of the carriage. "Some of our wagons will be used for passing reports. We have regular routes in that area, as you know, and soon we will have more."

She nodded, putting it all together. Then a thought struck her. She turned slowly and looked at her father. "I feel like I'm being tested again. First the Duke, now you. Just what is going on?"

"Very good, daughter. Would you like to help?"

"Of course." She shuddered. "As long as I don't have to go out into the forest with them."

He reached an arm around her, pulled her close. "Aleria, you have no idea how I feel every time I think of you, out there with those beasts of men. No matter what you think of him, I thank Raif every time that picture enters my head."

She clung to him for a moment, relishing the safe feeling. "I know, Father. I was so stupid."

"No, not stupid. You had no idea that a revolt would happen. No one did. Let us just be glad you survived."

After a moment she sat up. "So what do you want me to do?"

"Nothing complicated or dangerous. The information comes in on our wagons and has to be delivered to Raif. We assume that if there is any conspiracy they have spies in the capital. So we want you to make the deliveries. You are now socially connected to the Canah family. You just include Raif in your circle. That is, if it isn't too difficult for you."

I can do something useful! "No, it isn't too difficult. In fact, it sounds interesting. How will I get the deliveries? I suppose I'm going to have to take more of an interest in the business, aren't I?"

"I suppose you are. I had thought I would just hand the packages to you, but it would be better if you received them yourself. There may be verbal messages as well, and you could pass them on directly to Raif. Yes, I like that idea."

"So do I, even if it has nothing to do with spying. I have always wanted to get involved, but I didn't know whether you and Mother would approve."

"Well, I suppose we will have to now, won't we?"

She sat straighter, her breath coming quicker as she looked ahead out the carriage window. "Yes, you will."

23. The Arts of Battle

"It is good of you to help me with this equipment order, Aleria."

She shuffled the catalogues. "This is interesting. I have never seen so many implements of warfare and mayhem in one place. This one," she hefted a tome with an engraving of a beautifully crafted sustained-shot rifle on the cover, "is full of guns. All the most modern and up-to-date Mechanical weapons. I never knew there were so many kinds in the world. People certainly must like killing each other."

He reached over and removed the catalogue from her hand. "You are here to help with the equipment order for the Ladies' Academy Gymnasium, not have your young mind corrupted."

"And also because I have an ulterior motive." She picked up the next catalogue, one that showed gymnasium paraphernalia. She pretended to be leafing through it, but she glanced over to see the Battle Arts Master looking at her.

"Now, how did I already know that?"

She grinned. "I was hoping you might think it was to bask in the wisdom of the Master."

"But it was really...?"

She closed the book. "I was hoping to talk about how to solve my problem."

"The dreams."

"Yes."

"We have already discussed this when you returned from the rebellion, Aleria. Nightmares are a normal way for your mind to cope with a horrible experience, and they should fade with time."

"That's just it. They haven't. It's been weeks, now, and I think they're getting worse."

"I see."

"And I need a way to deal with them. You know me. I have to be moving. I need a plan of action."

"I don't see how I can help you, Aleria." Ogima's smooth brow showed wrinkles.

"You're the only one who can."

"Why?"

"Because you're the only one who understands. You deal in these matters, with fear and bravery and mental strength." Aleria found it impossible to sit, so she rose and paced around his office. "I'm not doing too well, Master Ogima. I thought I could handle fear, but I can't. It's ridiculous, isn't it?" she found a smile for him, "that the girl who did all those daring things back in school is the one who's afraid now."

"What form does this fear take?"

"It's at night, usually. I'll be lying there, not sleeping, thinking of nothing in particular, and then a thought will just slip in, and..." she stopped speaking and turned away to look out the office window at the school lawns, soft in the early summer sunshine.

He waited.

She turned back. "I haven't told anyone this."

"Why not?"

"I don't know. Oh, I told them I had nightmares. But not this. They all have their own problems, real problems. They don't need to be bothered with my imaginary ones."

"Fear is an imaginary problem."

She spun to face him. "What?"

He nodded. "Fear is in the imagination. Fear comes from imagining a situation that might cause pain. Those who have no fear have no idea of the connection between their actions and resulting pain. Those who fear too much imagine too much pain, where there is no pain."

"That's right! I can lie there in my bed in my father's house, and my imagination takes me back to that inn, and I think what would have happened if Raif hadn't found me. And I can't stop thinking about it...I just want to fall to pieces...I feel like I'm going to break down and scream or cry and I know it's all so stupid!"

"Not so stupid."

"I'm glad you think so."

"Oh, I do. Fear is a natural, positive response. You can be trained to fear, just as you can be trained to control fear."

She thought while she paced. "So the experiences I had during the rebellion taught me to fear."

"Quite correctly, you must admit."

"But now I have to re-train myself not to fear. How do I do that?

He shrugged. "I am not certain…"

"What?" She paced toward him. "You mean you have dumped all this smarmy philosophy on me, and you don't even have a solution?"

He smiled and shook his head. "Lady Aleria, you never change, do you?"

She frowned and allowed her voice to rise. "You can't duck by changing the subject. And don't call me 'Lady Aleria' in that fake-formal way. That's just hiding."

His hands came up in a helpless gesture. "All right, Aleria. Let us do some thinking. In the middle of the night, when you have one of these episodes, what do you do? Does anything work to calm you down, make you feel better?"

"Yes. If I work myself to exhaustion, then I sleep. Usually I do training exercises."

"Logical. You feel helpless, then you do something that prepares you to act. Then you do not feel helpless anymore. You have found your solution already. The one that soldiers use, when going into battle."

"And what is that?"

"Persuade yourself that, when the thing you fear happens, you can handle it."

"Well, that's pretty stupid. How can anybody run into a battle, truly believing that he's not going to get hurt?" She sat, picking up the catalogue again, riffling the pages.

The old man smiled. "Intelligence obviously has little to do with it. We make ourselves believe what we need to believe. Do you recall, once, saying that if a mercenary soldier attacked you, you would not have the power to defend yourself?"

Her cheeks went hot. "Were you listening to that?"

One side of his mouth lifted. "You do not have a soft voice. Do you still believe it?"

She nodded ruefully.

"Is that because you are just a girl, and weak?"

"No! It has nothing to do with being female. It's because I'm weak!"

He shook his head. "It has little to do with physical strength."

"What?"

"Of all the young men and women in your class, there are few, even the strongest of the boys, who would have the strength to follow through to the end. It is the mental strength you need. The physical is merely an advantage."

She thought a moment. "You said a few. Who?"

He shot her a calculating glance. "In a situation where you had decided that it was absolutely necessary? Two or three of the boys who come from military families. Perhaps Gita. Your little friend Mito, of course."

"Mito! She couldn't kill anyone. She's sweet. She's romantic. She's..."

"Mito has spent her life doing what she has to. Given the necessity, she will continue to act the same. With her, the difficulty would be in persuading her that it was necessary."

"Why?"

"Because she has been forced by circumstances to do what she would rather not, she will always be very sure that the situation is unavoidable before she acts.

"What about me?"

"Yes. What about you?"

She shook her head. "I saw too much of the reality. I don't ever want to be put in that situation, because I don't think I could."

"Too weak?"

"I suppose so." She sat, head in hands. "So here I am. Stuck in the poor, weak, victim role. That's why I have these dreams, I guess."

She turned the pages idly, but then something caught her eye. "Say, look at these."

"What?"

She showed him. "Look at the cost of these practice swords. There are never enough swords for the whole class. At this price, we could afford twenty new ones!"

He glanced down, shook his head. "Not possible."

"Why not?"

"At that price, they are certain to be mass made, in a Mechanical factory. Students at the Academy train only with hand-made weapons."

"These aren't weapons. They're just practice swords!"

"Nonetheless. The Board of Governors would not approve the purchase. No sense in even trying."

"But that's..."

His cautioning finger stopped her. "Perhaps it is. But you have not yet Completed your time here, and what you were about to say could be interpreted as unpatriotic, seditious, and by some people, even blasphemous."

"All right. I won't borrow any new trouble until I've solved the last batch." She frowned. "But do you think all these policies are doing any good? Here I sit in the Ladies' Academy, being protected from Mechanically made practice swords from Domaland, but my mind has been scarred far more deeply by the actions of the people of my own country."

He did not answer, merely turned the page for her. "The approved training weapons are on the next page. What is the price this year?"

She spun the catalogue on the desk so he could read. "Taking the rest of our list into account, we have 45 Crowns left. That means we can afford only five new swords. And for that price, we could buy exactly 20 of the cheap ones."

"Quick arithmetic." He wrote the numbers down.

She felt the need to get up and move again. "Master Ogima, what can I do? I hate being weak and helpless and afraid,"

"Strengthen yourself."

"What chance...wait a minute." She stopped her pacing and stared at him. "Are you trying to be obscure? Am I supposed to be reading something else into this?"

He slanted his head. "Not all our thoughts need be obscure. Sometimes the outcome of the simplest plan becomes hidden by variables beyond our control."

"Then let's make a simple plan, at least. What can I do?"

"I am not certain you can do it. I'm not sure you should even try."

"Now you're playing games with me. Tell me I can't do it, so I will?"

He stood, staring down at her. "I will not play games on a matter so serious. This would be very difficult, and not something a girl of your class ever does. You would have to train like a soldier. You would have to become a proficient fighter: barehand, sword, dagger, any other weapon you chose. You would have to both strike blows and endure them until you are unafraid of either. You would have to train hard and often, to strengthen your body and your mind to the point where you truly believed that you could put up a fight against another soldier. If you believed that, your fear would probably subside."

She frowned.

"Think of it as a story."

"What story?"

"What happened to you was a story that might have had a bad ending. Now you lie awake and tell the story over again and put the same bad ending on it. Thus you train yourself to fear."

"So I have to tell myself a story with a better ending."

"Yes, but it must be the same story and you must believe that the new ending could be true."

"Like the soldier who persuades himself, against logic, that he isn't the one who will get hit."

"Exactly. And it will make it easier to believe the story if your logic tells you that you are a good enough fighter to make the ending happen."

"I see."

"But it would, as I say, take a great deal of time and effort and it would change you."

"Change me? Of course it would. But that's what I want."

He shook his head. "Once you consider the use of violence to solve your problems, there is no going back. Violence will be one of your options for the rest of your life. You become a different person."

She was still for a moment, staring at him as the realization dawned. "You're going to let me do this, aren't you? You're going to help me."

He smiled. "What, set you up, then disappoint you and have you yell at me again? I do not think I am up to that twice in one day."

She jumped up and threw her arms around him. "Oh, thank you, thank you, Master Ogima."

He returned the embrace awkwardly, patting her shoulder. She stepped back, then realized that he was blushing.

"Oh, I'm sorry. I didn't mean…"

He shook his head, smiled. "No, no, that is quite all right. However," and he fixed her with the cold stare she was used to from practice, "this is not something you try for a while to see if it is fun. This is a commitment to a serious project for a great length of time. I will not waste my time!"

"I understand."

He nodded. "You must think on this. There is no hurry."

"Right. I will think on it. Tonight." She grinned. "When do we start?"

He shook his head. "Tomorrow, I suppose."

"I'll be here. I'll be ready."

"I sincerely doubt it."

* * *

By the next afternoon, she realized what he meant.

"I don't think I can do this much longer."

The Master glanced at her, then resumed his stoic gaze at the far wall of the training room. The silence continued.

"How much longer are we going to do this?"

"Until the lesson is learned."

She thought about that for a while. As well as she could think, as her legs, long past aching, burned with fatigue. She looked at the three other students, completely still in their deep fighting stances. The sweat streamed down her face, drenched her practice robe. Her left knee began to shake and she forced it to stop. She realized that in order to stop the shaking, she had to isolate the muscle that was fatigued, induce it to relax, and take the weight with the rest of her leg. It took some time and a great deal of concentration, but finally she managed it.

When she returned her attention to the rest of the room, she realized that considerable time had passed. She wondered if that was part of the lesson she was supposed to be learning

She couldn't help but notice that the others, all considerably senior to her, had not spoken for the last half hour. So that was the way. *Another lesson learned. I will not speak. I will not quit.* She dropped her stance a fraction, deepened her concentration as well. The clock in the corner ticked its slow, steady pace. The sweat ran into her eyes, reminding her of long, fearful days with a heavy pack on dusty roads. She looked around at friendly faces. *This is easy. Well, at least bearable.*

"That is sufficient. Aleria, rise slowly. Make no sudden movements."

She registered the Master's voice, considered. It had been close to an hour that they had been standing, legs deeply bent. She wondered how much longer she could have stayed there. After a moment's consideration, she decided that she could have gone on for some time. How long, she couldn't guess. Maybe that was another lesson. For now, she had done enough. Slowly, she straightened.

She copied the others, moving gently, stretching and relaxing each muscle.

"Twenty laps, slow jog."

They fell into line, Aleria at the end, and loped around the perimeter of the room. It felt good to be moving. She had always been a runner and knew she could pass the others, but she held herself in check. Who knew what abilities these older students possessed? *The last thing I want at this stage is to make a fool of myself.*

They walked the last lap, stretching their legs again.

"I believe we have abused our lower bodies enough for today. Let us finish the practice with a thousand punches. Aleria, will you start the count?"

Aleria assumed the forward attack stance, not too deep, and began. She made her count slow and measured, with enough feeling in her voice to encourage her fellows, but not enough to show off. She finished her count, then followed the next leader through his. While keeping most of her attention on her technique, she allowed a small part of her mind to consider her progress and register satisfaction. She had learned several lessons today. Obviously, her body had the ability to do things she had never dreamed it could. *I knew I was in decent physical shape, but to handle an hour of deep fighting stance on my first day of practice!*

It was her turn to take the count again and she focused on that task. She recalled her student days, when doing a thousand punches was considered a huge accomplishment. After the ordeal of the afternoon, the thousand punches went quickly and soon they were headed for the showers.

Correction. The shower. She had known that the Masters' dressing room was not segregated, but it wasn't until she walked through the door and the others started undressing that the import struck home. Another lesson to learn. Hoping no one had noticed her brief hesitation, she slipped out of her robe and strode to the nearest nozzle, trying to act as if showering with a group of men was something she did every day. Surprisingly enough, it seemed to work. Why wouldn't it?

As she was dressing, the man next to her turned her way. "You had good spirit today, Aleria. It will be a pleasure to have you practice with us."

She glanced at him. He was a stocky man of about thirty: dark hair, dark skin, work-roughened hands. She had been introduced to everyone by first names, and she struggled to remember.

"Rilke." He smiled to take any censure away.

"Thanks, Rilke. I think my mind was too busy with keeping my spirit strong to worry about names."

He nodded. "It is often that way."

"Another lesson to be learned."

He grinned. "The Master teaches us many lessons."

"Don't I know it," she tossed her cloak over her shoulder, "and often not the one we think we're getting."

The others chuckled at that, and as she moved towards the door they all called farewells. Before leaving, she bowed to Master Ogima.

"Thank you for practice."

"Thank you for your work. It would be best if you practise tomorrow."

"Yes. I know I will need to work out my legs. I'll see you then."

"I will see you then."

That was one lesson she had learned long ago. In order to maintain condition, two practices a week. To make progress, three. To make serious advances, four. Since she was working on both barehand and weapons techniques, she needed to make five practices a week. This meant leaving the wagon yard an hour early on three days, but it was unavoidable. She had started going in on Feastday mornings to make up the work.

24. Same Old Aleria

As the summer wore on, her hands and body hardened and her spirit, at least on the practice floor, strengthened as well. Now she thought nothing of an hour in any fighting stance. She could take punches and give them without a qualm.

One fall day when they were short of workers she surprised Spald, the yard foreman, by jumping in and helping to load a wagon train of lumber. The boards were not that heavy, and once she got the hang of it she swung them up without difficulty. As the last wagon cleared the gate, she flexed her shoulders.

"Not the kind of exercise I'm used to."

The foreman glanced down at her. "I imagine not, Lady Aleria."

"I'll probably be stiff tomorrow."

"Get one of the servants to give you a hot oil rubdown."

"Huh! My father doesn't believe in that kind of servants."

"Too bad. My wife does it for me."

"Well, thank you, Mr. Spald. That's the first good reason anybody has ever given me for getting married."

As she strode back into the office, she wondered what the dignified foreman would think if he knew that she was going to get a rubdown tonight from a thirty-year-old tavern keeper. By now she was used to working with everyone in the barehand class, a rotating group of ten men and two women, all busy people who came to practice whenever they could. Having her body handled, battered and treated by men who were neither servants nor doctors had taken some getting used to, but since they all regarded her and each other with a casual but unfailing respect, she had soon lost her reserve.

She found she enjoyed the weapons training the most. In spite of her growing confidence, she still had moments of unease in barehand practice, when one of the men had her in a submission hold or attacked too hard. There were times when she knew without a doubt that she was simply not strong enough to control the fight. With a sword in her hand she had no such feelings. Her mind and her skill counted much more with a weapon, and she worked hard and advanced rapidly as the winter passed.

* * *

She was running through a practice pattern in the garden just as the sun set one early spring evening, not concentrating hard, just enjoying the flicker of the dying light on her blade, when she noticed her father. He was standing in the portico, not doing anything, just watching her. When she lowered her sword, he sighed.

"Rough day, Father?"

"Not at all. I was just thinking. Normally, a man of my station is pleased to enter the garden in the evening to find his daughter playing music, reading poetry, or arranging flowers."

"I see. Am I a great disappointment to you, then?"

He smiled, but slowly. "No, just a bit of a surprise, sometimes."

Sheathing her sword, she took his arm and turned him towards the house. "Well, just to show you that I haven't lost my feminine skills, I will make and serve you a beautiful pot of tea, just the way you like it."

"With jasmine?"

She shook his arm. "Father, I said I was showing my feminine skills, not practicing to be a tavern cook. I will make you tea the way I think you like it. If you want something else, make it yourself."

He shook his head. "So much for normalcy."

"Oh. Sorry. Excuse me a moment, Father." Drawing her sword, she flicked it out, beheaded an assortment of blooms and gathered them. "There. Flower arranging. After the tea, I will read you a poem."

"I feel so reassured." Then he looked at her more gravely. "How are you, Aleria? How are the dreams?"

She rocked her hand in front of her. "Still there, but not the same."

"In what way?"

She considered. "My idea of seeing Raif seems to have worked. He is no longer in them. They are less specific to real events, now. More undefined terror than real situations. I don't know whether that's progress or not."

"I'm sure it is. I hope you have told Raif."

"Oh, yes. It wouldn't be fair not to."

"So that plan is working out? Seeing him, talking to him."

"That part of it is fine. You know, it's strange…"

"Yes?"

"I like him."

"You do?"

"I'm sure you've heard me complain about the boys in my class. How they're…you know…"

"Young, immature, callow, weak, boring, not serious enough…?"

"I guess you have heard me."

"Now and again."

"I know. And again and again. Because it's true. But Raif isn't like that. He's mature, he's serious, he's capable." She shivered. "A bit too capable, perhaps. He's been out there in the real world and he knows what it's like. And he survived."

"And so did you."

"Mostly. And I have a suspicion he's not completely unscarred either."

"So he sympathizes, and it means something."

"Now that I'm past the point of blaming him – not that I meant to, but some part of me must have – I realize what he went through as well. And he understands how hard it has been for me." She grinned. "When he's not traipsing off doing something completely hammer-headed, he's quite a decent sort."

She thought a moment. "And he treats Mito like a person."

Her father grinned. "What does that mean?"

247

She shrugged. "I don't know. It's just something I have noticed with people. The girls at school, of course, but also the teachers and other adults. It's because of her family problems. They are mostly over now, but when she came to school they must have been quite serious. People looked at her with a sort of calculation, and you could see what they were thinking. Would she be a problem? Could she be used to some advantage? Was she an easy target? Raif isn't like that. He just treats her like...well, like he treats me. Or anybody else. He even had sympathy for Slathe's soldiers – the poor ones with no other choices."

"Good for him."

"But if you always look at people as if they were tools to be used and treat them like that, then they will treat you the same way. You will never get to see anyone as a person. You never get to know if that person could be a friend. So you never have friends, you just have people who are convenient to you. What an empty way to live your life...why are you looking at me like that?"

"Because you have never said anything that makes me as proud of you as I am right now."

"Hmph. It was rather naïve, now that I heard myself say it."

He put an arm around her shoulders. "Well, you just keep being naïve, then. You'll live a much fuller life."

"If being naïve means not knowing about all the things there are to be afraid of, I wish I was."

"So you have solved your problem with Raif, but your dreams are still there."

"They come and they go, but yes, always there."

"So all your training has not been the solution you hoped."

She shook her head. "It didn't solve my predicament completely. But as I say, the problem has changed. I always think change means progress. Maybe this is a stage I have to go through."

He put an arm around her shoulders. "I wish I could give you some fatherly advice at this point, but I'm afraid you are quite beyond anything in my experience. Would you like to talk to the doctor again?"

She smiled. "He did a marvellous job of stitching that sword-cut I got last month, but I don't think he knows much more than you do about bad dreams."

"Then someone else. I hear there is a doctor at the University who is making a study of…"

Her scornful snort stopped him. "I am not about to let myself become the subject of some doctor's experiments."

"But it might help you."

"I'm doing fine, father. Has it ever occurred to you that many people must have this kind of problem? Lots of people have lived through all sorts of horrible experiences and they seem to be able to cope. They just don't weep and wail and wring their hands about their bad luck. I don't intent to, either."

"But your mother and I …"

"…worry about me. Of course you do. You're parents." She returned his one-armed hug as they entered the house. "And I expect you to continue to worry. You can ask me about it as much as you need, to feel that you're doing your parenting job right."

"This hasn't anything to do with thinking…"

"She's got you going again, hasn't she?"

Aleria grinned over at her mother, who was sitting in the family room reading the newspaper. "It was so easy, Mother. I couldn't resist."

"Well, don't take advantage."

Her father pushed her away, but not without a small extra tightening of his arm first. "Thank you for the timely rescue, my dear. She was playing the 'overanxious parent' gambit."

Leniema patted the sofa beside her. "Come and sit down and commiserate. She used it on me yesterday."

"Did she? Did you fall for it?"

"Only as much as I felt she needed."

"Good for you. I didn't have the same strength tonight."

Aleria stood, hands on hips, glaring at them. "You two are ganging up on me again."

"It seems a fair match, what with your advantages."

"Advantages?"

Her father joined in. "Yes. You know. The parental worries, that sort of thing."

"Ah. Those. I'll keep them in mind for the future. What's for supper, Mother?"

"Enough for even your appetite."

"Good." She half-drew her sword. "Need any help in the kitchen?"

"Not of the sort you would prefer to give. I'm sure the cook can keep everything under control until suppertime."

Aleria slid the sword back. "I'll be there."

She swung down the hall to her rooms, grinning. The next time she had a bad dream she should try to focus on the happiness in her life. Not many had what she had, and she knew it.

On the topic of happiness, she was pleased with how she was mastering that new circular riposte. She went through the complicated motion in her mind, feeling the slide of steel on steel when the contact pressure was right. It wasn't exactly right, though. She must work on that some more tomorrow.

* * *

And the next day, and the next day. Try as she might, the finish of the complex move escaped her. Finally, one day she threw her sword on the training room floor in frustration.

"I am just never going to get it! Never!"

Rilke, who had been training with her, stepped back, his sword wavering lower.

Master Ogima appeared at her elbow. "And what is it that you are never going to get?"

"The circular riposte you showed us last month. I can do it in practice. I can do it slowly. But the moment I try it in real-time, it just falls apart. Why can't I do it?"

"First, pick up your sword. It is not appropriate to treat your weapon so. I'm sure it is not to blame."

The heat rushed to her cheeks, and she bent to retrieve the sword. "Yes, Master. I know I should not give way to frustration." But then it boiled up again. "But it's just so damned frustrating! Why are you smiling?"

Master Ogima looked around at the rest of the class, who were politely ignoring her outburst, making her feel even smaller. "Who do you admire the most, here? Who is the best swordsman?"

"That's easy. Roeble."

"Master Cloete, will you join us?"

The hefty merchant strolled over. "What's the problem, Aleria? Sword bit you?"

She frowned, her embarrassment increasing.

"Roeble, will you demonstrate the circular riposte for us?"

"Why?"

Aleria's head came around. No one ever questioned the Master.

"I simply want you to show Aleria how it goes."

"That wouldn't be much good, would it?"

"And now it is my turn to ask why."

"You know very well, Master Ogima. Because the damned thing is well-nigh impossible. It only works decently against a left-handed opponent who holds his sword hand too far outside. Otherwise your blade just slips off. It's not worth the time to learn. At least, not for me. I'd sooner use my time perfecting my basics."

"Thank you Roeble. Better she hear it from you than from me."

"My pleasure, Master." With a grin at Aleria, he sauntered back to his opponent.

She glared at her instructor. "I suppose you think that's a great joke. Why didn't you tell us?"

"All sorts of questions, today. Because it was a lesson."

"And what am I supposed to learn from this?"

"I think enough questions. Perhaps you would like to return to a more productive exercise."

"Certainly, Master. Just a few more minutes on that riposte."

He did not respond, but she thought she detected a faint smile as he turned away.

Rilke raised his eyebrows but said nothing, only lifted his sword to the ready position.

She gritted her teeth and began the drill again, keeping in mind the new information she had learned. It didn't seem to help. It just felt awkward.

So Aleria was not in the best of moods when she racked her sword and left the practice rooms. She made the effort to be friendly to the other fighters in the dressing room, but inside she was still seething.

All right. I'm supposed to learn a lesson. Well, I'll learn it my way. Won't they be surprised when I do it right!

25. The Mess of Battle

She was so deep in thought that she missed her turning and found herself farther down the street than she usually walked. The homes were more tattered here, the shops even more rundown and seedy. Restricting herself to a ladylike curse, she was about to turn back when she heard voices coming from a nearby alley. Voices and unpleasant laughter.

Then there was a short, sharp, scream, cut off as if by a slap or a hand over someone's mouth.

Cursing her lack of a sword, she loosened her hideaway in its sheath and paced in.

A girl in a dirty dress was crouched on the reeking earth, her arm twisted behind her by a well dressed lad of about sixteen. Another youth lounged against a nearby building, a sneer on his face.

"I don't think she's worth it, Segre. She's ugly and stupid and probably hasn't bathed for a month."

His friend dropped the girl's arm and drove his knee into her back, sprawling her face down in the muck of the alley. "I suppose you're right. But we can't just leave her here. I think she needs a lesson to make sure she keeps her mouth shut."

A red tinge built up around the edges of Aleria's sight. The picture of the girl cringing, her hair covering her face, brought back memories that were just too much to bear. She strode forward. "I think someone else needs a lesson."

He looked up. "Who the hell are you? Keep your nose out of our business if you don't want to join her."

She remembered the lesson. *Bullies always expect to talk. They want to play the game, draw out their fun. Never give them time to learn their mistake.*

She attacked.

Three quick jabs to his nose drove the torturer away from his victim, and a sidekick to the stomach finished the task as she reversed her motion to face the second attack. A flailing fist caught her on the side of the head. Her vision filled with spots of light. She bored in, her fists driving into his ribs, and he gave way. She followed, but realized her mistake when she heard a heavy step behind her. Ducking aside and spinning around, she was surprised to see the first boy stumble past her, off balance. She glanced down to see the girl, her leg outstretched.

"Good work, kid. Now get out of here."

The girl scrabbled towards the alley mouth. Aleria twisted back, but it took too long. Her opponents had recovered and attacked together: one high, one low. Their combined weight staggered her and the enclosing arms gave her a moment of the old panic.

The face of the taller one loomed over her, a snarl twisting his lips. "Now we'll see who gets a lesson!"

With a tremendous wrench she freed one hand, speared her fingers towards his eyes, felt a satisfying squish. The boy reared back screaming, and the raised chin gave her the opening for an elbow to the throat. He collapsed with a gurgle.

There was the sing of steel, and she turned to see her other opponent jerk a dagger from his belt. The idiot held it wrong, his hand over his head, blade pointed down towards her. His move so perfectly mimicked the training position that she didn't even bother to pull her hideaway. As his dagger plunged down she grabbed his wrist and tugged him forward, turning her back to him and stooping under his arm. When he stumbled towards her she straightened her legs, throwing him over her head, to slam against the wall of the building opposite. Just before releasing she jerked upwards and felt something tear. He slid down, his head thudding to the dirt. He lay there, unmoving. Then he groaned and opened his eyes.

She walked over and picked up the dagger, flipped it end-for-end to catch it by the tip. A quick toss, and it arrowed into the ground beside his cheek. "I don't suggest you pick it up."

His eyes closed.

Without further speech, she turned and strode out of the alley. The girl was nowhere to be seen.

Reaction was not long in coming. Her father was called to the door while she was still at breakfast, two days later, and returned with a bemused look.

"Aleria, you have received an official document."

"I have?" She reached out. It was an envelope of heavy, cream-coloured paper. She glanced at the seal.

"The Office of the Royal Aribiter?" She used her dagger to break the seal, slipped out the document and scanned it. "Hmm. It seems I am invited to the Arbiter's office to help the police in their investigation of an assault on two young gentlemen of the Esteemed Class." She glanced at her father. "I wonder what kind of story they told." She frowned. "I wonder how they knew it was me. I've never seen either of them before."

Her father shook his head. "I'm afraid a lot of people know who you are, Aleria. In all sections of town."

"What kind of 'invitation' is this, father?"

"The kind you had better not decline. When are we going?"

"Are you coming with me? Stupid question. Of course you are." She glanced at the paper. "Tomorrow mid-morning. I'm allowed counsel, it says."

"Perhaps Master Ogima would like to know about the situation."

"I'll send him a message. I have to anyway. I'll be missing Weapons practice."

* * *

Master Ogima wanted more than information about the situation. The following morning he was there at the Royal Arbiter's office, his formal uniform bristling with ribbons. The Arbiter looked surprised.

"We don't usually see you here, Master Ogima. What interest do you have in this case?"

"The lady is allowed counsel, your Honour?"

"Of course."

"Well, then." The Battle Arts Master sat, and that was it. The Arbiter, a young man whose robe looked spanking new, cleared his throat and looked to Aleria. "You may sit, young lady."

"That would be 'my Lady,' your Honour."

Both Aleria and the young Arbiter looked at her father. His face was placid, but his stance unyielding.

"By all means. My Lord, my Lady, will you please be seated? This is only an informal investigation at the moment." His voice took on confidence as he moved into his official patter. "Nothing said at this time is considered to be under oath, although facts given here and later countered under oath could affect the veracity of your case," he paused, "if there should be a case."

Aleria nodded. "I understand." Otherwise she held her tongue. This was no time to be trying to take over.

The Arbiter laced his fingers before him. "Now, my Lady, we have a formal complaint from two young gentlemen of the Esteemed class, Segre Verades and Cervanne Scotney by name, that you did, three days ago in Lucnam Street, attack them and cause them grievous harm. What do you say to this?"

She glanced at her father, and he nodded. "Do they say what they were doing at the time of this supposed attack?"

"No, they do not."

"I see. And do they state the nature of the conversation that took place before the altercation?"

"No, they do not." He glanced at the papers before him. "They state that you attacked without warning."

"So the gist of their charge is that they were strolling along minding their own business when I suddenly ran upon them, attacked them and did them serious injury. Two young gentlemen, each half again my size."

"Lady Aleria, the presence of your Battle Arts Master here somewhat weakens that defence."

"I suppose. Why don't I tell you the story the way I experienced it?"

"That would be useful. Keep in mind the warning I gave you at the beginning."

"Don't worry. I'm not likely to be changing my story."

A grim smile played across his lips. "You would be surprised how many people tell me that, my Lady. The warning stands."

"Thank you, your Honour." She proceeded to give him a brief rundown of the events, skipping over the details of the fight except for the drawn dagger. When she was finished, the Arbiter steepled his fingers and looked at her for a moment.

"So your contention is that these two gentlemen had dragged a girl into the alley. They were seriously abusing her and promising to do more. When you intervened, they threatened you with the same. You felt it necessary to attack in order to protect the girl and yourself. They responded in kind. At one point in the altercation, the shorter of the two drew his dagger and attacked you with it. Is that correct?"

"You have the gist of it, your Honour. Do you wish to examine my bruises?"

"Thank you, Lady Aleria, but that will not be necessary." He thought some more, then looked up. His glance included the two men as well. "This is not an unexpected development. I will not be breaking confidence by telling you that we have had an increasing problem of this sort lately. The authorities are frustrated in our dealing with the situation because the perpetrators use their upper class to avoid responsibility, and the lower class victims close ranks likewise and refuse to aid us. We have been concerned at the escalating nature of the violence. Sooner or later, serious injuries might result."

He glanced down again. "Assorted bruises, two cracked ribs, broken nose, dislocated shoulder. One may lose the sight of his eye. The doctors won't know until the swelling goes down. That's pretty serious damage for a youngster like that."

"If I may say so, your Honour, it was a pretty serious activity they were engaging in."

"Are you absolutely certain of that? The young lady involved cannot be found."

"She was on her knees, and the taller one had her arm twisted up behind her into a vertical position above her head. Their conversation indicated that they were deciding whether to rape her or not. He then drove his knee into her back and slammed her face into the ground. There was blood on it when she rose. And he was threatening to do more, to persuade her not to talk. I suspect that if her father, her brothers, or her neighbours had come upon the scene, the damage would have been much greater."

"I am forced to agree with your interpretation of the facts, while I deplore the violence you have exhibited." He leaned forward. "I hope you don't feel that you have done anything to make this situation any better, young...my Lady. All you have done is accelerate the increase of the violence."

"With due respect, your Honour, there is one person who would disagree with you, even though she will probably never get the chance to speak."

"I cannot argue with that."

Then he sat straighter, returning to his formal pose.

Here it comes.

"Master Ogima, my Lord anDalmyn, the one benefit that may perhaps come of this unfortunate occurrence is that persons of your standing have become involved. Perhaps you can swing some weight in your circles towards finding a solution."

Her father nodded. "I do have a better understanding of your difficulties, your Honour, and you may count on me to work on your behalf in what I consider to be a worthy effort. Please feel free to contact me if the need arises." He glanced at the papers on the table. "What will become of this issue?"

"The same as all the rest." The Arbiter gathered the file together and slid it into an envelope, sealed it and dropped it on the table. "The perpetrators' social position protects them. The victim's social position hides her. Lady Aleria's Rank will keep her name out of it as well. She has not even been formally identified as a participant."

Master Ogima's voice cut in. "And Lady Aleria's chastisement of the two culprits will have little effect, because it only confirms in their minds the right of violence to hold sway."

The Arbiter rose. "I wholeheartedly agree with you, Master, although I am surprised to hear that sentiment from you."

Ogima smiled. "The greatest art of battle lies in avoiding one in the first place."

The Arbiter bowed; they rose, returned his courtesy and left.

As the carriage started out towards home, Aleria glanced at Master Ogima, then turned to her father. "Well, that was the easy part."

"It was?"

"Yes. She nodded towards the Battle Arts Master. "Now I have to talk to him."

Her father glanced at the stoic face across the carriage. "And do you need counsel for that meeting?"

"No, but it might perhaps ease your mind to attend."

"In that case, perhaps we should make it as soon as possible?"

Ogima nodded. "There is no better time than the present."

"Then please accept our hospitality. Can this ordeal be accomplished over food?"

Aleria batted her father's arm. "Oh, stop the fake formality. It's not going to be that bad. Will you come for lunch, Master?"

"The hospitality of anDalmyn…"

"Yes, yes, I know the proper expression. '…not to be passed up' and all that. Fine. We'll wait until you have been awed by the grace of my family and overwhelmed by the richness of the food. Maybe then you'll be easier on me."

"I am not the one who needs to be hard on you, Aleria."

"I am quite aware of that." She leaned back in her seat and stared out the window, wondering what she could possibly say. Finally, she sat up straight.

"Look, why don't we make this easy? I panicked. Master Ogima, you know what happens to me sometimes. When I am too heavily restrained, I panic. When both of them grabbed me, I lost control and performed an act equivalent to that of the boy drawing his dagger. Up until then, nothing in the fight was designed to do permanent damage. After my strike to the eye, the whole level of the fight changed, and whatever happened was caused by my action. My fault. They were just stupid kids and I should have been able to control the situation. If that boy loses his vision the responsibility is mine. I have a lot of learning ahead of me. Fair enough?"

Master Ogima glanced over at her father. "I could not have stated it more clearly." Both men nodded.

Aleria sat back, lost in thought, as the carriage pulled up at the Dalmyn front door.

"Do I gather I am still invited for lunch?"

Her father smiled. "I don't think we're going to get much out of Aleria. Come in and keep us company. Perhaps we have other concerns to discuss."

"I think we do."

26. Resolution

The next day Aleria took on her tasks with new enthusiasm. She grabbed her bag of training clothes and strode with purpose down the street. It felt good to be out doing something.

As she moved into the lower part of the city, she was surprised to see a rather well dressed figure approaching. Then her heart sank. There was something familiar about the set of those shoulders. She straightened her own and strode forward.

"Hello, Kalmein. What are you doing in this part of town?"

He greeted her with a touch more courtesy than required. "Just taking a short cut. What about you?"

"Master Ogima's practice rooms are at the end of the block."

"Of course."

"Do you have a moment?"

He regarded her with a frown. "Why?"

"Because we have some unfinished business, and I'm tying up loose ends this month."

"What unfinished business?"

She took him by the arm and steered him towards The Falcon. "Not out in the street. Let's be a little bit formal."

He followed, but in the doorway he hung back. "Um... Aleria, I don't know if this is the type of place to bring a young lady."

She looked around, trying to see the decor through his eyes. Scratched tables, broken chairs, torn curtains. "Oh. I suppose it isn't. We come here for a drink after practice quite often. Don't bother anyone and they won't bother you."

He looked dubious but followed her through the splintered door.

Inside, she directed their steps past the bar. "Just short mugs, Jems." The bartender nodded, and she led the way to a table by one of the few windows. She waited for Kalmein to sit before she joined him.

He looked around the dim room once, then focused on her. "So what unfinished business do we have that we can complete in a place like this?"

"That's good, Kalmein. Very sharp." She let her smile fade. "I have some explaining to do."

"That would be interesting."

"Are you still angry?"

"Not so much. Still disappointed in you, though."

"And yourself?"

His frown deepened. "This seems to be picking up where we left off."

She shook her head. "Not my intention. I want to explain what happened that day. It may or may not help, but I don't think it's right to leave you in the dark."

"So something was going on. I wondered."

She made a sour face. "Well, so did I. I just left it too late, that's all."

She shifted in her seat, and her eye caught movement up at the bar. She looked again, then muttered a soft curse.

"Look, Kalmein, I want to tell you about this, but there's something I've got to see to, first."

She was on her feet before he could question, strolling towards the pair at the bar. The taller of the two leered at her as she approached. His smile broadened as she moved closer, laid her hand over his on the bar. Then his face froze as she forced his little finger back, farther and farther. When she had his complete attention, she spoke calmly.

"I just came in here for a drink with my friend. I didn't have any plans to see anybody killed today. So what happens is all up to you."

She let go of his finger and brought her hands together in front of her, allowing her sleeve to fall back, sliding her right hand to caress the dagger hilt that was revealed.

His eyes slid around. "Tough girl, hey?"

"Maybe. I came over to deal with you before anything starts. I figured that way he," she tossed her head towards Kalmein, regarding them from his seat, "won't get involved. He doesn't want to have to hurt anybody so early in the afternoon. So you just have your drink, keep your head down, follow the rules and everything will be peachy-fine." She gave him a cold smile.

"Rules?"

"You're new around here, I can tell. Place like this," she ticked off on her fingers, "you keep to yourself, you don't bother anybody, and nobody will bother you. Got it?"

Once again, his eyes slid away, and she held her stare until his head dropped. "Yeah, I got it."

"That would be 'Yes, Ma'am, I got it,' don't you think?"

He glowered at her, muttered. "Yes, Ma'am. I got it."

She favoured him with a smile. "Well done. You learn real quick. You just might survive around here."

She turned and walked back to her table, followed by Jems with their drinks. She sat down, paid and winked at the barman. He smiled back. "No trouble from those lads?"

"I don't think so. If there is, they've been warned."

"Don't worry, Miss Aleria. You handled that smart. I was just tryin' to figure out how to wise them up without losin' a coupla customers."

"I'd keep an eye on them for a while. They might decide to take it out on somebody else."

"Don't worry. Enjoy your drinks." He nodded to Kalmein and strolled back to his post.

"Sorry about that." She raised her mug, tapped it against his, and they drank. "They serve good ale here."

He nodded, took another sip.

She put down her mug and leaned forward. "Now, as I was saying. The girls and I got into an argument one day. About losing our virginity."

She glanced up to appreciate the look on his face. "Truth. Girls talk about things like that. They were complaining about how hard it was." She raised her hand. "Don't even bother. I told them. I said they weren't trying hard enough. We went around that for a while and finally we concluded that the problem was losing it on our own terms."

He grinned. "I can see that. Did you decide what those terms were?"

She shrugged. "Different for different people, but mainly some kind of romantic situation with someone we liked a lot. Nobody was talking about love, but it we all decided it had to be someone a bit special."

He leaned back. "Is this the part where I'm supposed to start feeling better?"

She smiled, one side of her mouth only. "I hope so. Anyway, as I sometimes do, I made the challenge, and they took me up on it."

"I see. And I was the lucky subject of your plot?"

She glanced sideways at him. "I was young and foolish in those days. I always sort of thought…you know…"

He snorted. "Yes, well so did I."

"Right. So you were my choice. I guess you could tell."

"You were never known for your subtlety, Aleria."

"I always think that action gets results."

"Hmm."

"Right. So everything was going fine until the afternoon of the party. Then my father told me he trusted me not to do anything stupid."

"He said that? Clever man."

She smiled ruefully. "He is. Started me thinking. That's why it got all messed up, Kalmein. I wasn't treating you straight and I wasn't sure of myself, so I kept sending you the wrong signals."

He took a brief pull from his mug. "I thought the signals were pretty straightforward."

"That was the problem. I think I kept sending the signals, but inside I had already changed my mind. Then when it came to the actual moment…"

"You just couldn't go through with it, because you were not treating me fairly?"

She looked up at him. "Don't be so cynical. That was part of it, yes."

"I wasn't concerned about being treated fairly. Honest!"

"You can have your joke. You paid for it." She leaned forward, touched his hand. "But I messed up, Kalmein, and it's bothered me ever since. I'm sorry. I just thought if I explained it, you might not feel so bad about it."

"You mean I might not feel so bad about you."

She shrugged. "That, too. But that wasn't the important part. I realized that what I said mattered. I did want it romantic, with someone special. But not a set-up with everybody watching."

He nodded. "I can see that. I've spent a lot of time thinking about that night as well. I never figured out what was going on, because I didn't think you would treat me like that. It didn't seem like your way."

"Please believe me, it isn't. I can't stand women like that."

"So I've been going over it for a while, now, and I've changed my mind a bit."

"From what to what?"

"Well, something you said bothered me. About taking my share of the blame. At first, I couldn't see that. I was just doing what I was expected to do, and you were the one that threw everything into a mess."

"But...?"

"Well, I've been living a different life since I left school, and it opened my eyes to a lot of things. I realize I never should have pushed you. A lady has to have the right to change her mind, at any time, no matter what. You know why?"

"I know why I think so. Why do you?"

He grinned. "Because a man has to have the right to change his mind, too. At any time, no matter what."

She laughed out loud. "Some day you've got to tell me that story!"

He shook his head. "No, I don't think I ever will." Then he became serious. "But the fact remains. We were neither of us sober, we weren't playing straight with each other and we acted like a couple of silly kids."

"And we both got hurt."

"I think so."

"But, to set the record straight, you were the innocent party at the beginning. It was more my fault than yours."

He glanced at her. "But you paid more, didn't you?"

"What do you mean?"

His eyes dropped.

"No, go ahead. Say what you meant."

"Well, it was your chance. Romance and all that. I...I heard what happened last summer, Aleria. I'm truly sorry."

"What do you mean?"

He shrugged, rolled his shoulders. "Well, you know, what happened to you in that rebellion, and all."

"And just what happened in that rebellion?"

"I don't know much, Aleria, but there's all sorts of stories going around, and it sounds as if you had rough time." He took up his courage and looked her in the eye. "A very rough time, maybe."

'Oh. Oh, I see." She thought a moment. "Kalmein, can you be trusted to keep your mouth shut?"

"Of course. About...your...uh..."

"No, more important than that. I don't know what you've heard, but most of what's going around is based on the story the Army put out to cover some of the things that happened during the rebellion that they don't want any other rebels to hear about. Do you understand what I mean?"

She watched the light dawn. "Of course. Some people were saying that Slathe got wiped up pretty easily, and maybe he wasn't such a threat as they made him out to be."

"Don't worry. He was that bad, and worse. He just came up against someone smarter. And that's all you want to know. Got me?"

"Yes, I see. But you were there, and lived through it all. It must have been horrible for you. I'm so sorry."

"Thank you, Kalmein. I'm sure you mean that with all your heart. It's good to have friends who understand. But you're wrong about two things."

"I am?"

"You are. In the first place, I didn't get raped. I had a tough time, and I was beaten and humiliated, but not that. Does that make you feel better?"

"Not as much as I bet it made you feel. What was the other thing?"

She grinned at him. "I didn't miss my chance."

"You didn't?"

"No."

"You mean...before..." She could see his cheeks redden.

She nodded.

"Oh." His eyes widened. "Wow! You had a really busy summer!"

"Kalmein!"

He held up his hands in helpless defence. "I'm sorry, Aleria, please don't take it wrong, but..." His speech dissolved in laughter.

"All right, all right. Don't let's make a spectacle of ourselves." She glanced around. "Look what you've attracted now."

The approach of the two men from the bar brought instant gravity. Kalmein leaned forward to speak softly. "What did you tell them before?"

"I told them that I dealt with them because you didn't want to."

"I didn't want to? You told that right!"

"I didn't tell them why."

"Oh."

And then it was too late. Aleria looked up as the two approached.

"Excuse us, Miss..." In the light from the window, she could see that he was much younger than she had first thought. "The bartender...he told us who you were, Miss..."

"Oh. And now you're afraid my father's going to be upset with you?"

Puzzlement crossed the lad's face. "Who's your father?"

It was Aleria's turn to be unsure. "Just what did Jems tell you?"

"About...about last summer, Miss, and what...happened to you. I mean, we all heard the story, but I never thought I'd actually meet the lady what did it!"

"Did what?"

"Fought in the rebellion. We heard about you, Miss, 'n' how they treated you, and how you survived and beat them all at the end."

"Oh. I see."

"I just want you to know, Miss, that I think you did the right thing. I mean, no woman should be treated like that!" He seemed to think for a moment. "I hope you didn't think...I mean, I like lookin' at a pretty lady as much as the next man, but...I mean...I hope you don't think I'd ever treat a woman like that. I mean..."

She smiled up at him. "No, lad, I don't think that."

"Oh. Good. I mean..." A sudden thought seemed to strike him. "Will you do me a favour, Miss?"

"What kind of favour?"

"Well...if you'd just...stand up?"

"Stand up? That's all?"

He gulped, nodded.

She glanced at Kalmein, shrugged, and stood. The boy moved closer to her, turning towards his friend. "See! I told ya. She don't come up to my shoulder." He turned back to Aleria. "There you go, Miss. I told my friend, here. You don't even come up to my shoulder, and you had me shakin' in my boots a while back."

She grinned. "Well, maybe you were shaking in your boots because you deserved to."

"Oh, no, Miss. I told you. I wouldn't ever treat a lady like that."

"Or any other woman."

"Sure thing. Say, Miss..."

She shot another glance at Kalmein, who was trying to keep a straight face. "Yes?"

"Could my partner and me...well...could we buy you a drink? You and your friend, of course."

She shook her head. "Sorry, I'm on my way to Battle Arts practice, so we'll thank you and take our leave." She moved forward, and they stumbled over each other giving her room. "Nice meeting you, boys."

She held out her hand, and after a moment's hesitation they each grasped it then released, not sure exactly what was expected. Then she started towards the exit, Kalmein behind her. They followed, calling out farewells, rushing ahead to open the door for her, waving as she passed down the street.

She kept her poise until they turned into the doorway of Master Ogima's training rooms and Kalmein followed, both collapsing in laughter against the wall as soon as they were out of sight of the street.

"I have never…"

"Don't worry, Kalmein, neither have I."

Kalmein's face grew serious. "You have changed, Aleria."

"I suppose."

"I mean it. How you handled those two. They were afraid of you, weren't they?"

She shrugged. "Nothing surprising about that. I have a reputation, I guess, unearned though it might be. I do my best to live up to it."

His grin returned. "Well, I'm glad you're my friend, then."

She grasped his arm. "We still are, aren't we? Friends."

"We are." He waved his hand in a dismissive gesture. "All that, last year…"

"A mistake."

"On both sides."

"Fair enough." There was a moment's pause. "Well…"

"Yes. I was going…somewhere. You have your practice."

"See you again, then."

"Certainly."

He leaned forward and they touched cheeks. Then he spun away and strolled off down the street, kicking a stone ahead of him. A glow in her heart, she turned into the training rooms.

She was going to learn that circular riposte if she had to work at it until her arm fell off.

Epilogue

It was a beautiful fall day, and Aleria was glad to be on the road again. Her horses were also ready for exercise, and she took pride in her driving skills. This trip had held all sorts of unexpected bonuses.

She glanced back over her shoulder. Nobody. So much for her vaunted escort. She snorted. *No wonder Lord Fauvée is having trouble with bandits. Complete ineptitude. My two protectors forgetting their duty and haring off after some rabbit or other.* She reached down and patted the hilt of her sword, tucked close to hand under the wagon seat. *I can take care of myself.*

Then the two men stepped onto the road in front of her. Both hands busy with the reins, she had no time to reach for her sword before the smothering folds of blanket engulfed her from above.

Follow Aleria's progress "Into Trouble," Book Two in the "World of Change" series.

Please help out by putting your opinion into a review on Amazon.

About the Author

Brought up in a logging camp with no electricity, Gordon Long learned his storytelling in the traditional way: at his father's knee. He now spends his time editing, publishing, travelling, blogging and writing fantasy and social commentary, although sometimes the boundaries blur.

Gordon lives in Tsawwassen, British Columbia, with his wife, Linda, and their Nova Scotia Duck Tolling Retriever, Josh.

More from Gordon A. Long

Titles by Gordon A. Long available at <smashwords.com> and <amazon.com>:

"A Sword Called...Kitten?" – Romantic Comedy with an Edge
"The Cat with Many Claws" – "Sword Called Kitten" Book 2
"Why Are People So Stupid?" – Social Humour with a Point

Look for Gordon's books, selected reviews, poetry and short stories: <airbornpress.ca>

Gordon's opinions on humanity are at the "Are People Really That Stupid?" blog:
<airbornpress.ca/arewestupid/blogweb/index.php>

Find all his reviews and his ideas on writing at "Renaissance Writer:"   <airbornpress.ca/writing/blogweb/index.php>

"Sword Called Kitten Serial" Free online:
<airbornpress.ca/kittenserial>

Made in the USA
San Bernardino, CA
10 November 2014